The Art of Starting Over

Serenity Crossing: The Hartwell's
Book #3

Tara Baisden

STERLING RIDGE PRESS LLC

Printed in the United States of America

First Edition: March 2026

For permissions, contact: tara@tarabaisden.com or visit www.tarabaisden.com The Art of Starting Over © 2026 by Tara Baisden

This is a work of fiction. Names, characters, places, and incidents either are the product of the author's imagination or are used fictitiously. Any resemblance to actual persons, living or dead, events, or locales is entirely coincidental.

All Scripture quotations, unless otherwise indicated, are taken from the Holy Bible, New International Version®, NIV®. Copyright ©1973, 1978, 1984, 2011 by Biblica, Inc.™ Used by permission of Zondervan. All rights reserved worldwide. The "NIV" and "New International Version" are trademarks registered in the United States Patent and Trademark Office by Biblica, Inc.™

Cover designed by Sterling Ridge Press LLC

Published by: Sterling Ridge Press, LLC www.sterlingridgepress.com

ISBN: 978-1-966093-51-0

Dedication

I believe God brings the right people together at the right time.

You don't have to rush what He's building. You don't have to force the door open or worry yourself into a blessing that was already on its way to you. He knows what your heart needs, He knows when you're ready to receive it, and He knows the road that will carry you there, even when you can't see past the bend.

Be patient. Trust His timing. Even when the waiting feels long. Even when the road doesn't look the way you thought it would. Even when you're standing in a season you didn't choose and wondering if He's forgotten where you are.

He hasn't forgotten. He's working.

The love, the joy, the life He has for you will arrive in a way that proves His hand was on it the entire time, quietly preparing you for the moment you'd look up and find exactly what you didn't know you were ready for. It may come wrapped in an ordinary Tuesday. It may come through the laughter of a child or the steady kindness of someone who understands your heart because they've walked their own road to reach you. It may come so gently that you won't notice it's happening until you're already in the middle of it.

But it will come. And when it does, you'll know.

His hand was on it the whole time.

This book is for everyone who has ever stood in the space between what was and what's next, and trusted God to build the bridge.

Always Love,
Tara

"He hath made every thing beautiful in his time." — Ecclesiastes 3:11 (KJV)

Contents

Chapter 1

Lizzie Hartwell had her daddy's hand in a grip that suggested she intended to drag him through the entire Serenity Crossing Elementary School building, ready to explore this new adventure she was about to go on.

"Daddy, look," she said, pointing at a mural of a mountain range that stretched from the front office all the way past the water fountains. The mountains were bright green and cheerful, with a cartoon bear waving from behind a pine tree and a yellow sun wearing sunglasses in the corner. 'Welcome to Serenity Crossing Elementary School!' was written across the sky in big purple letters.

"That's pretty cool," Mike Hartwell said.

"The bear is waving at me."

"I think he's waving at everybody."

"No," Lizzie shook her head with the absolute certainty that only a six-year-old could pull off. "He's waving at me."

Mike smiled down at her. She was wearing the outfit she had picked out last night and laid across the chair in her bedroom with the care of someone preparing for a very important occasion—a pink T-shirt with a sparkly butterfly on the front, denim shorts, and her white sneakers with the little rainbow stripes on the side. Her blond hair was pulled back in two braids that his sister Rebecca had done this morning because, according to Lizzie, Daddy braids were fine for regular days, but today was a first-grade day, and first-grade days required Aunt Becca braids.

He hadn't argued with that logic.

Serenity Crossing Elementary was buzzing with families this Saturday morning, the annual Back-to-School Bash filling the hallways with parents carrying clipboards of forms and children running ahead to find their classrooms. A banner stretched across the main hallway that read, 'Back-to-School Bash—Meet Your Teacher!' and someone had tied blue and gold balloons—the school colors, to every door handle in the first-grade wing. The whole building had the kind of cheerful, slightly chaotic energy that happens when you put a couple hundred kids in one place and tell them to be excited about school.

Most of them didn't need the encouragement.

Lizzie had been talking about first grade since the last day of kindergarten in May. She had gone to kindergarten at this same school last year, half days in Mrs. Pruitt's class, and she had loved every minute of it. But kindergarten was only mornings. She had been home by noon every day, back at the Hartwell homestead with Mike's mom or sometimes with one of his other siblings, while Mike worked at the lumber mill. This year was different. This year was full days, five days of the week, and Lizzie had announced at Sunday dinner last weekend that she was "ready to be a real school kid now," while the rest of the Hartwells tried not to laugh at how serious she looked saying it.

Mike was ready too. He thought he was, anyway. The idea of Lizzie being gone all day still sat in a strange place somewhere in his chest—not worry, exactly, because Lizzie was the kind of kid who walked into any room as if she belonged there. More like an awareness that another piece of her growing up was clicking into place, and once it did, it wouldn't click back.

But today was not about any of that. Today was about finding Room 14, meeting Mrs. Sullivan, and letting Lizzie explore the classroom that would be her world five days a week starting Tuesday morning.

"Room twelve, room thirteen," Lizzie counted as they passed each door, reading the numbers the way she read everything now—out loud, with enthusiasm, and with the particular pride of someone who had discovered that letters made words and words were everywhere. "Room fourteen! Daddy, this is it!"

The door was propped open with a small wooden doorstop shaped like an apple, and a handwritten sign taped at a six-year-old's eye level read, 'Welcome to Mrs. Sullivan's Class!' with little hand-drawn stars around the border. Mike could see the classroom beyond the doorway—bright walls, low tables arranged in clusters, a reading corner in the far left with floor pillows in blue, green, and red scattered across a round rug printed with the alphabet. Cubbies lined the back wall, each one labeled with a name tag decorated with a different animal. Crayons, coloring pages, bins of picture books, a weather chart near the window—the whole room looked like someone had built it from the ground up to make a six-year-old feel like they had walked into a place that was theirs.

Lizzie tugged him forward.

Inside, a woman with long, wavy blond hair was standing near the front of the room, speaking with a couple—a tall man in a Volunteers baseball cap and a woman holding a toddler on her hip. The teacher was smiling as she talked, her hands moving in the relaxed, easy way of someone who was comfortable in conversation and comfortable in this room. She wore a navy-blue top and a lanyard around her neck with her ID badge and what looked like a small collection of keychain charms—the kind of thing a teacher accumulated over time from students who thought keychains were the best gift in the world. A few other families were scattered around the classroom. A dad with two boys was looking at the cubbies, pointing out their name tags. A mom was reading the daily schedule posted by the whiteboard while her daughter stood on tiptoe trying to see what was inside the art supply cabinet.

The children's activity area took up the right side of the room—two long tables pushed together and covered with coloring pages, cups of crayons in every color, sticker sheets, and a stack of construction paper. Two girls were sitting there, side by side, coloring with the kind of focus that meant the rest of the world had stopped existing for them.

Lizzie noticed them immediately.

Mike could see her watching the two girls as he guided her to an open spot along the wall where they could wait without crowding the teacher's conversation. The girls looked about Lizzie's age, and they were clearly twins—same dark brown hair pulled up in matching puffs, same round faces. One of the girls was leaning over her coloring page with her tongue poking out of the corner of her mouth in concentration, while the other one kept looking up from her page to watch the people coming in and out of the room. The watching twin had bright, curious blue eyes that swept across every new face as if she were cataloging the entire event for later.

"Daddy, can I go color?" Lizzie whispered, though her version of whispering was really just talking at a slightly lower volume.

"Sure," Mike said. "Go ahead."

She crossed the room with zero hesitation, walked right up to the table, and pulled out the chair next to the watching twin. "Hi," she said, the way she said hi to everybody—like they were already friends and just hadn't been introduced yet. "I'm Lizzie."

The watching twin grinned. "I'm Amber. That's my sister, Alicia." She pointed at the other girl, who looked up from her coloring page long enough to give Lizzie a small wave and a shy smile before going right back to her picture.

"Are you in this class too?" Lizzie asked, already reaching for a crayon.

"No, our mom is the teacher," Amber said, and the way she said it carried a note of obvious pride. "We're in Mrs. Fletcher's class next door, but we get to be in here today because Mommy said we could help her set up and be her helpers."

"That's so cool," Lizzie said with complete sincerity. "Your mom is my teacher?"

"Yep."

"Is she nice?"

"Super nice," Amber confirmed, and then leaned closer as if she were sharing classified information. "My mommy makes really good pancakes too."

Lizzie laughed—a bright, open sound that made Mike's chest warm from across the room—and just like that, the three of them fell into the easy, immediate rhythm that seemed to come so naturally to children. Within minutes, Lizzie was showing them her favorite crayon colors—purple, turquoise, and what she called "the fancy gold one"—and Amber was explaining that she always used the red crayon first because red was the best color and anyone who said otherwise was wrong. Alicia had quietly slid her coloring page closer to Lizzie's so they could compare pictures. They were sharing crayons, trading opinions about which colors went together, and leaning over each other's pages with the kind of instant familiarity that adults spent months trying to build and rarely managed.

Amber was the talker. That much was clear within thirty seconds. She led the conversation, made the declarations, asked the questions, and narrated her coloring choices like a sportscaster calling a game. Alicia was quieter, more watchful, but her smile came easily, and when she did speak, it was usually something specific and observant— "Your butterfly looks like the one on your shirt."

Mike leaned against the wall and watched the three of them. This was what he had hoped for—not just a good classroom, though the room looked great, but the feeling of Lizzie being at ease. She had friends at church, kids she had grown up seeing at family gatherings and town events, but school friends were different. School friends were the ones you sat with and whispered to and shared your crayons with, and watching his daughter slide into that so easily made the worry in him loosen up a little.

"Hello and welcome to first grade, Mr....?"

Mrs. Sullivan had finished with the family she had been speaking to and was walking toward him with a warm smile and her hand extended. She had friendly blue eyes and the kind of calm, open expression that made nervous six-year-olds and their parents feel like the world was a perfectly safe place.

"Hi," he said, shaking her hand. "Mike. Mike Hartwell. That's my daughter Lizzie over there—she's the one who has apparently already taken over your coloring station."

Mrs. Sullivan laughed, an easy, genuine sound. "I noticed that she walked in like she owned the place. I love that." She glanced at the table where Lizzie and the twins were now debating whether green or blue was a better color for a tree. "And she's already found my daughters, so she has excellent taste in friends."

"Those are your daughters?"

"Amber and Alicia," she said, nodding. "They're in Mrs. Fletcher's class this year, but they asked if they could come be my classroom helpers today, which mostly means they claimed the coloring table about an hour ago and have been holding court ever since."

Mike smiled.

"So, Lizzie's coming to us from kindergarten here at Serenity Crossing, right? Mrs. Pruitt's class?"

"That's right," Mike said. "She loved it last year. She's been counting down to first grade all summer."

"That's what I like to hear." Mrs. Sullivan smiled. "First grade is a big jump from kindergarten, especially the full-day schedule. Some kids take a week or two to adjust to the longer day, and that's completely normal. If Lizzie starts getting tired in the afternoons or seems a little overwhelmed at first, that's just her body and her brain catching up with the new routine. It usually sorts itself out pretty quickly."

"Good to know," Mike said. He hadn't thought much about the adjustment beyond the logistics—new drop-off time, new pickup time, packing a lunch instead of just a snack—but the way Mrs. Sullivan talked about it made it sound like she had walked a hundred families through this same transition and knew exactly what to expect.

"We'll do a lot of hands-on learning in this classroom," she continued, gesturing around the room. "Reading groups, math stations, art projects, science exploration—I try to keep things moving so nobody's sitting still too long, because asking a six-year-old to sit still for more than twenty minutes is asking for trouble." She said it with a wry little grin that told Mike she was speaking from experience. "And we have a reading corner over there that the kids absolutely love. That's usually where I lose them in an imaginary world for a little while."

He looked at the reading corner—the floor pillows, the low bookshelves stocked with books, and a lamp on a small table that gave the space a cozy, tucked-away feeling. He could already picture Lizzie curled up over there with a book, her legs folded underneath her the way she sat when she was really concentrating on something.

"Lizzie loves books," he said. "She's been reading everything she can get her hands on since she figured out how letters work."

"Then she and I are going to get along just fine," Mrs. Sullivan said, and the way she said it was so genuine and unhurried that Mike felt whatever last thread of new-school-year tension he had been carrying loosen and fall away. Lizzie's new teacher seemed like exactly the kind of person you wanted standing at the front of a classroom full of six-year-olds—patient, capable, kind, and clearly in love with what she did.

"Can I go say hello to Lizzie?" Mrs. Sullivan asked, tilting her head toward the table.

"Absolutely."

He watched her walk over to the three girls, and the shift was seamless—one second she was a professional having a conversation with a parent, and the next she was crouching beside the table, her voice bright and warm and pitched at exactly the right level for a six-year-old's world.

"Well, hi there," she said, and Lizzie looked up from her coloring page with a crayon in each hand. "I'm Mrs. Sullivan. I'm going to be your teacher this year. It looks like you've already met my two best helpers."

"I'm Lizzie," Lizzie said. "Amber and Alicia said you make really good pancakes."

Mrs. Sullivan looked over at Amber, who shrugged with a completely unapologetic grin. "I do make really good pancakes," she said, turning back to Lizzie with a conspiratorial smile. "Tell me something you like to do, Lizzie."

"I like drawing and coloring," Lizzie said.

"I can tell. That butterfly is beautiful."

Lizzie beamed. "It's purple and turquoise. Those are my favorite colors."

"Purple and turquoise are an excellent combination."

"That's what I said," Amber added from the next seat, nodding like this settled a matter of great importance.

Alicia leaned forward, turning her coloring page so her mom could see it. She didn't say anything, just held it up with a quiet, expectant look. Mrs. Sullivan took it in her hands and studied it with the kind of careful attention that made Alicia's whole face light up.

"Alicia, look at how you did the flowers. You kept all the colors inside the lines, and you used three different shades of pink. That takes real patience."

Alicia's smile was small and proud.

Mrs. Sullivan spent another minute with the girls, asking Lizzie about her favorite things to do at school, listening as Amber launched into a detailed explanation of why a coloring table should be a permanent fixture in every classroom, and complimenting Alicia on her color choices. She had the kind of presence that made the girls lean toward her without realizing they were doing it—warm, steady, fully present.

A new family appeared in the doorway—a mom with a little boy who was gripping a stuffed dinosaur and looking at the classroom with wide, uncertain eyes—and Mrs. Sullivan excused herself from the girls with a "You three keep creating those masterpieces" before straightening and walking back toward Mike.

"She's wonderful," Mrs. Sullivan said, stopping beside him and watching the table where Lizzie and the twins had already bent their heads back together over their coloring pages. "You can tell she feels safe in new places. That's a gift at this age."

"She comes by it honestly," Mike said. "She's never met a stranger."

"The best first graders never have." She paused and then turned to him. "Mr. Hartwell, have you had a chance to see the rest of the school yet? The cafeteria is serving cookies and lemonade, and the gym has bounce houses set up for the kids. It's worth the walk, especially if Lizzie has energy to burn."

"She always has energy to burn."

"Then the bounce houses were built for her." Mrs. Sullivan smiled. "If you have any questions before Tuesday, my email is on the welcome packet in Lizzie's cubby—the one with the little fox on the name tag."

"I'll grab that on the way out. Thank you, Mrs. Sullivan."

"Nicole," she said. "Mrs. Sullivan is for the classroom. Parents get to call me Nicole."

"Nicole," he repeated. "Thank you."

She gave him one more smile—easy, unhurried, the kind that made you believe she had all the time in the world even though there was another family waiting in the doorway—and then she turned to welcome the mom and the boy with the stuffed dinosaur, crouching down to the child's eye level before she said a single word.

Mike walked over to the coloring table and put his hand on the back of Lizzie's chair. "Hey, sweetheart. Are you ready to go see the rest of the school? I heard there are bounce houses in the gym."

Lizzie's head snapped up. "Bounce houses?"

"That's the rumor."

She was out of her chair in a flash, but then she stopped. She looked at Amber and Alicia with an expression that was equal parts excitement about bounce houses and genuine distress about leaving the coloring table.

"Will you be here when I come back?" she asked them.

Amber nodded. "We'll be here all day. Mom said we could stay the whole time."

"Okay, good. Save my seat."

"We will," Alicia said.

Lizzie grabbed Mike's hand and pulled him toward the door, already talking about how high she was going to bounce, but Mike paused at the threshold long enough to catch Nicole Sullivan's eye across the room. She was kneeling beside the nervous little boy with the dinosaur, pointing at something on the name-tag wall, and she looked up just long enough to give Mike a quick wave.

He lifted his hand in return, and then Lizzie was pulling him into the hallway, and the noise and color of the Back-to-School Bash swallowed them whole.

The school was even busier now than when they had arrived. Families streamed in both directions, some heading toward the cafeteria, following the smell of cookies that was getting harder to ignore, and others navigating the hallways with the same slightly lost expressions Mike had probably worn earlier. A couple of older kids, third or fourth graders by the look of them, raced past with lanyards bouncing against their chests, clearly on some kind of self-appointed mission. A teacher he didn't recognize waved at them from the doorway of Room 16 and called out, "Walk, please, gentlemen," with the tired affection of someone who had been saying that particular sentence for years.

Lizzie talked the entire walk to the gymnasium. She told him about the butterfly she had been coloring and about how Amber said red was the best color, but Lizzie thought purple was actually the best color. Amber said they could both be right, which Lizzie thought was very mature of her. She told him that Alicia was quiet but really good at coloring and that she kept all her colors inside the lines, which was really hard to do. She informed him that Mrs. Sullivan was nice, and that she liked the reading corner and the coloring table, and that the cubbies had animals on them.

Mike listened to all of it. He listened the way he always listened to Lizzie—with his full attention, nodding in the right places, asking follow-up questions—because her voice had been the best sound in his world for six years, and he had never once taken it for granted.

The gym was loud and bright and full of happy pandemonium that happened when you put inflatable bounce houses inside a room designed for sports. Lizzie let go of his hand and ran toward the nearest one before he could say a word, kicking off her rainbow-striped sneakers and climbing in with three other kids. She would probably know their names within five minutes.

Mike stood with his hands in his pockets, watching his daughter bounce. She was laughing, her braids flying, her whole face lit up with the simple, uncomplicated joy of being six years old and exactly where she wanted to be.

She was going to be fine. More than fine. She was going to love first grade the way she loved everything—all the way, holding nothing back.

He thought about the classroom they had just left. The reading corner with the soft pillows. The cubbies with the hand-drawn animals. The coloring table where three girls had decided within ten minutes that they were best friends.

And he thought, just for a second, that Mrs. Sullivan—Nicole—had a classroom that felt exactly the way a first-grade classroom should feel. Like it belonged to the kids the minute they walked in.

Lizzie launched herself so high in the bounce house that her braids touched the inflated ceiling, and her laughter rang out over the noise of the gym, bright and clear and fearless. Mike Hartwell stood there with his hands in his pockets and thought that first grade was going to be just fine.

Chapter 2

The peanut butter wasn't cooperating, and Mike was running ten minutes behind a schedule he'd only written down last night on the back of a receipt because his phone's calendar had felt too complicated at eleven o'clock at night.

He stood at the kitchen counter with a butter knife in one hand and a jar of creamy peanut butter in the other, trying to spread an even layer across a slice of bread without tearing a hole through the middle. The bread tore anyway. He set the knife down, pulled another slice from the bag, and started over. Lizzie sat at the kitchen table behind him, eating a bowl of cereal and talking non-stop, even though he'd only gotten her up forty-five minutes ago.

"Daddy, do you think Mrs. Sullivan will have the coloring table again today? Because Amber said they'd save my seat, but that was Saturday, and today is Tuesday, so maybe the seats are different now. Do you think the seats are different?"

"I think Mrs. Sullivan probably has a plan for where everyone sits," Mike said, carefully laying the peanut butter slice against a layer of strawberry jam on the other half. He pressed the two sides together, cut the sandwich diagonally the way Lizzie liked it, and slid it into a plastic bag. Sandwich done. He checked the mental list he'd been running since he woke up—sandwich, apple slices, a bag of Goldfish crackers, her water bottle, and a napkin with a smiley face drawn on it. He lined everything up on the counter next to her purple lunchbox and started fitting it all inside.

"But do you think Amber and Alicia will be there?"

"Well, sweetheart, here's the thing. Remember how Amber told you they're in Mrs. Fletcher's class?"

"Yeah, but that was just for Saturday. Today's the real day."

"Right, today's the real day. But they're going to be in Mrs. Fletcher's class on the real day too. That's their classroom for the whole year, just like Mrs. Sullivan's room is yours."

Lizzie's spoon stopped halfway to her mouth. A Cheerio slid off the edge and landed on the table. "But why can't they be in my class? Mrs. Sullivan is their mom."

"That's actually the reason," Mike said. He turned around and leaned against the counter so that he could face her. She was sitting in her chair with her legs swinging, wearing the outfit she'd picked out yesterday. A light blue dress with small white flowers on it, white sneakers, and a headband that she'd asked him to help her put on twice because it kept sliding back.

"When a teacher has kids at the same school where she teaches," he said, keeping his voice easy and matter-of-fact, "the school usually puts the teacher's kids in a different classroom. That way, the teacher can focus on her students during the day, and the kids get to have their own teacher, somebody who's just theirs. It wouldn't be quite the same for Amber and Alicia if their mom was also their teacher, right? They'd have to share her with the whole class."

Lizzie thought about this. She thought about it the way she thought about most things—seriously, with her eyebrows drawn together and her spoon frozen in midair, giving the idea the same weight she'd give any major life question. "I guess that makes sense," she said after a long moment. "Because if my daddy was my teacher, I'd want him to just be my daddy at school too, and that would be confusing."

Mike smiled. "Exactly."

"But I'll still see them, right?"

"You'll probably see them at lunch in the cafeteria and maybe on the playground during recess."

"Okay." She took another bite of cereal, chewing thoughtfully. "I'll find them."

He didn't doubt that for a second.

Mike turned back to the counter and zipped the lunchbox closed, then set it next to Lizzie's backpack by the front door. The backpack was light purple with a silver zipper and a little keychain of a horse that Rebecca had given her last week, and it was already packed with the school supplies from the list the school had provided. Pencils, crayons, a glue stick, a box of tissues, and a folder with pockets. He'd checked it twice last night and once more this morning, which was probably excessive, but the idea of

Lizzie showing up on her first day without something she needed bothered him more than he wanted to admit.

He glanced at the clock on the microwave as he walked back into the kitchen. Seven twenty-two. School started at eight, and the drive to Serenity Crossing Elementary took about fifteen minutes, which meant they needed to leave in the next ten to give themselves a cushion.

"All right, Lizzie girl," he said, pulling his keys off the hook by the door. "We need to get moving. Don't want to be late on day one."

She looked up from her cereal bowl with an expression of pure offense. "Daddy. I would never be late on the first day."

"Then finish that last bite and let's go."

She shoveled the remaining Cheerios into her mouth, hopped down from her chair, and carried her bowl to the sink with both hands, walking carefully so the milk wouldn't spill. Mike grabbed her lunchbox and her backpack and held the front door open while she ducked under his arm and bounded down the porch steps into the September morning.

The air had that early-fall quality that only happened in the mountains during the first week of September. Warm enough that you didn't need a jacket, cool enough that the warmth felt borrowed, like summer was still here but had already started packing its bags. The sky was clear and wide over the treeline, and somewhere in the distance, a rooster was crowing.

Lizzie climbed into the back seat of Mike's black F-150 and buckled herself in. Mike set her backpack and lunchbox on the seat beside her, checked her seatbelt, and climbed into the driver's seat. He looked in the rearview mirror and caught a glimpse of Lizzie in the back, sitting up straight with her hands folded in her lap. She had a look on her face that was equal parts excitement and the kind of focused seriousness that meant she considered this a very important day.

"Ready?" he asked.

"I've been ready since May, Daddy," she said.

He laughed and headed down the long road that wound through his property toward the main road into town.

***

The parking lot at Serenity Crossing Elementary was busier than Mike had expected. Minivans, SUVs, and pickup trucks lined the rows, and families were streaming toward the front entrance in a steady current of backpacks, lunchboxes, and children gripping their parents' hands with varying degrees of enthusiasm.

Lizzie was out of the truck and standing on the sidewalk before Mike had even locked the doors, her backpack on, her lunchbox in hand, her whole body angled toward the school like a compass needle pointing north.

"Come on, Daddy," she said, reaching for his hand and pulling him forward in a way that reminded him so much of Saturday's Back-to-School Bash that he almost laughed. The front entrance had a new banner—'Welcome Back, Serenity Crossing Stars! First Day of School!' — strung between two poles near the flagpole, and a couple of teachers he didn't recognize were standing near the doors welcoming families as they came in.

Inside, the school had the same floor-cleaner-and-fresh-paint smell from Saturday, but the energy was different now. Saturday had been a celebration, open and loose and full of bounce houses and fun. Today was real. Parents walked a little slower. Kids held their backpack straps a little tighter. The first-grade wing was buzzing with a particular kind of nervous excitement that hummed just under the surface of every conversation, every wave, every parent bending down to straighten a collar or tuck in a shirt.

Mike kept up with Lizzie as she navigated the hallway with the confidence of someone who'd already done this once and considered herself an expert. She counted the room numbers under her breath—twelve, thirteen—and when she reached the door of Room 14, she stopped.

The door was open. The classroom looked the same as it had on Saturday, but more organized, more ready—the coloring pages and sticker sheets cleared away, the tables arranged in neat clusters with blank name cards at each seat; the cubbies stocked with supplies, the reading corner waiting. A handful of kids were already inside. A few parents lingered near the doorway with the same expression Mike imagined was on his own face—pride and nervousness and something quieter underneath, something that recognized this was one of those ordinary mornings that would settle into memory.

Lizzie looked up at him. Her backpack looked enormous on her small frame, and her lunchbox dangled from one hand, and she had that look on her face—the one where her chin lifted just slightly and her eyes were bright and certain.

"I'll be fine, Daddy," she said. "You can go now."

It hit him somewhere between his chest and his throat, the way she said it. Just a six-year-old standing at the door of her classroom, telling her father with complete confidence that she was ready for this and that she had it from here.

He knelt down so he was at her level. "I know you'll be fine," he said. "I just want to make sure you've got everything you need. Lunchbox?"

She held it up.

"Backpack?"

She turned around and showed him, then turned back. "Daddy, you're being silly."

"Humor me, Lizzy… your good old dad is nervous for your first day of school. Now, do you remember where your cubby is?"

"The one with the fox on it. I checked Saturday, remember?"

"Right." He straightened up and put his hand on the top of her head, just for a second. "Okay. Go get 'em, Lizzie girl."

She grinned up at him, wide and bright, and then she turned and walked into the classroom as if she'd been doing it her entire life.

Mike stayed in the doorway. He watched her find her cubby, hang her backpack on the hook, and tuck her lunchbox onto the shelf underneath. She looked at her name tag and ran her finger over the hand-drawn letters before turning to survey the room. A group of kids was sitting on the large round carpet in the activity area near the reading corner, cross-legged and chattering. Lizzie walked over and sat down next to a boy in a green T-shirt who was showing the kid beside him something in his pencil box. Within ten seconds, she'd leaned over to look too, and whatever it was made her laugh.

She fit in, the way she always did, as naturally as water flowing in a river.

"Good morning, Mr. Hartwell."

He turned, and Nicole Sullivan was standing a few feet away with a clipboard in one hand and a coffee mug in the other, her lanyard swaying slightly as she stepped closer. She was wearing a yellow cardigan over a white blouse, and her smile was the same one from Saturday, warm and calming.

"Morning," Mike said.

She glanced past him into the classroom, her eyes moving to the circle on the carpet. "She didn't even look back, did she?"

"Not once."

Nicole's smile softened. "That's a good sign. The ones who jump right in on day one usually have the smoothest start to the school year." She paused, then looked at him with gentle steadiness. "She's going to have a wonderful day, Mr. Hartwell. I'll make sure of it."

"Mike," he said. "And I know she will."

He took one more look at the carpet. Lizzie was still talking to the boy in the green shirt, gesturing with both hands the way she did when she was explaining something she considered very important.

"All right," he said, more to himself than to Nicole. "I'll let you get on with your day."

"Have a good day, Mike... and relax... she'll be fine."

"I'm sure she will... not so sure about her daddy though," Mike said as he turned to look at Lizzie again.

The walk down the hallway felt empty without Lizzie beside him. Other parents were heading in the same direction, some in pairs, talking in low voices, and some alone with their hands in their pockets and their eyes forward. A mom near the front office was wiping her eyes with the back of her hand while her husband rubbed her shoulder. Mike looked away because he understood it and didn't need to watch someone else carry it too.

He pushed through the front doors into the September sunshine and crossed the parking lot to his truck, climbed in, pulled his door shut, and reached for the ignition.

Then he stopped.

The cab was quiet. He glanced in the rearview mirror out of habit and saw the empty back seat. The space where she normally sat, where she told him about her day and asked him questions and sang along to whatever was on the radio, was just a seat now.

Mike sat with his hands on the steering wheel and let the quiet settle around him.

This was it. This was the new shape of things. Five days a week, September through May, from the morning bell to the afternoon bell, for the next twelve years. His daughter was in a building and under someone else's care. She was fine—more than fine; she was thriving; she was probably sitting on that carpet talking to other kids she'd met this morning and laughing—and he was out here in a parking lot realizing that the part of his life that had been his normal for years, had ended.

She was growing up. She'd been growing up every day since the moment she was born, but there were mornings when it moved at a pace you could feel, and this was one of them.

Mike turned the key, let the engine rumble to life, and sat there for another moment with the truck idling, staring at the school, thinking about going back inside just to make sure she was okay.

Mike shook his head and put the truck in gear, pulled out of the parking lot, and headed toward the mill.

Chapter 3

Seventeen first graders were sitting on the carpet in front of her, cross-legged, wide-eyed, and buzzing with restless energy, and Nicole Sullivan loved every second of it.

She'd watched the last parent disappear through the doorway about four minutes ago—a dad who'd lingered near the cubbies pretending to adjust his son's backpack until Nicole had gently caught his eye and given him the smallest nod that said, *He's going to be just fine, I promise.* The dad nodded back, squeezed his son's shoulder, and left the way they all left on the first day—walking forward but looking back. Now the classroom door was closed, the hallway noise was muffled, and Room 14 belonged entirely to the seventeen children arranged in a loose semicircle on the big round carpet in the reading corner, looking up at Nicole like she was about to reveal the secret to the entire universe.

She sat down on the carpet with them, folding her legs the same way they did. She'd learned a long time ago that the fastest way to make a nervous six-year-old feel safe was to meet them at their level—literally. Standing above them was for later, when the classroom felt more like it was theirs and she was just the person who kept things running. Right now, on day one, she needed to be close enough that they could see her face and hear her voice without feeling like they were looking up at something big and unfamiliar.

"Good morning, everyone," she said, letting her voice fill the space. "My name is Mrs. Sullivan, and I'm going to be your teacher this year. Some of you I got to meet on Saturday at our Back-to-School Bash, which was so much fun, and some of you I'm meeting for the very first time today, and I'm so happy you're all here."

A few kids smiled. A boy in the front row with red hair and freckles was already fidgeting with the Velcro strap on his sneaker. A girl near the back with two long braids sat perfectly still with her hands in her lap, watching Nicole with the serious, careful attention of someone taking mental notes. Lizzie Hartwell was sitting near the middle of the group, her legs crossed and her hands on her knees, looking around at the other kids with the open, interested expression Nicole remembered from Saturday.

"So here's what we're going to do this morning," Nicole said, resting her hands on her knees and leaning forward slightly. "First, we're going to go around the circle, and everybody will have a chance to tell us a little about yourself—your name, what you like to do, maybe something that makes you smile. You don't have to if you don't feel like it, but I really hope you will, because I want to get to know every single one of you. I want you all to get to know each other, too. After that, I'm going to read a story, and then we're all going to pick which desk you'd like to sit at for the year. Sound good?"

A chorus of nods and scattered "yeahs" rippled through the group.

A hand shot up near the middle of the carpet.

"Yes, Lizzie?"

"Ms. Sullivan, where are Amber and Alicia?"

Nicole smiled. She'd been expecting this question—not specifically from Lizzie, though it didn't surprise her one bit. Amber had talked about Lizzie the entire drive home after the Back-to-School Bash, and Alicia had drawn a picture of three girls at a coloring table and taped it to the fridge.

"That's a great question," Nicole said. "Amber and Alicia are my daughters, and they're in Mrs. Fletcher's class right next door. Because I'm their mommy and also a teacher here, it's best for them to be in another teacher's classroom so they can have their own special teacher who's just for them, and so I can be the special teacher who's just for you guys. Does that make sense?"

Lizzie's face fell a little, the way a six-year-old's face falls when they're processing something disappointing but trying to be okay with it. "So they won't be in here at all?"

"Not during class time, no. But you'll see them at lunch in the cafeteria, and you'll see them on the playground during recess, and I have a feeling you three are going to find each other every single day, Lizzie."

That worked. Lizzie's expression shifted from disappointed to determined, and she nodded once like she'd already made a plan for exactly how she was going to track down Amber and Alicia the moment the cafeteria doors opened.

"Okay, Daddy said the same thing this morning." Lizzie said. "I'll find them at lunch."

"All right," she said. "So, I'll start us off this morning so you can see how this works. My name is Mrs. Sullivan. I love reading books, I love being outside, I love baking, and my favorite thing in the world is being a teacher, which is why I'm so happy to be sitting right here with all of you today." She paused and smiled at them. "See? Easy… right? Now, who wants to go first?"

About half the hands in the circle went up immediately. The other half stayed down, some tucked into laps, some wrapped around ankles, some simply waiting, watching, and deciding. Nicole noted every one of them. The kids who raised their hands would do fine. The kids who didn't were the ones she'd keep her eye on today and tomorrow and the next day, making sure they knew the room was theirs at whatever speed they needed.

"How about you?" Nicole said, pointing to the boy in the front row with the red hair and the Velcro sneakers.

The boy grinned like he'd just won a prize. "I'm Curt," he said. "I have a dog named Biscuit, and he's a beagle, and he can shake hands and roll over, and he almost caught a squirrel one time, but the squirrel was faster, and my dad said that's probably for the best."

The circle of children erupted in laughter, and Nicole grinned because Curt had delivered his introduction with the deadpan timing of someone who had no idea he was being funny.

"Curt, I love that," Nicole said. "Biscuit sounds like an amazing dog. Thank you for sharing that with us."

Curt beamed and went right back to fidgeting with his Velcro strap, perfectly content.

"Who's next?" Nicole asked, and three more hands went up. She pointed to the girl with the two long braids who'd been sitting so still and serious near the back. "How about you, sweetheart?"

The girl straightened her posture and spoke in a clear, precise voice. "My name is Sophia. I like math. I can count to a thousand, and I don't like waking up so early in the morning."

She said it as a simple fact, the same way someone might say the sky was blue, and then she folded her hands back in her lap and looked at Nicole as if to say, That will be all.

"Sophia, that's very impressive," Nicole said. "I think you and I are going to have a lot of fun with math this year."

Sophia gave a single, satisfied nod.

Nicole pointed to a boy sitting next to Lizzie, who'd been bouncing slightly on the carpet since the moment he sat down, like sitting still was something his body had strong opinions about. "How about you?"

"I'm Tyler!" he said, loud enough that the girl sitting next to him flinched and then giggled. "I like trucks, and I like dinosaurs, and my grandma makes the best biscuits in the whole wide world, and she said I could tell everybody that because it's true!"

"Tyler, I believe your grandma one hundred percent," Nicole said.

She called on three more children—a quiet girl named Maya who said she liked drawing rainbows, a boy named Jackson who told everyone he'd lost two teeth over the summer and showed the gaps to prove it, and a girl named Harper who said her family had just moved to Serenity Crossing from Nashville and she was "still figuring stuff out," which Nicole filed away as something to pay gentle attention to in the coming weeks.

"Lizzie," Nicole said. "Your turn."

Lizzie sat up a little taller, and her face broke into a wide, easy grin. "I'm Lizzie Hartwell," she said, and her voice carried through the circle with the natural confidence of a kid who'd never had a reason to be unsure of herself. "I love to draw, and I love to go fishing with my daddy, and I love playing outside, especially in the woods behind our house. I love my Daddy, and I love my Grammy and Poppa."

She paused, just for a beat, and then she added, "And my mommy is in heaven, so she's not here, but I know she still loves me."

She said it the way a child says something that is simply part of their world, not sad, not searching for a reaction, and not asking for anything. Just true. Just the shape of her life, laid out alongside the fishing and the drawing and the people she loved, because to Lizzie it all belonged in the same sentence.

Nicole kept her expression steady. She kept her smile in place and her eyes on Lizzie, and she said, "Lizzie, thank you so much for sharing that with us. It sounds like you have a wonderful family, and I know your mommy would be so proud of you."

Lizzie smiled. "She is... Daddy says so."

Nicole nodded, and then she looked to the next child in the circle, a boy named Eli who'd been holding his hand up patiently for the last thirty seconds, and said, "Eli, you're up. Tell us about yourself."

Eli launched into a detailed account of his summer camping trip, and the circle leaned in, and the morning kept going.

But Nicole's eyes drifted back to Lizzie while Eli talked.

Lizzie was watching Eli with her chin resting on her hand, engaged and attentive, perfectly fine. She hadn't said what she'd said for sympathy or attention. She'd said it because it was real and a fact and part of her normal world.

Nicole watched her, and something quiet moved through her chest.

This little girl with the easy laugh and a daddy she clearly adored was walking through the world without a mother, and she carried it so lightly that you'd never know unless she told you. She carried it the way children carry big things, folded into everything else and not separate from it. It was part of who she was, not all of who she was.

And Nicole knew exactly what that looked like, because in the classroom next door, her own daughters were sitting in Mrs. Fletcher's classroom carrying the same kind of weight at the same gentle angle.

Amber, who talked about her daddy sometimes at bedtime with a voice that went soft and careful in a way it never went at any other time. Alicia, who still kept one of Derek's old T-shirts folded under her pillow, hadn't said why and didn't need to.

Eli finished his camping story; the circle clapped, and Nicole smiled. She called on the next student, and the morning moved on, full of introductions and laughter and the slow, careful work of turning a room full of strangers into a room that belonged to all of them.

But she carried Lizzie's words with her through every minute of it, turning them over the way you turn over a stone you've picked up on a walk—not because you need it for anything, just because it fits in your hand and you aren't quite ready to set it down.

My Mommy is in heaven.

Seventeen first graders, and one of them knew something about loss already at such a young age.

Nicole called on the next child, and the next, and she smiled, and she listened, and she did what she did best—she made the room feel safe. But somewhere beneath the warmth and the professionalism and the yellow cardigan, a quiet thought had taken root, and it wasn't going anywhere.

She and Mike Hartwell had more in common than a classroom.

Chapter 4

The sidewalk in front of Serenity Crossing Elementary was shoulder-to-shoulder with parents by two-fifty in the afternoon. Mike had positioned himself near the flagpole, where he'd have a clear line of sight to the front doors and enough room that he wasn't standing in anybody's pocket.

A row of yellow school buses idled along the curb, their engines rumbling in that low, familiar way that sounded exactly the same as it had when Mike was a kid climbing onto one of them years ago. Drivers leaned out of their windows, chatting with each other or scrolling their phones, waiting for the three o'clock bell the same way the parents were.

A few moms near the bike rack were talking in a loose circle, and a dad Mike recognized from church, Tom Beckett, gave him a nod from a few yards away.

Mike nodded back and checked his watch. Two fifty-three.

The afternoon was warm, the kind of early September heat that still had summer's vibes behind it even though the calendar said fall was coming. The mountains were visible above the tree line to the east, green and layered and hazy in the distance, and the air smelled like freshly cut grass from a field behind the school where somebody had been mowing.

The bell rang at three o'clock sharp, a loud, old-fashioned buzzer that echoed through the open windows, and the front doors swung open like floodgates.

The first graders came out first, two classes walking in loose, wobbly lines led by their teachers. Mike spotted Nicole at the front of one line, guiding her students toward the sidewalk with the calm, easy authority of someone who'd done this before and could probably do it in her sleep. The other first-grade teacher walked beside the second line. Some kids peeled off toward the buses, guided by aides with clipboards. Others scanned the sidewalk for their parents, eyes wide, backpacks bouncing.

"Daddy!" Lizzie yelled as she broke from the line and ran toward him across the grass. Her purple backpack thumping against her shoulders with every stride, her entire face was lit up with a grin. She hit him at full speed, wrapping her arms around his waist, and he caught her with one hand on her backpack and the other on the back of her head.

"Hey, Lizzie girl. How was your day?"

She pulled back and looked up at him with eyes that were practically vibrating. "It was the best day ever."

He laughed, took her hand, and they started walking toward the truck. The parking lot was a slow-moving river of minivans and SUVs, parents waving at each other through windshields, kids climbing into back seats with their lunchboxes and the crumpled artwork they'd made that day. Mike's truck was parked near the back row, and Lizzie talked the entire walk there without pausing to breathe.

"We picked our desks, and I sit by Tyler; he's really funny, and we did reading groups, and Mrs. Sullivan read us a book about a bear who goes to school, and it was so good, Daddy, and then we did art, and I drew a picture of our cabin, and Mrs. Sullivan said it was beautiful, and she put it on the wall, Daddy. She put it right on the wall where everybody can see it— "

"That's great, sweetheart."

"—and then at lunch I found Amber and Alicia, Daddy. I found them in the cafeteria just like you said, and we sat together at the same table, and Amber said we should sit together every day, and I said yes, and then at recess we played on the monkey bars, and Alicia can do four in a row without stopping, and I can do three, but I'm going to practice— "

She stopped walking. Mike looked down at her.

"Daddy," she said with sudden gravity. "I want to ride the school bus."

That caught him off guard. He'd assumed that he'd just keep driving her to school and picking her up, the same way he'd done for kindergarten.

"The school bus?" he said.

"Most of the other kids ride it. Tyler rides it, and Curt rides it, and Sophia rides it, and they said it's so much fun, and you get to sit with your friends."

He opened the back door of the truck, and she climbed in, swinging her backpack off and dropping it on the seat beside her before buckling herself in. Mike stood in the open doorway and looked at her.

"You really want to ride the bus?"

"Yes... more than anything. Please, Daddy?"

He wasn't sure why such a small thing hit him so hard in the chest. It was a school bus. Kids rode them every day. But somewhere in the back of his mind, the image of Lizzie climbing the steps of a yellow bus and disappearing into a seat where he couldn't see her face felt like one more piece of life that was moving just a little faster than he was ready for.

"All right," he said. "We can try it. But you'll need to get up a few minutes earlier in the morning because the bus comes at a set time, and if we're not at the end of the road when it gets there, it's not going to wait."

"I'll get up earlier."

"We'll see about that on a cold morning in November."

She grinned as if she'd won a negotiation, which Mike realized she had.

He closed her door, climbed into the driver's seat, and pulled out of the parking lot while Lizzie picked up right where she'd left off—telling him about the weather chart on the wall and the reading corner and how Ms. Sullivan let them pick their own books during quiet time and she'd picked one about a horse, which was the best book in the whole corner, and did he know that Amber and Alicia live on a farm?

"I didn't know that," Mike said, turning onto the two-lane road that led out of town toward his parents' house.

"They do. They live with their grandma and grandpa on a real farm with animals and everything. Amber said they have horses and goats and chickens and dogs, and two cats."

"That sounds like quite a farm."

"It's a sanc... sancchew... or something like that," Lizzie said. "That means the animals live there because they need a happy home."

"Sanctuary, Lizzie, you almost had it."

She was quiet for about three seconds, which was a record, and then: "Daddy, can I tell Grammy and Poppa about my day when we get there?"

"I think they're counting on it."

The drive from town to the Hartwell homestead took about twelve minutes on the winding road that climbed gradually through the foothills, the pavement narrowing from two lanes to one and a half as the trees closed in on both sides. Mike had driven this road so many times he could do it by feel—the curve past the old Dawson mailbox, the dip where the creek ran under a culvert, the long straightaway before the turnoff that led to his parents' property. The mountains rose ahead of them, green and solid and unhurried, the way they'd been rising for as long as anyone could remember.

He turned onto their drive and followed it through a corridor of hardwoods and pines until the trees opened up and the Hartwell homestead came into view—his parents' home, a large modern log cabin that sat on cleared acres of landscaped property with the mountains stacked up behind it like a painting somebody had hung on the world's biggest wall. The wrap-around porch stretched across three sides of the house, and the old red barn sat off to the left near the tree line.

Mike had barely put the truck in park when his mom, Olivia Hartwell, stepped onto the porch with a dish towel over one shoulder and a smile that could've lit up the whole valley. Lizzie had her seatbelt unbuckled and the back door open before Mike had even turned off the engine. She hit the ground running and took the porch steps two at a time—which was impressive given that her legs were about two feet long—and threw herself into her grandmother's arms.

"Grammy!"

"There's my girl," Olivia said, catching her granddaughter and pulling her into a hug that lifted Lizzie's sneakers off the porch boards. "Tell me all about your first day of big girl school."

Mike climbed out of the truck and walked toward the porch while Lizzie launched into what promised to be a very long and very detailed account of every single thing that had happened between eight o'clock this morning and three o'clock this afternoon. Olivia listened with her full attention, her hands on Lizzie's shoulders, her face reflecting every emotion Lizzie's face showed. She was fifty-seven years old, with silver threading through her brown hair.

She'd spent twenty years as an elementary school teacher before retiring three years ago, which meant she knew exactly what the first day of first grade felt like from every possible angle.

She caught Mike's eye over the top of Lizzie's head and smiled at him while Lizzie continued talking.

Mike smiled back and followed them inside.

The Hartwell home was the kind of house that felt like a hug the minute you walked through the door. The big kitchen opened directly into the family room in an open-concept design that Olivia had insisted on when they'd built the place twenty-five years ago, back when six kids running in different directions meant you needed to see everything from one spot. The walls were covered with family photos, decades of Christmases, graduations, fishing trips, Sunday dinners, and her only grandchild, Lizzie, in various stages of joy. The furniture was comfortable and meant for use, not for display. A pot of coffee sat on the counter, as always. And Olivia had already set out a plate of apple slices with peanut butter and a glass of milk on the kitchen table.

Bill Hartwell was standing at the counter, pouring himself a cup of coffee when they walked in.

Mike's dad was the kind of man whose presence filled a room without making any noise about it. He was fifty-eight, broad-shouldered and solid, with hands that had run the Hartwell Lumber Mill for over thirty years and managed two hundred acres of mountain property on top of it. His hair had gone mostly gray at the temples, and he wore the same thing he wore every day—work boots, jeans, and a flannel shirt with the sleeves rolled to the elbows.

He didn't talk much. He didn't need to. When Bill Hartwell spoke, people listened, because he'd spent a lifetime making sure his words were worth hearing.

"Poppa!" Lizzie ran to him, and Bill set his coffee down just in time to scoop her up with one arm, holding her against his side like she weighed nothing.

"Hey, little bit," he said, and his voice was low and warm in that quiet way of his. "Heard you had a big day."

"The biggest day," Lizzie said, and she was off again—telling Bill about the reading corner and the art wall and the monkey bars and Tyler's grandma's biscuits and everything in between. Bill listened patiently, nodding in the right places, his eyes crinkling at the corners when something she said struck him as funny, which was often.

He set her down at the table in front of Olivia's snack, and Lizzie ate apple slices and talked at the same time. Mike pulled out a chair across from her and sat down. Olivia brought him a cup of coffee and settled into the chair beside him.

Bill leaned against the counter with his own mug and watched the scene with the quiet contentment of a man who understood that the people in this house were the only things that mattered.

"And then," Lizzie said, dipping an apple slice into the peanut butter with the focus of a surgeon, "at recess, I played with my two best friends. Amber and Alicia. They're twins, and they're in Mrs. Fletcher's class, but we ate lunch together, and we played together at recess, and their mommy is my teacher."

Olivia's eyebrows rose. "Their mommy is your teacher? That's fun. Tell me about your new friends."

"They're the best," Lizzie said. "Amber talks a lot, like me, and she's really funny, and Alicia is quiet, but she's really good at coloring, and she can do four monkey bars in a row. They live on a farm with their grandma and grandpa, and they have horses and goats, chickens, and a donkey too."

"That does sound like a wonderful farm," Olivia said.

"It's a sanctuary," Lizzie said proudly. "And guess what, Grammy? Amber and Alicia are like me."

"What do you mean, sweetheart?" Olivia asked.

"They have a mommy, but their daddy is in heaven. So they don't have a daddy, and I don't have a mommy, and Amber said that makes us the same kind of special."

The kitchen was quiet for a second. The coffee pot clicked on the counter. Somewhere outside, a bird called from the direction of the barn.

Mike stared at his daughter. He'd known, in a distant and theoretical way, that some other kids out there in the community had lost a parent. He'd talked to Lizzie about it more than once—gently, carefully, always following her lead—and she'd always handled it with the same open, uncomplicated honesty that seemed to be woven into who she was. But hearing her say it like this, hearing that Nicole Sullivan's daughters were walking through the same world as Lizzie was walking through, from the other side of the same kind of loss—that landed somewhere deep in his chest and hurt.

Olivia looked at Mike. Just a glance, just a second, but it carried years of motherhood in it. Then she looked back at Lizzie.

"Honey, what's your teacher's name again?"

"Mrs. Sullivan."

Olivia nodded slowly. "And what's her first name? Do you know?"

"Nicole. She told Daddy to call her Nicole on Saturday."

Olivia's eyes came back to Mike, and this time they stayed. "Mike, do you know who Nicole Sullivan is?"

"Lizzie's teacher."

"She's Adam and Tabitha Hanshaw's daughter, Mike. The vet and the animal sanctuary out on Ridge Road. Those are her parents."

Mike knew of the Hanshaws by reputation and from church. Adam Hanshaw was one of two veterinarians in the area, and his wife, Tabitha, ran the animal sanctuary. He hadn't connected the Hanshaws to Nicole Sullivan because of the difference in last names.

"You've probably seen her at church," Olivia said.

"I don't remember seeing her at church."

"Well, she's been there, son, for the past couple of months. Tabitha told me Nicole moved back to Serenity Crossing in June. She's been living with her parents since then." Olivia paused. "She lost her husband some time ago. I don't know all the details, but Tabitha mentioned it when Nicole first moved back. She's raising those two girls on her own."

Mike looked at his coffee and didn't say anything as he processed this new information. His mom was watching him with the gentle, careful expression she wore when she was letting her children process something at their own speed.

"Daddy," Lizzie said, pulling him back to the table with the unerring instinct children have for choosing the exact moment an adult has drifted too far into their own head. "I forgot to tell you the most important part."

"What's the most important part?"

"Amber and Alicia said their grandma is going to teach them to ride a horse. A real horse. And they said maybe I could come too." She looked at him with the kind of hope that was so big it barely fit on her face. "Daddy, can I learn to ride a horse? Can I please, please, please learn to ride a horse?"

Mike opened his mouth and then closed it again because the number of new things that had come at him in the last thirty minutes was starting to stack up in a way that made his head swim. His daughter's teacher was a widow. Lizzie's new best friends had lost their father. His daughter wanted to ride the school bus. And now she wanted to learn to ride a horse.

"What if you get hurt?" he said, because it was the only thing his brain could find.

"I won't get hurt."

"You don't know that."

"Poppa," Lizzie said, turning to Bill with the instinct of someone who knew exactly when to bring in reinforcements. "Tell Daddy I won't get hurt."

Bill took a slow sip of his coffee. "Can't promise that, little bit. But I can tell you I learned to ride when I was about your age, and I turned out all right."

"See?" Lizzie said, as if that settled everything.

Olivia put her hand on Mike's arm. "It couldn't hurt to give Tabitha a call," she said. "If she's teaching her granddaughters to ride, she might be happy to have one more."

Mike looked at his mom, then his dad, and then Lizzie, who was gripping the edge of the table with both hands and staring at him with an expression that suggested his answer to this question might be the most consequential decision he'd ever make.

"I'll call," he said. "But I'm not making any promises. Mrs. Hanshaw might not want to take on another student."

"She will," Lizzie said with breezy confidence. "Amber and Alicia said their grandma teaches all kinds of people to ride horses. And they have goats, Daddy. And chickens. I want to meet all of them."

Mike leaned back in his chair and rubbed a hand over his face. This morning, his biggest concern had been getting peanut butter on a piece of bread without tearing it. In the span of eight hours, his daughter had informed him he could leave at the door to her classroom, requested a change in transportation, learned her new best friends were without a daddy, and asked to learn an entirely new skill involving an animal that weighed a thousand pounds.

He looked at his mom, who was watching him with the kind of smile that mothers get when they can see something their children can't yet—the shape of what's coming and the puzzle pieces of life fitting together and growing bigger.

"Welcome to first grade, son," she said.

Bill chuckled and didn't say a word.

Chapter 5

The Hanshaw farm sat at the end of Ridge Road on fifteen acres of rolling green pasture that backed up against the tree line at the base of the foothills. Mike pulled his F-150 into the gravel parking area beside a white fence just before two o'clock on Saturday afternoon with Lizzie in the back seat, who hadn't stopped talking about horses since Tuesday.

The property was nicer than he'd expected, which probably said more about his expectations than the farm itself. A modest farmhouse sat up on a gentle rise—white clapboard, green shutters, a wide front porch with hanging baskets of purple and yellow flowers—and a large red barn stood to the right, connected to a fenced riding ring by a gated path. Beyond the ring, the pastures stretched out in sections divided by white rail fencing, and Mike could see animals scattered across the fields. A few horses grazing near a water trough, a cluster of goats bunched together under the shade of an oak tree, and what looked like a donkey standing by itself near the far fence, watching the truck with mild interest.

The air smelled like hay and something earthy underneath—the honest smell of a working farm on a September afternoon. The sun was high and warm, and the mountains rose behind the property like a postcard somebody had tucked behind the barn.

"Daddy, I see horses," Lizzie said.

"I see them too."

"There are two. No, three. There's one behind the barn, I think. Can I get out?"

He'd barely said yes before she was unbuckled and out the door, her sneakers hitting the gravel at a run. She was wearing jeans and a T-shirt and the boots his mom had bought for her. Olivia had insisted that you didn't learn to ride a horse in sneakers, and Mike had learned a long time ago not to argue with his mother.

A woman was walking toward them from the direction of the barn. She was tall and sun-weathered, with dark hair streaked with gray that was pulled back in a loose ponytail. She wore jeans, work boots, and a denim shirt with the sleeves rolled up, and she moved with the unhurried confidence of someone who'd spent most of her life around animals and wide-open spaces. Mike recognized her as Tabitha Hanshaw as she got closer.

"Mike, good to see you," Tabitha said, extending her hand with a warm, direct smile. "Lizzie, are you ready for your big riding lesson?"

Lizzie looked up at her with wide eyes. "Are you Amber and Alicia's grandma?"

"I sure am. And they've been waiting for you all morning. They're in the barn with their mama right now, helping me get Clover ready."

"Who's Clover?"

"She's the sweetest mare you'll ever meet, and she's going to be your teacher today as well."

Lizzie turned to Mike with an expression that suggested this was the single greatest moment of her entire life, and he put his hand on her shoulder and said, "Ready to learn to ride a horse, sweet pea?"

"Yes, Daddy... a million... No, a trillion times yes!"

Tabitha led them toward the barn, and Mike fell into step beside her while Lizzie ran ahead, her boots scuffing the gravel with every step. The barn doors were open wide, and as they got closer, Mike could hear voices inside—a woman's voice, warm and familiar, and the high, chattering sounds of children.

Nicole was standing in the center aisle of the barn near a stall where a chestnut mare stood patiently while two small hands brushed her neck. Amber was on a step stool, working a soft brush across the horse's coat with enthusiastic strokes that probably did more rearranging of the hair than actual grooming. Alicia stood to the side, holding a brush and watching her sister's technique with the careful, observational expression Mike remembered from the coloring table last Saturday.

Nicole was wearing jeans and a flannel shirt. Her hair was pulled back in a ponytail, and she looked up and smiled when they walked in.

"Hey there," she said. "Right on time."

"We've been ready since six this morning. Lizzie dragged me out of bed because she was so excited," Mike said.

Nicole laughed. "Mine were up at five-thirty."

"There should be a law against waking up that early on a weekend," he said with a grin.

Lizzie was staring at Clover with the kind of reverence most people reserved for Christmas morning. "She's so pretty."

Amber spun around on the step stool so fast she nearly toppled off it. "Lizzie!"

And just like that, the barn filled up with chatter and giggles, the sounds of three six-year-olds who were about to learn to ride a horse and considered this the most important event in recorded history.

Tabitha took charge of the lesson with calm, easy authority. She led Clover out to the riding ring and spent the first ten minutes just letting the girls stand near the horse, touch her, and learn where to put their hands and where not to. She showed them how to approach from the side, how to keep their voices steady, and how to read Clover's ears to know if she was relaxed or alert. Mike watched from behind the fence as all three girls listened with intense focus.

Lizzie went first. Tabitha helped her up into the saddle, adjusted the stirrups, and showed her how to hold the reins—not tight, just steady, like holding a friend's hand. Then Tabitha walked beside her, one hand on the lead rope, guiding Clover in slow, wide circles around the ring. Lizzie sat up straight in the saddle with a look on her face that Mike would remember for the rest of his life. Part thrill, part concentration, and part pure, uncomplicated joy of a child doing something she'd dreamed about doing.

He leaned forward on the fence rail as Nicole appeared beside him, settling her arms on the top rail about two feet to his left.

"She's a natural," Nicole said, nodding toward Lizzie.

"She's fearless," Mike said. "Which is wonderful unless you're the one responsible for keeping her in one piece."

Nicole smiled. "I know exactly what you mean. Amber tried to climb on Clover by herself last weekend before Mom was ready, and I aged about ten years in three seconds."

They watched Tabitha guide Lizzie through a second loop around the ring, then gently bring Clover to a stop so Lizzie could dismount and Amber could take her turn. Amber climbed up with bold energy, gripping the saddle horn and announcing, "I'm ready," before Tabitha had even finished adjusting the stirrups.

"How's the first week of school treating you?" Mike asked.

"Good," Nicole said. "Busy. The first week is always a sprint, honestly. Getting seventeen six-year-olds into a routine when half of them have been running wild all summer takes some doing." She smiled. "But I love it. Every year it takes me about a week to remember why I chose this job, and then by the second week I can't imagine doing anything else."

"This is your first time teaching at Serenity Crossing Elementary, right?"

"First year here, yes. I taught second grade in Maryville before I moved back in June. What about you? How's the adjustment going with Lizzie being in school full-time now?"

He thought about that for a second. "Honestly? It's been a bigger change than I expected. Not for her—she's taken to it like she was born for it. For me." He leaned further on the rail and watched Amber trot past on Clover, waving at them with one hand, while Tabitha called out, "Both hands on the reins, sweetheart," with the practiced tone of someone who'd said it a thousand times. "I rearranged my whole schedule at the lumber mill this week. She wanted to ride the school bus, which she informed me about approximately thirty seconds after I picked her up from school on Tuesday. So now she takes the bus in the morning, and the bus drops her off at the mill in the afternoon. She hangs out with me there for an hour or so until we head home."

"She rides the bus to the mill?"

"Yep. I just had to call the school administration office and get it all set up. The stop's right at the entrance. So now Lizzie gets off the bus, walks into the office, and does her homework at the conference table while I finish up for the day." He paused. "She's actually reorganized the pencil cup on my desk. Twice. She's filled my office notes board with about 20 different pages of her schoolwork, and she's decided that she's now my secretary's assistant."

Nicole laughed. "I can just picture that."

"I give her another week, and she'll be scheduling lumber deliveries."

They fell into the easy rhythm of two people who had enough in common to keep a conversation going without effort. Nicole told him about the reading groups she'd set up in her classroom and how Lizzie had already finished three books from the reading corner in the first week, which didn't surprise Mike at all. He told her about the morning routine he was still figuring out—how he'd burned the toast Thursday because he had been focusing on ironing her shirt, and how Lizzie had looked at the blackened bread and said, "Daddy, that's not toast anymore, that's charcoal," with the deadpan delivery of a forty-year-old comedian.

Nicole told him about Amber's latest declaration that she was going to be a veterinarian like her grandpa when she grew up, and how Alicia had quietly corrected her by saying "you said that last week about being an astronaut," which had resulted in Amber deciding she would be an astronaut veterinarian who took care of animals in space. Mike told her about Lizzie's ongoing campaign to convince him that they needed a dog, which had been going on for a year now and showed no signs of slowing down.

None of it was remarkable. None of it was heavy. It was just two parents standing at a fence rail on a Saturday afternoon, watching their kids learn to ride a horse and talking about the ordinary things that made up their ordinary lives. The sun warmed the fence rail under Mike's arms. Hay dust floated in the air near the barn. The mountains sat green and steady in the distance. And the conversation kept going the way good conversations did—without anyone steering it.

At one point, while Alicia was taking her turn in the saddle and Tabitha was walking beside her with steady encouragement, Nicole was telling Mike about the classroom pet she was thinking about getting—a hamster, maybe, or a fish tank—and she tucked a loose strand of hair behind her ear while she talked, a small gesture that she probably didn't even notice. Mike noticed, though—just for a second, just enough to register that Lizzie's teacher looked different out here than she did in a classroom. More relaxed. Less careful. Like the flannel shirt and the ponytail were closer to who she actually was than the cardigans and the lanyard.

He filed the observation away and turned his attention back to the riding ring. Alicia was sitting perfectly still in the saddle with her hands in exactly the right position and her back straight. Her face wore an expression of such quiet, focused contentment that Tabitha looked over at Nicole and mouthed, "She's a natural."

The lesson lasted about an hour, and by the end, all three girls had ridden multiple times around the ring with Tabitha. They'd learned how to mount and dismount and how to signal a stop, all of which they did with a seriousness that suggested they considered it a sacred duty. When Tabitha finally said, "All right, ladies, that's our lesson for today," the three of them ran straight for Mike and Nicole at the fence.

"Daddy, did you see me? Did you see me ride all by myself?" Lizzie grabbed the fence rail with both hands and looked up at him, her cheeks flushed, hay in her hair, and her boots covered in dust.

"I saw every minute of it."

"Can I stay and play? Please? Amber said they have baby goats, and I haven't met them yet, and Alicia said there's a donkey named Earl, and he's really sweet, and —"

"Please, Mr. Hartwell?" Amber said, appearing beside Lizzie at the fence with the seamless solidarity of a co-conspirator.

Alicia stood slightly behind her sister, her eyes on Mike with the quiet, hopeful intensity of someone who'd learned that sometimes the best strategy was to let other people do the talking and just look as sincere as possible.

It was devastatingly effective.

Mike opened his mouth to say something about how they had plans—because they did, sort of, in the vague Saturday-afternoon way that fishing counted as plans—but before he could form the words, Nicole stepped in.

"Girls, I'm sure Lizzie and her daddy have things to do this afternoon. You can't just put people on the spot like that."

"But we don't have plans," Lizzie said, turning to Mike with cheerful honesty. "We were just going to go fishing, and you always say we can fish any old time."

He'd said that. More than once. And now his own words were being used against him by a six-year-old negotiator with hay in her hair and two pairs of puppy-dog eyes backing her up.

Nicole looked at him with an apologetic half-smile. "Mike, truly, if you had plans, please don't feel like — "

"We didn't really have plans," he said.

"Lizzie's welcome to stay and play this afternoon. I was just go-ing to have a fun day with the girls around the farm anyway—play with the baby goats, check on Earl, and maybe see if the chickens laid any eggs. Nothing fancy, just fun."

Three small faces turned to him in unison.

Mike looked at the three of them—his daughter and her two best friends, dusty and flushed and vibrating with energy—and he realized that saying no would require a level of heartlessness he simply didn't possess.

"I'll stay too," he said. "If that's all right. I'd like to see the farm myself."

"Of course," Nicole said. "The more, the merrier."

Tabitha had walked up while they'd been talking, her gloves tucked into her back pocket and Clover's lead rope coiled over her arm. "I'm going to get Clover settled and check on the back pasture," she said, looking at Nicole. "Sounds like you have an adventure planned for this afternoon. You good if I leave you to the farm tour? Or would you rather I came along?"

"We're fine, Mom," Nicole said. "Go check on your animals. We'll manage."

Tabitha smiled and headed toward the barn with Clover walking calmly beside her.

Nicole turned to the three girls, who were standing in a tight cluster of barely contained excitement, and put her hands on her hips with the theatrical seriousness of someone about to announce a mission of great importance. "All right, ladies. Where do we start? The donkey or the goats?"

"Goats!" all three of them yelled at the same time, and then they were off, running toward the pasture gate with the kind of speed that suggested the baby goats had approximately ten seconds before their quiet afternoon was over.

Nicole jogged after them, calling, "Wait at the gate, please," in her teacher voice, and Mike stood by the fence and watched them go—four figures crossing the green pasture in the warm September sun, three small and fast and one taller and steady, all of them headed toward a cluster of goats who had no idea what was coming.

He stood there for a second longer than he needed to, his hands on the warm fence rail, taking in the whole picture. His daughter was on a farm with her new best friends and their mother, who happened to be her teacher, who happened to be someone he'd been having an easy conversation with for the better part of an hour without a single awkward pause.

This was new territory. All of it. The riding lessons. The Saturday afternoon at someone else's home. He had been standing at a fence talking to a woman he barely knew about burned toast and bus schedules while their daughters learned to ride a horse. Mike's world had always been the mill, the cabin, his parents' home, and church. Lizzie's friends had always been the kids she saw at family gatherings or after the Sunday service—church families, the same circle they'd orbited since she was born.

This was something else. This was playdates and coordinating schedules with another parent. This was his daughter's world expanding past the edges of his own, pulling him into spaces he'd never had reason to enter and conversations he'd never had reason to have.

He pushed off the fence and followed them toward the goats.

Somewhere between the riding ring and the pasture gate, it occurred to him that this was probably just the beginning.

Chapter 6

The baby goats were one week old and approximately the size of house cats. All three girls were sitting cross-legged on the straw-covered floor of the goat pen with one tiny animal in each lap, their faces wearing identical expressions of complete and total wonder.

Nicole leaned against the gate beside Mike and watched the scene unfold. The goat pen was inside the barn, a roomy stall with clean straw, a water trough, and a low wooden feeding rack along one wall. Five adult goats milled around the space: three Nubians with long, floppy ears and two smaller Pygmy goats that Tabitha had rescued from a farm in western Tennessee last spring. Her mom had been very hands-on with the baby Nubian goats since they'd been born, and they were so accustomed to humans that they climbed into any available lap the moment someone sat down.

"This one's licking me," Lizzie said, giggling as the smallest baby goat nuzzled its nose against her palm and then proceeded to nibble on her fingers with soft, toothless gums. "Is this okay? Is she eating me?"

"She's not eating you," Nicole said. "She's tasting you. Baby goats explore everything with their mouths, kind of like human babies do."

"Grandma says they like the salty taste of our skin," Amber announced. The baby goat in her lap had climbed up her chest and was standing on her shoulder, its tiny hooves pressing into her shirt. She was holding it with both hands and looking at Nicole with a grin that said she considered this the greatest achievement of her life. "She thinks I'm a mountain, Mommy."

"You probably are a mountain to a baby goat," Alicia said from where she was sitting perfectly still with the third baby goat curled in her lap, its eyes half-closed, its little body tucked against her stomach. Alicia had a way with animals that Nicole had noticed since the day they'd moved to the farm—she didn't grab or chase or squeal the way most kids did. She sat still and let them come to her, and they always did.

Mike was watching Lizzie with the expression of a parent who was seeing a new experience his child was enjoying and didn't want to miss a second of it. He'd stepped inside the pen when the girls had, crouching down to let one of the adult goats sniff his hand before it lost interest and wandered back to the feeding rack. Nicole could tell he wasn't entirely sure what to do with himself in here—he stepped carefully around the straw, treating the whole space with respectful caution, not entirely certain how the rules of life applied to baby farm animals.

But he was rolling with it. She'd give him that.

"Daddy, I want one," Lizzie said, looking up at Mike with the baby goat still licking her hand.

"Nope."

"But she loves me."

"She loves everybody. She's a week old. Her standards are very low."

Nicole pressed her lips together to keep from laughing, because the delivery had been so dry and so immediate that it caught her off guard. Lizzie didn't seem offended. She just looked back at the goat and whispered, "He doesn't mean it," into its ear, and Nicole had to turn away for a second so nobody saw her laughing.

They spent another ten minutes in the goat pen before Nicole led them out through the barn toward the fenced paddock where Earl lived. Earl was a donkey who'd come to the sanctuary two years ago when his elderly owner had passed away and the family hadn't known what to do with him. He was gray and stocky and one of the most patient animals on the property.

"This is Earl," Nicole said, opening the paddock gate and waving them through. Earl stood near the fence post, chewing slowly, watching them with his soft brown eyes and his enormous ears tilted slightly forward.

Lizzie approached him from the side, slowly, with her hand out and her voice calm. "Hi, Earl. I'm Lizzie."

Earl blinked at her. Then he lowered his head and nudged his nose against her palm, and Lizzie's face lit up like someone had plugged her into a wall socket.

"He likes me."

"Earl likes everybody," Amber said, walking up to the donkey and wrapping her arms around his neck in a hug that Earl tolerated with the patience of a saint. "But he especially likes treats. Mom, did you bring treats?"

"I didn't bring treats," Nicole said. "You can give him some hay from the rack over there."

All three girls went to the hayrack and pulled out handfuls. Earl accepted every offering with the slow, dignified chewing of an animal who understood that this was his kingdom and these children were guests.

Mike stood beside Nicole at the paddock fence, his arms resting on the top rail. "How many animals does your mom have out here?"

"It changes," Nicole said. "Right now we've got six horses, four miniature horses, the goat, Earl, chickens, two barn dogs, and my mom's house dog, a golden retriever named Sunny. Some of the animals are permanent residents, like Earl. He's too old to be re-homed, and he's happy here, so he stays. A couple of the horses are boarders. The miniature horses were all rescues—people bought them thinking they'd be easy pets and then realized minia-ture doesn't mean low-maintenance. The barn dogs are Hank and Rosie, both older dogs. Both of them just showed up one day, actually. Walked out of the woods and sat down in front of the barn like they'd scheduled an appointment."

"And your mom just kept him."

"My mom has never turned away an animal in her life. Or a person, for that matter."

Mike smiled at that, a small, easy smile. "Sounds a lot like my mom."

"From what I've heard about your mom, I'd say they're cut from the same cloth."

They moved on from Earl's paddock toward the horse pasture, where six horses grazed in the late-afternoon sun. Clover, whom the girls already knew from the riding lesson, along with two older quarter horses named Rusty and Belle, a Tennessee Walker named Jasper, and two younger mares that were boarding while their owner was overseas for work. The four miniature horses occupied a separate fenced area next to the main pasture, and when the girls saw them, the reaction was immediate and loud.

"They're so tiny!" Lizzie said, pressing her face against the fence. The minis were grazing near the water trough, compact and round and roughly the height of a large dog, with thick manes that hung over their eyes. "Are they babies?"

"They're fully grown," Nicole said. "They're miniature horses. They'll stay this size forever."

"Forever?" Lizzie said as she turned to Mike. "Daddy, these could fit in our cabin."

"We're not putting a horse in the cabin."

"But they're little."

"Still no."

Nicole watched the exchange and bit the inside of her cheek to keep a straight face. Mike caught her eye and shook his head slowly, the expression of a man who'd been fielding impossible requests from his daughter all afternoon and was running out of diplomatic ways to say no. She gave him a look that said, Welcome to my world, and turned back to the girls.

After the miniature horses, they walked the path that looped behind the barn toward the chicken coop—a sturdy wooden structure with a fenced run that her dad had built the year Nicole's mom decided she wanted fresh eggs. A dozen hens scratched and clucked inside the run, and a large rooster named Captain sat on top of the coop, watching everything with the suspicious, territorial expression of an animal who took his job very seriously.

"Can we go in?" Amber asked.

"You can, but watch out for Captain. He gets cranky."

All three girls entered through the gate, and within thirty seconds Alicia had found two eggs in the nesting boxes and was holding them up carefully with both hands, her face glowing. Amber was trying to catch a hen that clearly didn't want to be caught. Lizzie was standing very still near the fence, watching Captain with the cautious respect of someone who'd correctly identified the one animal on this farm that might not be friendly.

"He won't bother you unless you bother him," Nicole said.

"I'm not going to bother him," Lizzie said, without taking her eyes off the rooster. "I'm going to stay right here, and he's going to stay right there, and we're going to have a good long talk."

Mike laughed out loud at that—a real, full laugh that Nicole heard over the clucking and the scratching and Amber's ongoing negotiation with the hen. It was the kind of laugh that came from somewhere genuine, the sound of a man who was completely amused by his daughter and not trying to hide it.

As if on cue, Hank and Rosie appeared from around the corner of the barn—two old dogs, one a scruffy brown mutt with a graying muzzle and the other a black Lab mix with a limp in her back left leg, both of them moving at the unhurried pace of animals who'd earned the right to take their time. They sniffed Mike's boots, accepted a scratch behind the ears from Nicole, and then padded toward the chicken coop to supervise the girls with the seasoned disinterest of dogs who'd seen it all.

The last stop was the veterinary building—a small, clean structure at the far end of the property that her dad used for his mobile practice and for treating the sanctuary animals. Nicole led them through the front door into the small reception area, which smelled of antiseptic, hay, and coffee, and her dad was at the desk with his reading glasses on, writing in a chart.

Adam Hanshaw looked up when they walked in, and his face broke into the easy, comfortable smile of a man who spent his days with animals and liked people just fine too. He was tall and lean, with dark hair going gray at the temples.

"Well, hey there," he said, standing up and pulling off his glasses. "I was wondering when the tour would make it over here."

"I see you talked to Mom... Dad, this is Mike Hartwell. I'm not sure if you two have met before," Nicole said. "And his daughter, Lizzie, who's in my class this year."

"Mike." Adam extended his hand, and the handshake between them had the comfortable familiarity of two men who'd been in the same church for years. "Good to see you. I think we've waved at each other about a hundred times but haven't gotten the chance to talk much lately, just passing hello."

"That sounds about right," Mike said. "I think the last time we chatted was at the Christmas potluck last year, and I'm pretty sure your wife's green bean casserole made my mom jealous."

Adam laughed. "Don't tell Tabitha that. She'll make it every Sunday for the rest of the year."

Lizzie was already exploring the space, looking at the framed photos on the wall—Adam with various animals, a horse, a calf, a parrot that was sitting on his shoulder in one picture—and the glass cabinet of veterinary supplies. She examined everything with the focused curiosity of a child who'd just discovered an entirely new category of interesting things.

"Mr. Hanshaw, do you take care of all the animals on the farm?" Lizzie asked.

"Every single one of them," Adam said. "And about half the animals in the county, if I'm being honest."

"Even Captain?"

"Especially Captain. He's my most difficult patient."

Lizzie nodded solemnly, as though this confirmed everything she'd already suspected about the rooster.

They visited for a few minutes longer, Adam showing Lizzie and Mike the exam room and telling them about the mare he'd treated that morning for a sore hoof, before the girls began to orbit the door with the particular fidgety energy that meant they were done standing still and ready to move.

"Mom," Amber said, tugging on Nicole's sleeve. "Can we go play on the swing set?"

"Lizzie," Alicia said, turning to her with those quiet, hopeful eyes. "We have a swing set behind the house. Grandma and Grandpa built it. It has four swings and a slide, and it's really fun."

Lizzie looked at Mike.

"Go ahead," he said.

The three of them were out the door in a flash, their voices echoing across the yard as they ran toward the farmhouse. Nicole and Mike followed at a pace that suggested neither of them was in any hurry, walking side by side along the gravel path that curved past the barn and the garden and around the house to the backyard.

The swing set was a solid wooden structure that her parents had built the month after Nicole and the girls had moved in—four swings, a slide, and a small platform at the top with a railing. It sat on a flat patch of grass behind the house with the pastures stretching out behind it and the mountains rising in the distance, and the three girls had already claimed their swings and were pumping their legs with the concentrated effort of children who believed that with enough momentum, they might actually go over the top.

Nicole and Mike stood in the yard and watched them swing. The late-afternoon sun was warm on Nicole's shoulders. The only sound was the creak of the swing chains and the girls' laughter carrying across the yard.

"Mike," Nicole said after a minute, her voice even, her eyes on the girls. "Can I tell you something? It's a little more personal, and I don't want to overstep."

He looked at her. "Sure."

She took a breath. "On the first day of school, I had the kids introduce themselves to each other. Just a little icebreaker—their name, what they like to do, things like that. And when it was Lizzie's turn, she told the class that she loves to draw, and she loves fishing, and she loves her daddy and her grammy and poppa." Nicole paused. "And then she said that her mommy is in heaven."

She watched his face as she said it. The shift was subtle—not dramatic, not a flinch—more like something behind his eyes went still for a second, the way a person goes still when they hear something they weren't expecting to hear right now.

"She said it so naturally," Nicole continued, keeping her voice steady and gentle. "Like it was just another part of who she is, right alongside the drawing and the fishing. She wasn't upset. She wasn't looking for a reaction. She was just being honest the way kids can sometimes be."

His jaw tightened, just slightly, and then relaxed. "Yeah," he said. "That sounds like Lizzie." He watched the swings for a few seconds. "Her mom, Jenny, passed away three years ago."

Nicole nodded. "I wanted to bring it up because I'm also..." She paused because the words still caught in a place she couldn't quite get around, even now. "My husband, Derek, passed away about ten months ago. The girls' father."

Mike turned to look at her. "I'm sorry. I know you've probably heard that a million times, but I mean it. I've been where you are."

"Thank you." She swallowed. "I'm telling you this because I want you to know that when it comes to Lizzie, I understand. I'm not just a teacher who's read about childhood grief in a textbook. I'm living it. My girls are living it. And if Lizzie ever has a hard day, or says something in class that seems like she's working through something, or acts a little different from usual, I'll handle it. I'll handle it carefully, and I'll call you, and we'll figure it out together. I just want you to know that."

Mike didn't answer right away. He stood there looking at the swings, his hands in his pockets, and Nicole could see the weight he was carrying in the set of his shoulders and the way his gaze lingered on Lizzie.

"I appreciate that," he said finally.

They stood there for a moment, side by side, watching their three daughters swing higher and higher against the September sky.

"Push me, Mama!" Amber called from the swing, her legs pumping, her voice carrying across the yard with the particular volume that was Amber's default setting.

Nicole smiled. "Coming."

She walked over to the swings and positioned herself behind Amber, giving her a push that sent her sailing forward with a shriek of delight. Mike followed and stepped behind Lizzie's swing. Alicia, who'd been pumping steadily on her own, looked over at both of them and smiled her quiet, contented smile.

They pushed the girls for a while, and the afternoon wound down the way good afternoons do—slowly, without anyone trying to rush it. The girls traded swings. They went down the slide. Amber tried to see if she could swing standing up, and Nicole told her absolutely not. Lizzie asked Mike to push her higher, and he did, and when she came back down laughing, he caught the swing with both hands and held it still just long enough to kiss the top of her head before letting go again.

"Mama, I'm thirsty," Alicia said, slowing her swing to a stop.

"Me too," Amber said.

"Me three," Lizzie added.

"I'll go get juice boxes," Nicole said. "You three stay with Mr. Hartwell and don't run out of this yard while I'm gone."

"We won't," all three of them said in unison.

Nicole turned and walked toward the back porch, the girls' voices and laughter fading behind her as she crossed the yard. She climbed the porch steps and reached for the screen door, and then she stopped.

She stood there with her hand on the door handle and let out a long, slow breath.

The conversation with Mike was still sitting in her chest—not the words themselves, but the look on his face when she'd told him about Lizzie saying her mommy was in heaven. The way his jaw had tightened. The way he'd said Jenny's name, plain and steady, like he'd trained himself to say it without letting anything underneath come up too far. She knew that voice. She knew exactly what it cost to keep it level.

And when she'd said Derek's name out loud, standing there in the warm September air on a perfectly ordinary Saturday afternoon, something had moved in her chest that she hadn't been ready for. Not a wave. Not a crash. Just a soft, persistent ache that reminded her it was still there, and that ten months was long enough to learn how to carry it but not long enough to stop feeling it either.

Her eyes stung. She blinked once, twice, three times, fast and deliberate, and pressed her lips together and breathed in through her nose and held it.

Not here. Not now. No tears today.

She blinked one more time, straightened her shoulders, and pulled open the screen door.

"We're okay," she said quietly to the empty kitchen. "We're doing just fine."

And she went inside to get the juice boxes because three little girls were thirsty, and that was the kind of thing she knew exactly how to fix.

Chapter 7

Clover was trotting in slow, steady circles around the riding ring with Alicia in the saddle. Nicole was leaning against the fence rail, watching her daughter sit taller than she'd sat last week, her small hands holding the reins exactly the way Tabitha had taught her.

"Mommy, look!" Alicia called. "I'm doing it by myself!"

"You are, baby," Nicole called back. "You're doing great."

Alicia smiled and turned her attention back to the horse. Amber and Lizzie were sitting on the fence rail a few feet away, their boots hooked on the lower rung, watching Alicia ride with restless patience. Amber was narrating Alicia's performance like a sportscaster— "She's going around the turn now, she's doing so good, oh she's going to speed up, I bet" —while Lizzie listened and nodded and added her own commentary.

Mike was standing beside Nicole at the fence, leaning against it with his sleeves rolled to the elbows. He'd been mid-sentence when they'd been interrupted with Alicia's excited comment—something about how the elementary school's parent website portal had sent him the same welcome email four times this week and he still hadn't figured out how to log in.

"My mom finally called the school office for me," he continued, picking the thread back up. "Which is embarrassing for a twenty-eight-year-old man, but in my defense, the password requirements were unreasonable. Uppercase, lowercase, a number, a symbol, and apparently it also needed to contain a haiku."

Nicole laughed. "I cannot tell you how many parents I've helped log in to the system, and I'll tell you a secret—half the teachers have had issues as well."

"That makes me feel slightly better."

"It should. You're in good company."

The September afternoon was warm and unhurried, the kind of late-season warmth that felt like a gift because you knew it wouldn't last much longer.

This was the girls' second riding lesson. And already it felt like a routine—Mike's truck pulling in at two o'clock, Lizzie jumping out before the engine was off, the three girls finding each other within seconds and picking up whatever conversation they'd been having at school on Friday as if no time had passed at all.

Nicole enjoyed talking to Mike. Not in the way some people were easy to talk to, where the conversation stayed on the surface and skipped from topic to topic without ever landing anywhere. Mike listened. He responded to what she actually said, not what he thought she was going to say. He asked follow-up questions that showed he'd been paying attention, and when he didn't have anything to add, he was comfortable just standing there and watching the girls without filling every second with words. She appreciated that more than she could have explained, because for the last ten months, most of the conversations she'd had with other adults had been either professional, awkward, or cautious—the kind of conversations where people chose their words carefully around her because they knew her story and didn't want to say the wrong thing. Talking to Mike didn't feel like that. It just felt like talking.

"So, how are you settling in?" he asked. "You've been back since June, right? Are you finding Serenity Crossing feeling a little more like home again?"

"June, yes. It's been good." She paused, watching Tabitha guide Alicia through a turn at the far end of the ring. "Honestly, some days it still feels new. I grew up here, but everything's a little different when you come back as an adult. There are shops I don't recognize and families I don't know or remember. And the town feels smaller than it did when I was a kid, which I think means I got bigger, not that the town got smaller."

"I've never left Serenity Crossing, and even I notice the changes. A new coffee shop opened on the square last spring. The bookstore moved two doors down. My brother's hardware store started selling candles for some reason."

"Candles?"

"I believe that was his fiancée Grace's idea. Apparently, she thinks candles and a few other more feminine things in a hardware store could grab the attention of any females coming in to shop or be a way to jar a man into considering buying a gift for his better half."

Nicole smiled. "That's either the most Serenity Crossing thing I've ever heard or the most depressing commentary on the state of home repair."

Mike's laugh was quick and genuine, and it caught Nicole off guard.

In the ring, Tabitha brought Clover to a stop and helped Alicia dismount, and Amber was off the fence rail before Alicia's boots hit the ground.

"My turn, my turn," Amber said.

Lizzie stayed on the fence, swinging her boots, waiting with the focused patience she'd been developing over the past two weeks. When Amber was settled in the saddle and Tabitha started walking her around the ring, Lizzie cupped her hands around her mouth and yelled, "You've got this, Amber!"

Amber waved with one hand, and Tabitha called out, "Both hands, sweetheart."

Amber rode two full laps with increasing confidence, and then it was Lizzie's turn. She hopped off the fence and jogged to the mounting block, and when she was up in the saddle and Tabitha had adjusted her stirrups, Lizzie turned and found Mike at the fence.

"Daddy, watch this," she said. "I'm going to trot."

"I'm watching," Mike said, and he was—fully, completely, with the same undivided attention Nicole had seen him give Lizzie from the very first day he'd stepped into her classroom during the Back-to-School Bash. His eyes tracked his daughter as Tabitha clucked her tongue and Clover picked up the pace from a walk to a gentle trot. Lizzie bounced in the saddle twice before finding the rhythm and settling into it with a grin that could've been seen from the next county.

"She's trotting," Mike said, and there was something in his voice—pride, wonder, the particular disbelief of a parent watching their child do something they couldn't do before—that made Nicole look at him instead of at Lizzie for just a second.

He was a good dad. She'd known that since the Back-to-School Bash, since the way he'd stood and watched his daughter color with the kind of attention that most parents reserved for recitals and ball games. But watching him here, at the fence, leaning forward every time Lizzie rounded the far turn—that wasn't just good parenting. That was a man who showed up. Every time. Without being asked. She could feel the love he had for his daughter.

Derek had been like that.

The thought arrived unexpectedly, the way those thoughts always did—not with a crash, but with a quiet slide, like a drawer opening. Derek, standing at the edge of the sandbox at the park, clapping every time Amber dumped a bucket of sand, recording it on his phone like it was a championship performance. Derek, lying on the floor of the nursery at two in the morning with Alicia sleeping on his chest because she wouldn't sleep anywhere else, his hand on her back, his eyes barely open, staying exactly where he was because she needed him there.

Nicole blinked a few times and looked back at the ring.

Lizzie was trotting confidently, her braids bouncing, her face bright. Amber and Alicia were cheering from the fence.

"They're happy," Nicole said. "All three of them. They're so happy right now and in the moment. That's one of the best feelings in the world, knowing a child is feeling joy."

"They are," Mike said.

"I worried about that. When we moved here. I worried the girls would have a hard time adjusting to a new town and home after losing their dad. That they'd pull back, or act out, or that something would come up at school or at home that I wouldn't know how to handle. But so far they've been..." She searched for the right word. "They've been themselves. Just themselves, which is the best thing I could've hoped for."

Mike nodded.

Nicole stood there for a moment, watching Tabitha slow Clover to a walk.

"Mike," she said. "Does it ever get easier?"

He didn't answer right away. He watched the ring, where Lizzie was walking Clover along the fence line with the easy posture of a girl who'd decided this horse belonged to her now.

"It changes," Mike said finally. His voice was low and even, as if he were choosing each word carefully. "It doesn't get easier the way you hope it will, where one day you wake up and the weight isn't there anymore. The weight's always there. But you get stronger under it. Or maybe you just get more used to carrying it, and at some point you stop noticing the difference."

Nicole listened.

"The sharpness goes away," he said. "That's the first thing that changes... at least for me it did. The first year, everything is sharp. You walk into a room and something catches you—a smell, a song on the radio, the way the light comes through the window at a certain time of day—and it just cuts right through you. That dulls. Not all the way, but enough that you can breathe through it instead of having to stop and sit down."

He paused. In the ring, Tabitha was helping Lizzie dismount, and all three girls were gathering near the mounting block, chattering about who did what and who went faster.

"Lizzie was three when Jenny died," Mike said. "She doesn't remember much, but she knows her mom loved her very much... I've made sure of that. But there was a time, maybe six months after, when Lizzie did something funny at the dinner table—I don't even remember what it was—and I laughed. Really laughed for the first time in months. And then I felt sick about it. Like laughing meant I was forgetting, or moving on, or that I didn't deserve to feel good because Jenny wasn't there to feel good with me."

Nicole swallowed. She knew that feeling. She knew it in her bones.

"And then one day," Mike said, "probably a year later, Lizzie said something hilarious—she told my dad his coffee smelled like a tire on fire, and his face was priceless—and I laughed, and I didn't feel terrible afterward. And that was its own kind of grief. Realizing I was moving forward. Realizing the guilt was fading a little and not being sure I wanted it to."

He turned his head and looked at Nicole with the honest, steady gaze of someone who'd been where she was standing and wasn't going to pretend it was simple.

"I still feel like there's a hole," he said. "Right here." He put his hand flat against his chest, just for a second, and then dropped it back to the fence rail. "Like something's missing that used to be there, and no matter how good things get, that spot stays empty. But the rest of your life fills in around it. The good stuff doesn't replace what's gone. It just grows next to it."

The ring was quiet now. Tabitha was leading Clover toward the barn. The girls were walking toward the fence, their voices carrying across the dirt.

Nicole nodded. She didn't trust herself to say much, but she wanted him to know she'd heard him, all of it, and that it had landed exactly where she'd needed it to.

"Thank you," she said. "For being honest about it."

"You're doing better than you think you are," Mike said. "I know it doesn't feel like it some days. But you are."

She looked at him, and for a second, something moved through her that she didn't have a name for—not sadness, not relief, not gratitude, though all three were in there somewhere. Just the quiet recognition of being understood by someone who didn't need an explanation.

Then Amber's voice cut through the moment like a foghorn.

"Mommy, did you see me trot? I trotted SO fast. Faster than last week. Way faster."

"You were wonderful, baby," Nicole said, and just like that, the world was loud and bright again. Three dusty, flushed, horse-smelling six-year-olds were talking over each other with the urgency of children who had been doing something amazing and needed every adult within earshot to know about it.

Lizzie was telling Mike about how Clover had sneezed while she was trotting, and she hadn't even flinched. Alicia was standing beside Nicole, quietly brushing hay off her jeans with the methodical care of someone who liked things neat. Amber was demonstrating her riding posture on the ground, which mostly involved walking in circles with her arms out and saying, "Look at my form," to no one in particular.

Mike knelt down and brushed the dust off Lizzie's shoulders while she talked. "Daddy, can Amber and Alicia come with us to the Pizza Palace?"

Mike's hand paused on her shoulder.

Nicole watched the half-second of hesitation cross his face—not reluctance, not annoyance, just the quick mental calculation of a man who was realizing that this afternoon was about to become something bigger than a riding lesson. She understood the hesitation because she'd have felt it too. Riding lessons at the farm were one thing. Going out together to a restaurant as a group—that was a different step.

"What's the Pizza Palace?" Amber asked immediately, spinning toward Lizzie with laser focus.

"It's the best pizza place in the whole world," Lizzie said with the absolute authority of someone who'd eaten there approximately forty times and considered herself the leading expert. "They have pepperoni and cheese, and they have this game where you put a quarter in and try to get the claw to pick up a stuffed animal, and there's a jukebox that plays real music, and the breadsticks are SO good."

Amber and Alicia turned to Nicole in unison, their faces identical portraits of raw, unfiltered hope.

"Can we go, Mommy?" Amber asked. "Please?"

"Please?" Alicia added.

Nicole looked at Mike over the tops of three small heads. He met her eyes, and there was a wordless exchange in that look, and then Mike gave a small nod that was barely more than a tilt of his chin.

"I don't see why not," Mike said, looking down at Lizzie. "If it's all right with Mrs. Sullivan."

"It's fine with me," Nicole said. "I think we've all earned some pizza after that lesson."

The noise that erupted from the three girls was somewhere between a cheer and a shriek. Amber grabbed Lizzie's hand, and Lizzie grabbed Alicia's hand, and for a moment the three of them were bouncing in a tight circle of celebration like they'd just been told Christmas was coming early.

"We should take separate vehicles," Nicole said, while the girls continued their victory lap.

"Works for me," Mike said. "You know where the Pizza Palace is, right?"

"I do. I haven't been in there in ages."

Lizzie nodded, satisfied that the situation was under control, and ran toward Mike's truck with Amber and Alicia close behind before Nicole reminded them that only Lizzie was riding with Mr. Hartwell and the twins were riding with her.

The girls sorted themselves out with a maximum amount of drama and a minimum amount of speed. Nicole buckled Amber and Alicia into the back seat of her SUV while Mike helped Lizzie into his truck across. She closed the back door and walked around to the driver's side, and as she reached for the handle, she glanced across the gravel and caught Mike looking at her. He threw up his hand in a wave, and she lifted her hand in return.

Then she climbed in, started the engine, and followed his truck toward town, with two chattering girls in the back seat asking her what she thought pizza at the Pizza Palace was going to taste like. Nicole told them that when she was younger, it had been the best pizza in the world, and it probably still was.

Chapter 8

The noise level in The Pizza Palace was loud enough that you had to lean across the table to hear the person sitting across from you, and that was before you factored in three six-year-olds who hadn't stopped talking since they'd walked through the front door.

They were seated in a big corner booth near the back. The remains of two medium pizzas sat between them—one pepperoni, one cheese—along with a basket that had held breadsticks, which had been demolished in under ten minutes. Lizzie was sitting between Amber and Alicia on one side of the booth. Mike and Nicole were across from them, and the table looked like a small tornado had passed through it, which was accurate because three small tornadoes had in fact been eating there for the last thirty minutes.

The Pizza Palace hadn't changed much over the years; the same colorful murals covered the walls—cartoon chefs tossing pizza dough, a bear in a chef's hat riding a skateboard, and the Serenity Crossing skyline painted along the back wall with the mountains behind it. The jukebox near the front still glowed with neon lights, though it played from a digital screen now instead of actual records. The arcade area bled sounds through the entire restaurant—the electronic chime of a racing game, the mechanical claw of the prize machine dropping and missing, and the muffled thump of a Skee-ball rolling up a ramp. And through a wide archway decorated with strings of lights, the play area waited—complete with a ball pit, tube slides, a climbing structure, and a foam pit—humming with the shrieks and laughter of kids who'd reached the post-pizza, pre-sugar-crash energy peak.

"Okay, so after we finish, we go to the play area," Lizzie said, pointing toward the archway with a breadstick like a general pointing at a map. "There's a ball pit, which is the best part, and tube slides that go all the way up to the ceiling, and a climbing wall and a foam pit thingie where you jump off a platform." She paused for emphasis. "But you have to take your shoes off first. That's the rule. Right, Daddy?"

"That's the rule," Mike confirmed.

"And you have to finish your pizza first," Lizzie added, looking at Amber and Alicia's plates with the evaluative eye of a quality inspector. "You can't go in there with food."

Amber picked up her last slice of pepperoni and took the biggest bite Mike had ever seen a six-year-old attempt. Alicia, who'd been eating at a careful pace, looked at her remaining half-slice and then at the play area archway and began eating noticeably faster.

"Girls, slow down," Nicole said, reaching over to put a hand on Amber's arm. "The play area isn't going anywhere. Chew your food."

"But Mommy, Lizzie said there's a ball pit."

"It'll still be there when you finish eating."

Mike took a drink of his iced tea and watched the three girls buzzing with impatience while Nicole calmly negotiated the speed of pizza consumption. Breadstick crumbs were everywhere; napkins were balled up, and the remains of a meal that had been eaten with more enthusiasm than technique. The booth was crowded and messy and loud, and something about it—the fullness of it, the noise of it, the simple fact that there were five people at this table instead of two—settled in a place he tried not to examine too closely.

"Okay," Amber announced, holding up her empty plate like a trophy. "I'm done. Lunch is over."

"Me too," Alicia said, folding her napkin neatly beside her plate.

"Me three," Lizzie said.

Nicole looked at Mike. "I think we've been outvoted."

"I think we were outvoted before we sat down."

The girls scrambled out of the booth with the coordination of a fire drill and made a beeline for the play area. Lizzie led the charge, stopping at the entrance to kick off her boots with the ease of someone who'd done this a hundred times.

"Shoes off," she instructed Amber and Alicia, pointing at the shoe shelf along the wall. "Shoes go on the shelves; if you throw them on the floor, they get lost, and then it takes Daddy twenty minutes to find them."

"You are correct, Lizzie," Mike said.

Amber yanked off her boots and dropped them on the shelf. Alicia placed hers side by side, perfectly aligned, and then the three of them were gone into the tube slides with a collective shriek.

The play area was brighter than the restaurant because of the fluorescent lights and primary-colored foam padding on everything. A few other parents sat at small tables spread throughout the room, scrolling on their phones or talking quietly while their kids bounced and climbed overhead.

Nicole sat down across from Mike and tucked a strand of hair behind her ear. "I forgot how much I loved this place," she said, looking around at the murals and the neon, and the organized mayhem of the play area. "I used to come here all the time when I was in school."

"Same," Mike said. "After basketball games, mostly. The whole team would pile in here and take over the back booths in the dining room and be way too loud and eat way too much pizza."

"Friday nights after football games for me," Nicole said. "My friends and I would grab a couple of booths and feed quarters into the arcade machines for hours. I was terrible at every game except Skee-ball. I could beat anyone at Skee-ball."

"Skee-ball's a legitimate skill."

"I've always thought so."

Mike smiled. It was strange, sitting here with Nicole in a place they'd both been to when they were kids, realizing they'd probably been here at the same time at one point or another without ever noticing each other. Serenity Crossing was small, but not so small that everyone knew everyone personally. He'd been a basketball player. She'd been an academic. Different circles, different orbits.

"We graduated the same year," Nicole said, as if she'd been tracking the same thought. "I don't think we ever had a class together, though, and I don't recall ever hanging out together. "

"I don't recall ever having a class together. I took the classes the school required, and the others I took were solely for fun. I was not a good student; I did enough to pass my classes and stay on the basketball team. I was mostly in the gym or the wood shop class during free time or after school."

"I was mostly in the library or the lab during free time."

"And now we're both sitting in the Pizza Palace watching our kids go down tube slides."

Nicole laughed. "Life is weird."

"Life is very weird."

A shriek erupted from Lizzie in the tube slides, followed by Amber's voice echoing through the plastic tunnels: "That was AMAZING. Again!"

Mike shook his head. "Lizzie has one volume when she's having fun."

"Amber came out of the womb at that volume. The nurses in the delivery room jumped." Nicole paused, and her smile shifted. "That feels like a hundred years ago."

"I remember the day Lizzie was born. It was one of the best but scariest days of my life, knowing that a little human was depending on me," Mike said as he watched the play area, then turned to look at Nicole. "Just think… it's been ten years since we were seniors in high school. Hard to believe how much has happened since then."

He said it easily, the way you say things that are true without thinking about how much truth is in them. But the words landed heavier than he'd intended, and he saw it cross Nicole's face—not sadness exactly, not a flinch, but something that moved behind her eyes for just a second, like a cloud passing across a clear sky. The shadow of everything that had happened in those ten years, passing through and moving on.

"Daddy! Daddy, come on!"

Lizzie was leaning over the edge of the ball pit, waving at him with both arms, her braids hanging down and her face flushed red with exertion. "You have to come in! It's so deep! Bring Mrs. Sullivan too!"

Mike looked at Nicole. She raised an eyebrow.

He stood up, walked to the edge of the play area, and sat down on the padded bench to pull off his boots.

Nicole was right behind him. She slipped off her shoes, set them beside his, and followed him to the ball pit without a word.

The ball pit was about four feet deep and roughly the size of a small swimming pool, filled with thousands of plastic balls in red, blue, yellow, and green. Lizzie, Amber, and Alicia were already submerged up to their chests, throwing balls at each other with the accuracy of children who had no accuracy whatsoever, which meant Mike took a ball to the shoulder the moment he stepped in.

"Direct hit!" Lizzie yelled.

Mike waded into the pit, the balls shifting and rolling under his feet in a way that made walking feel like navigating a very colorful swamp, and immediately three six-year-olds turned on him with the unified focus of a pack of wolves who'd identified the weakest member of the herd.

"Get him!" Amber shouted.

The barrage was instant and relentless. Balls from every direction. Mike raised his arms to block the incoming fire while Lizzie tunneled through the balls on her stomach like a submarine and launched a handful at his knees. He picked up a yellow ball and tossed it gently at Lizzie, who dodged it with a dramatic dive that sent balls spraying in every direction.

Nicole had waded in from the other side and was crouching down when Amber hit her square in the shoulder. Alicia, with a grin that showed she'd been planning this, whipped a ball directly at Nicole about six inches away.

"Traitors," Nicole said, and then she grabbed a ball in each hand and fired back, and the ball pit erupted into full-scale war.

For a few minutes, everything else disappeared. The conversation. The weight of the afternoon. The quiet, honest things they'd said at the fence rail. All of it fell away, and what was left was just five people in a ball pit, laughing and throwing plastic balls and being ridiculous together. Lizzie was shrieking. Amber was yelling tactical commands that nobody followed. Alicia was methodically ambushing anyone who turned their back on her. Mike took a ball to the face and laughed so hard he nearly lost his footing. Nicole caught Amber mid-throw and tickled her until she dropped her ammunition.

The madness peaked when all three girls launched a coordinated assault on both adults simultaneously. Mike and Nicole both ducked at the same time, turning toward each other to shield themselves, and suddenly they were face-to-face in the middle of the ball pit. The balls shifting under their feet and the girls' laughter ringing off the surrounding walls.

Nicole's face was right there in front of him—flushed from laughing, her hair coming loose from its ponytail, her eyes bright and startled and close. Close enough that he could see the gold flecks in her blue eyes and the small freckle near the corner of her left eyebrow that he'd never noticed before.

A current of awareness moved through him—quick and startling and completely involuntary—that went through his chest like someone had opened a door he didn't know was there and let a gust of wind through.

He pulled back. She pulled back. At the same second, both with the same instinct.

Mike picked up a ball and whipped it at Lizzie, who caught it against her chest and screamed with delight. Nicole turned to the twins and announced that the war was over and everyone needed to surrender immediately, which Amber rejected with a dramatic "NEVER" that echoed through the entire play area.

The moment was over. Seconds. That's all it had been.

But Mike's hand was tingling where it had braced against the ball pit wall, inches from where Nicole's had been, and something in his chest that had been still for three years was no longer entirely still.

He threw another ball at Lizzie and tried not to think about it.

He tried not to think about it while they climbed out of the ball pit ten minutes later. Mike tried not to think about it while the girls put their shoes back on, Lizzie supervising the process with her usual authority. He continued trying not to think about it while they walked through the arcade area, and Lizzie pointed out the claw machine, the racing game, and the Skee-ball lanes to Amber and Alicia. It was still on his mind while they said goodbye in the parking lot; the girls hugging each other like they were parting for war instead of seeing each other at school on Monday.

"Drive safely," he said to Nicole as she buckled the twins into her back seat.

"You too," she said, and her smile was the same warm, easy smile she always gave him.

He loaded Lizzie into the truck; she buckled herself up, and she leaned her head against the seat. Her eyes were heavy, her cheeks still pink, her boots dusty from the farm, and her hair a mess from the ball pit.

"That was the best day ever, Daddy," she said, her voice already going soft with the drowsy, contented tone of a six-year-old who'd spent every drop of energy she'd been carrying all day.

"It was a pretty great day," Mike said.

"Can we do it again next Saturday?"

"We'll see."

"That means yes," she said, her voice barely there, and her eyes were closed before he reached the end of the parking lot.

Mike pulled onto the main road and drove. The cab was quiet except for Lizzie's soft breathing from the back seat and the hum of the engine, and the tires on pavement. The mountains were vivid in the late-afternoon light; the sun had dropped to just above the ridgeline, and the road ahead was empty and familiar and his.

In the quiet of the cab with his daughter sleeping behind him, he let himself sit with what he had felt earlier. The jolt, the current, and the sudden awareness of a woman's face close to his in a ball pit full of plastic, and the way something inside him had responded to it before he'd had any say in the matter.

He didn't name it. He didn't chase it. He didn't know what to do with it.

But he didn't pretend it hadn't happened either.

Chapter 9

The twins had spotted Lizzie before Nicole even finished settling into the pew, and the whispering started approximately two seconds later.

"Mommy," Amber said, tugging on Nicole's sleeve from the left side where both girls were seated. "Lizzie's right behind us."

"I see that," Nicole said, opening her bulletin and glancing down at the order of service. Sterling Ridge Community Church was filling up the way it always did on Sunday mornings—families filing in, finding their usual spots, and exchanging greetings across the aisle with the comfortable ease of people who'd been sitting in the same pews for years.

Her parents were seated to her right—Tabitha with her Bible open on her lap and Adam beside her, his reading glasses perched on his nose, studying the bulletin like it contained vital intelligence. Nicole had been coming to this church since before she could walk and had rejoined the congregation as soon as she had moved back home, and the rhythms of Sunday morning were as familiar as breathing—the organist warming up with something soft, and the low hum of a hundred quiet conversations blending into something that sounded like home.

"Can Lizzie come sit with us?" Alicia asked, leaning across Amber to look up at Nicole with those quiet, hopeful eyes.

"That's up to her daddy," Nicole said.

Both girls turned around in the pew. Nicole could hear the negotiation happening—Amber's whispered, "Lizzie, come sit with us," Alicia's softer, "please," and then Lizzie's voice, slightly louder than a whisper: "Daddy, can I?"

Nicole turned. Mike was seated directly behind her, with Lizzie on his left. The rest of the Hartwell family filled the pew beside him and spilled into the one behind.

Mike had that half-second of hesitation on his face, the quick internal calculation of a father deciding whether to hold his daughter close or let her go. She understood that look. She wore it herself more often than she'd admit.

"It's fine with me," Nicole said.

Olivia Hartwell put her hand on Mike's shoulder. "Let her go sit with her friends, sweetheart."

Mike looked at Lizzie, who was already halfway out of the pew with the anticipatory lean of someone who'd decided the answer was yes regardless of what came out of his mouth.

"Go ahead," he said.

Lizzie slipped around the end of the pew and wedged herself between Amber and Alicia. Amber immediately opened a small book bag she'd brought and pulled out coloring books and a pack of crayons, distributing them.

Nicole watched the three of them settle in and opened her bulletin again. She could feel Mike's presence behind her the way you feel someone standing close in a quiet room. Not intrusive. Just there.

Pastor Warren Davis stepped up to the pulpit at ten o'clock sharp. He was a tall, unhurried man with silver hair and a voice that carried without ever needing to be raised. He looked out over the congregation the way he always did—with the patient warmth of someone who knew every face and carried every story.

"Good morning, family," he said, and the sanctuary settled.

He opened his Bible. "Ecclesiastes 3:1. 'To every thing there is a season, and a time to every purpose under the heaven.'"

He closed the Bible and rested his hand on the pulpit.

"There's something about this time of year," he said, his voice easy and conversational, the way he always preached—like he was talking to you across a kitchen table. "Late September. The air begins to shift. Mornings come a little cooler. The trees haven't fully turned yet, but you can tell they're thinking about it."

Nicole listened. Beside her, Amber was carefully coloring a picture of a horse, and Alicia was showing Lizzie something in a picture book, their heads close together, their whispers barely audible.

"Most people don't struggle with understanding that life has seasons," Pastor Warren continued. "They struggle with accepting the one they're currently in. When life feels heavy, we want relief. When things feel uncertain, we want clarity. When we've been waiting, we want movement." He paused, the way he always paused when he wanted something to land. "But Scripture doesn't say we get to choose the season. It says there is a season... and there is a purpose in it."

Nicole's hands stilled on the bulletin in her lap.

She'd been in Serenity Crossing for three and a half months. She'd started a new job. She'd enrolled her daughters in school. She'd unpacked boxes, hung pictures, and built routines. From the outside, her life looked like it was moving forward in a straight, steady line, and most days it felt like it too. But there were mornings—quiet ones, usually, before the girls woke up—when she sat at her parents' kitchen table with a cup of coffee and felt the gap between how her life looked and how her life felt. The gap was wider than she wanted anyone to know.

"Some seasons look full and bright," Pastor Warren said. "Easy to recognize as good. Others are quieter. Seasons of rebuilding. Seasons of learning how to carry something you didn't ask for. Seasons where your life looks steady on the outside, but inside you're still sorting through things."

He let the words sit.

"Those seasons count too. They're not wasted time. They're not pauses in the story. They are part of it."

A rustle from the pew beside her pulled Nicole's attention. The whispering between the three girls had escalated from a murmur to something approaching actual conversation volume, and Amber was demonstrating something with her crayon that required sound effects.

Nicole leaned forward and put her finger to her lips.

At the exact same moment, Mike's hand appeared over the back of the pew, tapping Lizzie lightly on the shoulder.

All three girls went quiet instantly, with the immediate compliance of children who knew exactly which line they'd been approaching and had just been reminded where it was.

Nicole sat back. She didn't look at Mike. She didn't need to. But something in her registered the parallel—two parents, same instinct, same timing, no coordination required. The kind of thing that happened between people who parented the same way. Quietly. Firmly. With love.

It was a small thing. It shouldn't have mattered. But it settled somewhere in her chest like a stone dropping into still water, and the ripples spread in directions she fought not to think about.

Pastor Warren had moved on, his voice carrying through the sanctuary with the same unhurried cadence.

"A farmer doesn't expect to harvest in the same season he plants. There are seasons when God is planting something new. Strengthening roots. Clearing what no longer belongs. Preparing something that isn't ready yet." He looked out over the congregation. "And if you try to live outside of the season you're in, you'll miss what God is doing right in front of you."

Nicole glanced back, just a natural turn, and Mike's eyes were on her and then quickly shifted to the girls.

Warmth moved through Nicole's chest, a feeling like the sun on your face when you step outside after being in a cool room for too long. Simple and physical and startling in its plainness.

She didn't want warmth. She wasn't ready for warmth from anyone. She knew that the way she knew her own name, and she folded her hands in her lap and looked at Pastor Warren and listened.

"It's easy to look around and feel like everyone else is in a different place," he was saying. "Someone else's life seems settled. Someone else seems to be moving forward. Someone else looks like they've already arrived somewhere you're still trying to reach." He paused. "But you're not called to live in someone else's season. You're called to be faithful in yours."

"Faithfulness doesn't always look big," Pastor Warren continued, his voice gentler now, easing toward the close. "Sometimes it looks like getting up and doing what needs to be done. Caring for the people God has placed in your life. Taking one steady step when you're not sure what comes next."

Nicole looked at her daughters. Amber was coloring with her tongue poking out of the corner of her mouth. Alicia was reading quietly, her finger tracing the words on the page. Lizzie was leaning against Alicia's shoulder, watching the book too, perfectly content.

"You don't have to have the whole picture," Pastor Warren said. "You just have to be willing to live the day you've been given."

He brought it back to the verse, his voice settling into the quiet authority of a man who'd delivered a thousand sermons and knew when to stop talking.

"'To every thing there is a season... and a time to every purpose under heaven.'" If the season you're in right now doesn't look like what you expected, that doesn't mean God has stepped away from your life. It may just mean He's doing something you can't fully see yet."

The organist began to play, and the congregation rose.

The familiar shuffle of Bibles closing, purses being gathered, and children released from their best behavior filled the sanctuary with the bustling energy of a Sunday morning reaching its end.

The three girls were already standing, and Amber—bold as she was about everything—turned around to face Mike and said, "Mr. Hartwell, can Lizzie come get ice cream with us?"

Nicole turned, half-smiling, half-apologetic. "Amber, you can't just invite people to things without asking me first."

"I'm asking now," Amber said, with the ironclad logic of a six-year-old who saw no flaw in her approach.

Mike was standing, his Bible tucked under one arm, and he looked at Nicole with the quiet, easy expression of a man who was getting used to being ambushed by three little girls with big plans.

"We're heading to Frosty Tips," Nicole said. "You and Lizzie should come."

"Please, Daddy?" Lizzie said.

"Please?" Alicia added.

Mike looked at the three of them, then at Nicole. "Ice cream it is."

"We'll meet you there," Nicole said.

She herded the twins toward the aisle, pausing to hug Olivia, who told her the girls looked beautiful today.

The parking lot was bright and warm, the September sun sitting high and generous in a sky so blue it looked painted. Nicole walked across the asphalt with Amber on one side and Alicia on the other, both of them talking about ice cream flavors with the serious deliberation of diplomats negotiating a treaty.

"I want chocolate with sprinkles," Amber said.

"You always get chocolate with sprinkles," Alicia said.

"Because it's the best. What are you getting?"

"Strawberry."

"You always get strawberry."

"Because it's the best."

Nicole laughed. The sun was warm on her face. Her daughters were beside her. The morning had been good; the sermon had been wonderful and held great meaning for her, and she was walking across a parking lot toward ice cream on a Sunday afternoon in the town where she'd grown up. For the first time in longer than she could remember, the day didn't feel like something she was getting through.

It felt like something she was living.

She unlocked the SUV, opened the back door for the girls, and stood there for a moment with her face turned toward the sun, enjoying the warmth on her face.

Whatever season this was, it was hers. And right now, standing in the sun with her girls chattering about sprinkles, it felt like enough.

Maybe even a little more than enough.

Chapter 10

The great ice cream debate had reached a critical stage, and Mike was losing badly.

"Butter pecan is a classic," he said, holding up his cup like a piece of evidence. "It's been around forever. It's sophisticated. It has depth."

Three six-year-olds stared at him with the unified contempt of a jury that had already reached its verdict.

"Daddy, that's an old person flavor," Lizzie said, and the seriousness in her voice was impressive.

"She's right," Amber said. "Strawberry is the best flavor. It's pink, it's sweet, and it has real strawberry pieces in it."

"Mint chocolate chip," Alicia said. "The chocolate chips are the best part, and the mint makes it even better. It's the best flavor in the whole wide world."

Nicole, who was sitting beside Mike on the other side of the table from the girls, pressed her lips together and looked at him with the expression of someone who was trying very hard to re-main neutral and failing. "I think you might be outnumbered."

"I'm beginning to think you might be correct."

Frosty Tips was a small ice cream parlor on Maple Street that had been serving Serenity Crossing for years. The place had the kind of worn-in charm that came from decades of sticky fingers and Sunday afternoon crowds—a black-and-white checkered floor, a long glass display case with twenty-four flavors behind the counter, several small tables with mismatched chairs, and a hand-painted mural on the back wall of a cartoon cow wearing a top hat and holding an ice cream cone. The cow had been there since at least the eighties and showed no signs of leaving. A small brass bell rang every time someone walked in, and on a Sunday morning after church, it was getting a workout.

They'd been here about ten minutes, and the table was already a landscape of ice cream drips, crumpled napkins, and the general destruction that happens when you give three children ice cream. Lizzie's face was a masterpiece of chocolate chip cookie dough. Amber had somehow gotten strawberry ice cream on her elbow and in her hair. Alicia was the only one eating with anything resembling precision, spooning her mint chocolate chip in small, deliberate bites.

Mike was mid-bite of his butter pecan when the brass bell above the door rang again, and Nicole looked up.

"Rick!" she said, her face brightening. She was already on her feet, moving toward the door.

"Hey, sis," Rick replied as he hugged Nicole.

Mike recognized Rick Hanshaw immediately—he'd know his mill foreman anywhere, even out of work clothes. Rick was thirty, built solid, with the same dark hair as Nicole and an easy, open face that made him the kind of guy everybody at the mill liked working with. His wife, Felicia, was beside him—shorter, with curly dark hair and a warm smile—carrying three-year-old Courtney on her hip while five-year-old Caleb held Rick's hand and scanned the ice cream case with the wide-eyed intensity of someone approaching a crucial decision.

Mike stood and extended his hand as Rick approached the table. "Hey, man. Good trip?"

Rick shook it with a grin. "Two weeks in Destin was sheer heaven on earth. We got back last night. I'm pretty sure we brought back a quarter ton of sand in the SUV and that I left half my sunscreen budget on the beach."

"You look like a lobster," Mike said.

"I look like a man who fell asleep on a beach towel and woke up a different color." Rick glanced at the table—at the three girls, at Nicole, at Mike—and something quick and curious passed across his face, gone almost before it registered. "Didn't know you two knew each other."

"Mike's daughter is in my class," Nicole said, pulling a second table over to butt up with theirs while Mike grabbed chairs. "And the girls are inseparable now, so Mike and I have been doing the parent thing—riding lessons, pizza, the usual."

"The usual," Rick repeated, and there was a note of amused interest in his voice that Mike decided to ignore.

Felicia got Rick, and the kids settled, and within minutes the table had doubled in size and volume. Caleb had climbed into a chair next to Lizzie and immediately began telling her about the jellyfish he'd seen in Florida. Courtney was focused primarily on the chocolate ice cream Felicia had ordered for her as she sat on Felicia's lap and watched the older kids with the detached curiosity of a toddler who had her own priorities.

"So how was Florida, really?" Nicole asked, leaning toward Felicia while the kids sorted themselves out.

"Wonderful," Felicia said, "and exhausting. Courtney ate sand on the first day. Caleb tried to catch a seagull. Rick got sunburned on his shoulders so badly he couldn't wear a shirt for two days." She smiled at Rick with the affection of a woman who'd been married long enough to find her husband's failures endearing. "We had the best time."

"She's underselling it," Rick said. "The condo was right on the beach. The kids didn't want to leave. Honestly, neither did I, but somebody's got to pay the mortgage." He looked at Mike. "How's the mill? Everything survive without me?"

"Barely. The whole operation nearly collapsed. I had to sharpen my own pencils."

Rick laughed. "The horror."

"Seriously, though, it all went fine. Your crew handled everything great. I'll catch you up Monday."

"No work on Sundays," Felicia said, pointing a spoon at both of them.

"Yes, ma'am," Rick said, and Mike held up his hands in surrender.

The expanded table settled into the kind of easy, overlapping conversation that happens when family and friends share space. Rick told a story about Caleb trying to build a sandcastle that was taller than himself and the engineering challenges that followed. Felicia asked Nicole about the school year and how her classroom was going. Mike listened and laughed in the right places and occasionally fielded a question from Lizzie about whether they could go to Florida too, which he answered with a diplomatic "we'll see."

The kids, meanwhile, had formed their own conversation at their end of the table, and it was louder and faster and covered significantly more ground.

"Are you going to the Harvest Festival?" Lizzie asked Amber and Alicia, her spoon frozen in midair with a glob of cookie dough ice cream hanging off the end.

"What is it?" Amber asked.

"It's the best thing ever. There's pony rides and pumpkin painting and a hayride and craft stuff and rides, and it's so much fun."

"You forgot the face painting," Caleb added. "I got a dragon on my face last year. It was awesome."

"Is there ice cream?" Courtney asked from Felicia's lap, and the question was so perfectly on-brand that every adult at the table smiled.

"There's ice cream," Rick confirmed.

"Then I want to go," Courtney said and returned to her chocolate ice cream.

Amber turned to Nicole. "Mommy, can we go to the Harvest Festival? Can Lizzie come with us? Can we do the pony rides?"

"We'll definitely go," Nicole said.

The conversation between the kids continued at full speed, and for a moment, the adults just listened. Lizzie was describing the hayride in vivid detail. Amber was asking whether you could paint a pumpkin to look like a horse. Caleb was telling Courtney about the dragon face paint again, and Courtney was telling Caleb she wanted a butterfly, not a dragon, because butterflies were prettier.

Then Caleb, who'd been following the conversation the way five-year-olds follow conversations—partially, with detours—looked across the table at Amber and Alicia and said, with the blunt, guileless directness that only a young child could produce: "Wait. I thought your daddy was in heaven."

Alicia looked at Caleb with her quiet, steady eyes. "He is."

Caleb processed this. His eyebrows scrunched together, and his gaze moved from Alicia to Nicole and then to Mike, and the wheels behind his eyes turned with the visible effort of a child connecting dots he'd just noticed.

"Then why is your mommy here with my daddy's boss?" Caleb asked. "Is he going to be your new daddy?"

Mike's hand tightened around his ice cream cup as he sat very still. His whole body was locked in the particular stillness of a man who'd just heard a question that nearly knocked the breath out of him by a five-year-old.

Rick's spoon stopped halfway to his mouth. Felicia's eyes went to Nicole. Nicole's face stayed calm—Mike could see it in his periphery, the teacher in her holding steady, her expression open and patient, her body language loose and unbothered even though every adult at the table had paused.

Amber looked at Nicole, then at Mike, then back at Caleb. "I don't know. Maybe. He would make a good new daddy."

Lizzie looked at Nicole, then Caleb, and said without hesitation, "I think Mrs. Sullivan would make a good mommy. I need a mommy."

Mike couldn't move.

His daughter's voice hung in the air between the dripping ice cream cups and the cartoon cow on the wall, and it sounded exactly the same as it always sounded—bright, clear, and matter-of-fact—because to Lizzie, she'd stated something as obvious as her name. Something she believed the way she believed in gravity or Tuesday or the fact that purple was the best crayon color.

She wanted a mother.

Mike's throat tightened. He stared at his daughter's face—open, unbothered, already turning back to her ice cream like she'd said nothing more remarkable than "pass the napkins"—and the enormity of her simplicity chipped away at his heart.

Three years. He'd spent three years trying to be enough. Three years of making sure Lizzie never felt the absence of what she didn't have, and she'd just told a table full of people that she felt it anyway.

"You know what, girls?" Nicole said. "Your daddy will always be your daddy, Amber and Alicia. And Lizzie, your mommy will always hold a special place in your heart too; she'll always be your mommy. Nobody can ever replace them. But it's a really wonderful thing to have people in your life who care about you. And you three have a lot of people who care about you very much."

Amber nodded. Alicia nodded. Lizzie scooped another bite of cookie dough and nodded too, satisfied with that answer.

Rick cleared his throat. Mike felt his friend's eyes on him, and when he glanced sideways, Rick was looking at him with an expression that held no judgment, no teasing. Just the quiet understanding of a man who knew Mike well enough to see what was happening under the surface and cared enough not to make it worse.

"Kids have a way of making everything sound so simple, don't they?" Rick said.

Felicia smiled. "If Courtney had her way, every problem in the world would be solved with chocolate ice cream and a nap."

"That's not the worst approach," Nicole said, and the table laughed, and the moment passed without a backward glance. The kids were already talking about the Harvest Festival again. Adult conversation resumed.

Mike sat in the middle of all of it and didn't say much for the rest of the visit. He laughed when he was supposed to laugh. He answered when he was spoken to. But inside his brain, a sentence was playing on a loop that he couldn't pause and couldn't turn off.

Rick and Felicia gathered their kids first, Courtney already half-asleep against Felicia's shoulder. Hugs were exchanged. Plans were loosely made for the Harvest Festival. Rick shook Mike's hand on the way out and held it for an extra second, and then they were gone.

Nicole wiped down the table with the efficiency of a woman who'd been cleaning up after small children for years. The goodbye in the parking lot was brief and normal. Nicole thanked him for coming. Mike said he'd had a good time. The girls hugged as if they were parting for a year instead of probably seeing each other at school tomorrow. Nicole loaded the twins into her car. Mike loaded Lizzie into his truck.

He pulled out of the parking lot and turned onto the main road toward his parents' home.

"Daddy, do you think Amber and Alicia can come to the Harvest Festival with us? I could show them everything and we could do the pony rides together and— "

"We'll figure it out, Lizzie," Mike said.

"That means yes."

"That means we'll figure it out."

She moved on to the hayride and whether you could bring your own pumpkin or if you had to buy one there, and Mike answered on autopilot—short, steady responses that kept her talking while his mind was somewhere else entirely.

The road wound through the foothills, the mountains green and close and solid on both sides, and the truck climbed the familiar curves toward home. Lizzie's voice filled the cab the way it always did, warm and constant and the best sound in his world.

I think Mrs. Sullivan would make a good mommy. I need a mommy.

He gripped the steering wheel and continued driving on autopilot.

Chapter 11

The roasted chicken was making its second trip around the table, and Olivia Hartwell's biscuits were disappearing at a rate that suggested a third batch might be required for the next family dinner. The Hartwell dining room was full of laughter and conversation, as it always was on a Sunday evening.

Mike sat between his brother Dave and his sister Sarah at the long table that stretched across the dining room. The table had been built to expand, and tonight it was at full stretch—ten chairs, ten place settings, platters of chicken, roasted potatoes, green beans, corn on the cob, and a basket of biscuits that Olivia kept replenishing from the kitchen like she'd set up a factory in there. A bowl of coleslaw sat near his brother Jim's end of the table. Grace, Jim's fiancée, had brought a sweet potato casserole that was already half gone.

Lizzie was sitting across the table between his sisters, Rebecca and Anna, perched on the cushion she always sat on to give herself a few extra inches of height. She was holding court in a way that suggested the adults at this table were her audience and she'd prepared a lot of material.

"Jim, pass me those potatoes before Dave eats all of them," Sarah said from Mike's left, leaning forward and pointing across the table.

"Hey now, sis, go easy on me; I'm a growing boy," Dave said.

"You're a full-grown man, and you've had three servings already."

"They were small servings."

Jim picked up the bowl and passed it down the table with the easy, long-suffering expression of a man who'd been refereeing his siblings' food disputes for years. Grace was watching the exchange with the amused patience of someone who'd been part of this family long enough to know that dinner-table negotiations were a spectator sport.

"How's the store been this week?" Mike asked Jim.

"Busy, actually," he said, buttering a biscuit with the focus of a man who took his biscuits seriously. "Sold out of the fall garden supplies by Thursday. And Grace's candle display is outselling the power tools section, which I'm still processing emotionally."

"As you should be," Grace said, smiling.

"Nobody needs that many candles," Jim said.

"Your sales numbers say otherwise."

Rebecca laughed from across the table, and the sound carried over the overlapping conversations the way Rebecca's laugh always did—bright and impossible to ignore. She was Mike's twin, and she and Lizzie shared the same tendency to say exactly what they were thinking at the exact moment they thought it. She was sitting beside Lizzie, one arm draped casually over the back of Lizzie's chair, and every few minutes she'd reach over and tuck a stray strand of hair behind Lizzie's ear.

Bill was at the head of the table, eating his chicken with the same methodical patience he brought to everything, his eyes moving around the room, watching his family the way he always did—like a man taking an inventory of the things that mattered most and loving every moment of having his family all together around his table. He'd been quiet all dinner, which was Bill's default setting, and his presence anchored the table the way it always had. You didn't need to hear Bill Hartwell talk to feel him in the room.

Olivia sat at the other end, and she was everywhere at once—refilling the biscuit basket, asking Grace if the casserole needed to be reheated, pouring more iced tea for Dave, and keeping one ear on every conversation while maintaining her own with Anna about the Harvest Festival planning committee, which Anna was coordinating through the Chamber of Commerce.

"We've got the layout finalized for the town square," Anna said. She was the youngest of the six siblings, and she ran the Chamber of Commerce events with the kind of organized energy that made everyone around her feel simultaneously impressed and exhausted. "Craft booths on the north side of town, food vendors along the south end of town, and a stage in the center of the square near the gazebo. Pony rides are confirmed, the hayride is confirmed, and pumpkin painting will be set up in the square."

"Aunt Anna," Lizzie said. "Are there going to be bounce houses?"

"Yes, sweetie, the bounce houses will be there again this year."

"How many?"

"Three."

Lizzie nodded, satisfied with this number.

"So, Lizzie," Jim said, leaning back in his chair and looking across the table at her. "How's first grade treating you? You've been at it a couple of weeks now."

Lizzie set down her fork, which was the first sign that the answer was going to be long, because Lizzie never voluntarily stopped eating unless she'd decided she had something important to say.

"It's so good," she said, and her voice shifted into the gear Mike recognized—the one she used when she was about to deliver a comprehensive report on every aspect of her life and expected full attention from everyone in the room. "My teacher, Mrs. Sullivan, is super nice, and she lets us pick our own books during quiet time, and I've already read like ten books from the reading corner. And I sit next to Tyler, who's really funny, and Sophia, who can count to a thousand too, just like me, and there's this boy named Jackson who brought a frog to school in his lunchbox on Wednesday, and Mrs. Sullivan had to call his mom."

Everyone around the table laughed.

"My best friends are Amber and Alicia," Lizzie continued. "They're twins, and their mommy is my teacher, and they live on a farm with their grandma and grandpa, and they have six horses and baby goats and a donkey named Earl and a rooster named Captain who Amber says can be a meany."

"That's a lot of animals," Rebecca said.

"It's a sanc… chew… sanctuary," Lizzie said. "That means the animals live there because they need a happy home. And Tabitha teaches horseback riding, and yesterday was my second lesson, and I trotted, and Amber trotted, and Alicia is really good at it too."

"You trotted?" Anna said, genuinely impressed. "That's amazing, Lizzie."

"It's so cool," Lizzie said with zero false modesty. "And then after the lesson yesterday, we all went to the Pizza Palace—me and Daddy and Amber and Alicia and Mrs. Sullivan—and I showed them everything because they'd never been there before, and we played in the ball pit, and Daddy and Mrs. Sullivan did too, and it was the best day ever."

Mike felt the shift at the table the way you feel a change in the wind. Nobody moved. Nobody said anything obvious. But he could feel the attention realign and see the quiet recalculation happening behind his siblings' eyes as they assembled the picture Lizzie was painting.

"And then today after church we went to Frosty Tips," Lizzie continued. "Me and Daddy and Amber and Alicia and Mrs. Sullivan, and their Uncle Rick and Aunt Felicia and Caleb and Courtney. I had chocolate chip cookie dough, and Daddy had butter pecan, which is an old person flavor."

Jim laughed. Sarah pressed her napkin to her mouth. Rebecca was looking at Mike with an expression that was seventy percent amusement and thirty percent something else.

"Butter pecan is hands down the best ice cream flavor," Mike said.

"It's an old people ice cream, Daddy. Everybody says so."

"Everybody is wrong."

Lizzie shrugged in the way that six-year-olds shrug when they've decided an argument is over and they've won and went back to her chicken.

The table was quiet for about ten seconds longer, which was how long it took for the Hartwell siblings to process everything Lizzie had just laid out.

Sarah spoke first, like she were asking about the weather. "So you and Lizzie's teacher have been hanging out?"

Mike picked up his iced tea and took a drink. "It's not like that. The girls are best friends. They want to be together all the time, and the riding lessons are at Nicole's mom's farm. We're just parents whose kids are attached at the hip."

"Nicole Sullivan," Rebecca said from across the table. "She came into the salon a few weeks ago, actually. I did her hair."

"Okay," Mike said.

"She's lovely. Really lovely. And I remember her from when we were in high school. She was a quiet one, always in the library, always studying. But she's just as sweet now as she was then, maybe even more so." Rebecca paused. "She seems like a really great person, Mike."

"She is a great person," Mike said. "She's Lizzie's teacher, and she's great with the kids. End of discussion."

The sentence was a door closing, and every Hartwell at the table heard the lock turn. Jim looked at his plate. Sarah glanced at Dave, who gave the smallest shake of his head. Anna looked like she wanted to say something and then decided against it. Grace kept her expression perfectly neutral and reached for the sweet potato casserole.

Mike turned to Jim. "So what's the plan for this week? Dad mentioned something about the Henderson order moving up, and you need us to deliver his order sooner?"

Jim accepted the redirect without hesitation, and the conversation shifted to lumber deliveries and supplier timelines, and the table relaxed into the familiar rhythms of family talk that covered ground without digging too deep.

But Mike could feel his mother's eyes on him.

He didn't look at her. He didn't need to. He knew what he'd see—the same expression she'd worn when Jim had announced his divorce years ago, the same expression she'd worn when Sarah had started dating Ethan and tried to act as if they were just friends and nothing more. The expression that said, I know something's going on with you, and I'll be here when you're ready to talk about it.

He focused on his plate. He laughed when Dave made a joke about Jim's candle empire. He answered Lizzie when she asked if they could go ride the rides at the Harvest Festival.

But underneath all of it, under the banter and the Sunday evening warmth of his parents' dining room, a sentence kept playing in a voice that belonged to his daughter, and it wouldn't stop.

I think Mrs. Sullivan would make a good mommy. I need a mommy.

Chapter 12

The rocking chairs on the front porch creaked in the easy, unhurried rhythm of a peaceful Sunday evening. The September sky was turning the mountains purple against the last light of the day, while Lizzie's laughter carried up from the front yard like a bell.

Mike sat near the porch rail with a mug of coffee he'd been holding for ten minutes without drinking. Bill and Olivia were in their usual chairs to his right, Bill's boots crossed at the ankles and Olivia's hands wrapped around her own mug. Rebecca was on the porch swing, one leg tucked underneath her, rocking it gently with her foot.

The dinner noise had faded. Jim and Grace had gone home. Dave had left shortly after, mentioning something about an early morning at the office. Sarah and her fiancé, Ethan, were in the yard with Lizzie and Anna, playing some kind of tag game that seemed to have rules only Lizzie understood and that changed every thirty seconds. The front yard sloped gently down toward the tree line, and fireflies were just starting to appear in the space between the grass and the first row of pines.

"Anna said the Harvest Festival setup starts early Thursday morning this year," Olivia said, looking out at the yard. "She's got the whole committee working double shifts. That girl could organize a war and have it done ahead of schedule."

"She gets that from you," Bill said.

"She gets the organizing from me. The stubbornness she gets from you."

Bill took a sip of his coffee and didn't argue, which was its own form of agreement.

"Mike, are you taking Lizzie to the festival on Saturday?" Rebecca asked from the swing.

Mike nodded. "Yeah. We'll be there."

Rebecca waited. When nothing else came, she tilted her head and continued watching him.

"What's going on with you tonight?" she asked.

Mike looked at his coffee and then at Lizzie, who was running in circles with Anna chasing her. Sarah was standing off to the side with Ethan, laughing at something.

"Something happened today," he said. "At Frosty Tips."

Olivia's rocking slowed. Bill's eyes moved to Mike's face and stayed there.

"The kids were all talking," Mike said, and he kept his voice even. "Lizzie and Amber and Alicia, and Rick's boy, Caleb. They were going back and forth about the Harvest Festival, and then Caleb asked the twins why their mommy was there with his daddy's boss. He asked if I was going to be their new daddy."

Rebecca's foot stopped rocking the swing.

"And Amber—she thought about it for a second and said maybe, and that I would make a good new daddy." He paused. "And then Lizzie said she thought Mrs. Sullivan would make a good mommy."

His throat tightened, just slightly, just enough that he needed a second before the rest of it came out.

"She said she needs a mommy."

The porch was quiet. Somewhere in the yard, Lizzie shrieked with laughter.

Rebecca set her coffee mug down on the porch railing. Olivia's hand found Bill's knee, and Bill covered it with his own without looking.

"She said it so plainly and easily," Mike continued. "Like it was the most obvious thing in the world. She wasn't upset. She wasn't sad. She just said it and went right back to her ice cream, and I sat there and couldn't move."

"Has she ever said anything like that before?" Olivia asked.

"No. Never." Mike stared at the mug in his hands. "And that's what's getting to me. It's not that she said it. It's that she said it so easily. Like she'd been thinking it for a while and just hadn't had a reason to say it out loud until today."

"How did you respond?" Rebecca asked.

"I didn't. I froze." He shook his head slowly. "Nicole handled it. She was calm and steady and said something to the girls about how their parents, who've passed, will always be their parents and that having people in your life who care about you is a good thing. She was perfect. And then Rick changed the subject, and the kids moved on as if nothing had happened. And I drove home, and I haven't stopped thinking about it since."

Olivia rocked her chair slowly, once, twice, and then she looked at Mike with the quiet certainty of a woman who'd raised six children and had watched every one of them go through doubt, confusion, love, and anger in their lives.

"Mike, she's six years old," Olivia said. "She sees the world simply. She sees a woman who's kind to her and patient with her and spends time with her, and she thinks, 'I want that in my life.' That's not a crisis, sweetheart. That's a child being a child."

"But what if it's not just Lizzie being Lizzie?" Mike said. "What if she meant it?"

"Well... she might have meant it," Olivia said. "And that's okay. It doesn't mean you failed her. It means she has the kind of heart that's big enough to love what she has and still want more. You raised that heart, Mike."

He didn't answer. He took a drink of his coffee and stared at the yard, where Lizzie had climbed onto Ethan's back and was pointing in a direction that suggested she was now giving tactical commands.

"Mike," Rebecca said. "I watched you at dinner tonight. I watched you manage every question about Nicole like you were navigating a minefield. You deflected, Sarah. You shut down the whole table with one sentence. And the fact that you did that tells me this isn't just about Lizzie."

He looked at her.

"I spent about three hours with Nicole, giving her a complete makeover for the new school year when she was in the salon a few weeks ago. She's warm, she's genuine, she's easy to talk to, and she has the kind of quiet strength that you don't notice until you realize she's carrying more than most people could handle and she's still standing. She's a lovely person." Rebecca paused. "Do you like her?"

Mike looked at his coffee. "Yeah. I like her."

"I like talking to her," he continued. "I like how she is with the girls. I like how steady she seems. I like standing at the fence rail on Saturdays and watching the kids ride a horse and talking about nothing important and having it feel like the most natural thing in the world." He paused. "I like having her as a friend. It's easy. It makes sense."

"But?" Rebecca said.

"But I haven't thought about dating in years...not once." He set his mug on the porch rail and leaned forward with his elbows on his knees. "After Jenny died, I put my head down. I raised Lizzie. I worked at the mill. That was my life. Romance wasn't something I avoided. It just didn't exist. It was like a door I walked past every day and never noticed was there."

He looked at his hands.

"And then there was this moment at the Pizza Palace yesterday. In the ball pit, of all places." A rough exhale of a laugh escaped him.

"We were playing with the kids, and we both ducked at the same time, and she was just—right there. Like... close. And something went through me that I haven't felt in a really long time, and I didn't know what to do with it, and I still don't."

Rebecca was quiet for a moment. "What if you asked her to dinner? Just the two of you. Not a playdate. Not a riding lesson. Just a man and a woman having a meal together."

"She's Lizzie's teacher, Becca."

"I know."

"She lost her husband ten months ago. She's in the hardest season of her life. I know what that season looks and feels like. I lived it. The last thing she needs is someone coming along and complicating things."

"Or," Rebecca said, "maybe what she needs is someone who understands exactly what she's going through. Someone who's been there and came out the other side."

Bill shifted in his rocking chair. "Son. You've been a good father. Nobody can question that or say any different." He paused. "But being a good father and being happy aren't the same thing. And I don't think Jenny would've wanted you to confuse them. It's okay to want something more in your life, Mike. Being a single father isn't a one-lane road for the rest of your life."

Bill held his gaze for a long moment, and then he looked out at the yard. "I think you need to sit back and really look at your life and decide if it might be time to take a step forward. And I'm not talking about Mike, father to Lizzie. Not Mike the boss at the lumber mill, but Mike away from those things."

Olivia reached over and put her hand on Mike's arm. "You don't have to figure this out tonight," she said. "But take it to God, Mike. He already knows what you're feeling. You might as well talk to Him about it."

Mike nodded. He didn't trust himself to say anymore, so he just nodded and looked at the yard, where Lizzie had climbed down from Ethan's back and was now chasing fireflies with her hands cupped. She ran from one blinking light to the next with the pure, uncomplicated joy of a child who didn't know that the world was anything other than good.

They sat there for a while longer as the evening became full of the sound of crickets and the last calls of birds settling into the trees.

Then Lizzie came running up the porch steps, out of breath, her cheeks flushed, and her hair a mess. Her eyes were bright with the particular wildness of a six-year-old who'd been running until she couldn't run anymore. She crossed the porch in three steps and climbed into Mike's lap, and she leaned against his chest and caught her breath.

"Daddy, Aunt Anna said I caught the most fireflies. I got seven."

"Seven is a lot."

"It's a record."

He wrapped his arm around her and held her. She fit against him the way she'd always fit—perfectly, like she'd been designed to occupy exactly this space in his life.

Rebecca caught his eye over the top of Lizzie's head and smiled.

Bill and Olivia sat together in their rocking chairs, Bill's hand resting on Olivia's, watching their son hold their granddaughter on the porch of the house where he'd grown up, and the evening settled around all of them—quiet and warm and full of things that had been said and things that hadn't, and the space between was patient.

Mike pressed his lips to the top of Lizzie's head and breathed her in.

"I love you, Lizzie girl."

"I love you too, Daddy."

She closed her eyes and tucked herself closer, and Mike held her. The fireflies blinked in the dark, and somewhere on the other side of Serenity Crossing, a woman he was only beginning to understand was putting her own daughters to bed, and the world kept turning the way it does—slowly, steadily, carrying everyone in it toward whatever comes next.

Chapter 13

The pizza box was empty except for two slices. Mike stood at the kitchen counter, sliding them into a container while the faucet ran hot water over the plates in the sink.

Friday night. End of the week. The kind of evening where he settled into the welcome rhythm of relaxation—no school errands, no mill schedules, no place to be, and nobody waiting on him for a decision. It was just him and Lizzie and the low murmur of cartoons drifting in from the living room. He rinsed the plates, loaded them into the dishwasher, and wiped down the butcher-block countertops with a damp cloth. The pizza box was folded flat and slid into the recycling bin by the garage door. The leftover container went into the fridge beside Lizzie's juice boxes and the half-gallon of milk they'd go through by Monday.

He hung the dish towel over the oven handle and walked into the living room.

Lizzie was on her stomach on the hardwood floor in front of the stone fireplace, her legs bent at the knees and swinging slowly behind her. An art supply basket lay open beside her, with its contents scattered across the floor. Crayons in every color fanned out around Lizzie like a rainbow that had fallen apart. The TV was on above the fireplace—a cartoon she was half-watching, the volume low enough that it was background noise, not entertainment. Her attention was on the large sheet of white paper spread flat in front of her and the crayon in her hand, which was moving across the paper with the focused intensity of someone doing important work.

Mike walked over and sat down on the floor beside her.

"Whatcha coloring?" he asked.

"I'm making art, Daddy," Lizzie said without looking up.

"My mistake. What kind of art?"

"Look."

He leaned over slightly to look at what she was making.

It was a crayon drawing. The kind of picture that existed in a world where proportions were suggestions, perspective was optional, and colors were chosen based on emotional truth rather than visual accuracy. Two tall figures stood in the center of the page. Three shorter figures stood beside them, clustered together. A red house sat behind them all, with a triangle roof and a chimney with a curly line of smoke coming out the top. A blue truck was parked in the yard. Something four-legged and brown stood near the truck. A large yellow sun filled the upper right corner of the sky.

And behind everything, a line of green, jagged triangles ran across the top of the page. Mountains.

Mike looked at the drawing for a long moment.

"Tell me about your picture," he said.

Lizzie pointed with her crayon, narrating each element as if she were giving a tour of a place she'd already built. "This is you, Daddy." She tapped the tall figure on the left, which had dark hair and very long arms. "And this is Mrs. Sullivan." She tapped the tall figure on the right, which had yellow, wavy hair that went past her shoulders and a pink shirt. "And this is me, and this is Amber, and this is Alicia." The three smaller figures stood between the adults, holding hands in a line, each one drawn with a different colored dress and a wide U-shaped smile.

"And that's our house," she said, pointing to the red rectangle. "And that's your truck."

Mike pointed to the four-legged brown figure near the truck. "Who's this?"

"That's Baxter. He's our dog."

She said it with the casual certainty of a child who'd already decided this dog existed and was simply waiting for reality to catch up with her vision.

Mike sat there for a moment, looking at the drawing. Two adults standing side by side. Three small girls between them. A red house. A blue truck. A dog named Baxter. Mountains in the background and a big sun in the sky.

His daughter had drawn a family. Not the one she'd been given. The one she wanted.

"Hey, Lizzie. Remember last Sunday at Frosty Tips, when you said you thought Mrs. Sullivan would make a good mommy? That you need a mommy?"

Lizzie nodded and continued coloring.

"Can I talk to you about that?" Mike asked.

"Okay."

He chose his words carefully. "Mrs. Sullivan is a really great teacher. And she's a really kind person. And I'm really glad that we've all become friends—you, me, Amber, Alicia, and Mrs. Sullivan. That's been one of the best things about this school year so far for me."

Lizzie nodded again, adding a flower to the bottom of the drawing near the red house.

"But I want to make sure you understand something," Mike said. "Liking someone and spending time with them doesn't automatically mean they become your mommy. Being friends with someone is a really good thing all by itself. You know that, right?"

Lizzie considered this as she tilted her head. "But she could be."

He looked at the drawing on the floor. "Tell me something. You really like Mrs. Sullivan and Amber and Alicia, right?"

Lizzie's face lit up as she looked at him. "I love them, Daddy. Amber is so funny, and she's brave. She climbed the hay bales at the farm, and she wasn't even scared. And Alicia is really nice, and she's the best at drawing, even better than me, and she always saves me a seat at lunch even though I'd find her anyway."

"And Mrs. Sullivan?"

"Mrs. Sullivan reads the best stories. And she smells really pretty all the time, like flowers but not too much flowers. And she's always happy when she sees me, like really, really happy, not just teacher happy. And when she talks, I like listening because she sounds like sunshine."

Mike listened, and she continued to talk. She told him about the books Mrs. Sullivan read to the class and about how Amber had announced on the playground yesterday that the three of them were going to be best friends forever and had made Lizzie and Alicia pinky-swear on it. She told him Alicia had given her a drawing she'd made of the three of them on horses, and Lizzie had put it in her desk at school so it was always there for her to look at.

He heard everything she was saying, and he heard everything underneath it, too. Lizzie wasn't sad. She wasn't grieving. She was hoping. She'd drawn a picture of a life that included more people in it, and she wanted that picture to be real. She wanted the noise and the laughter and the presence of a woman and two girls who'd walked into her world three weeks ago and made it bigger.

And underneath the drawings and the stories and the easy way she talked about Nicole, there was something quieter. A want she didn't have words for quite yet, but Mike could hear it in every detail she chose to share.

It didn't break his heart. It filled it, and the filling ached, and the ache was complicated, and he let it sit.

"Are you excited about the Harvest Festival tomorrow?" He asked, guiding the conversation to easier ground.

Lizzie snapped out of her narration as if she'd been hit by a bolt of electricity. "Tomorrow? It's tomorrow?"

"After the riding lesson."

"I almost forgot... Amber and Alicia are coming, right? They said today they were."

"We'll ask Mrs. Sullivan at the lesson tomorrow and make sure."

"Good," Lizzie said. She turned back to her drawing and began adding what appeared to be a second dog near Baxter. "This one is Baxter's friend. He doesn't have a name yet."

Mike smiled. "One imaginary dog at a time, Lizzie."

"He's not imaginary, Daddy. He just doesn't live here yet."

He shook his head and stood up from the floor. "You wanna watch a movie?"

Lizzie looked up. "Can I pick?"

"You always pick."

"Because I pick better movies."

He grabbed the remote from the coffee table and sat down on the couch while Lizzie climbed up beside him. She tucked herself against his side the way she always did, small and warm, her feet pulled up underneath her, her head resting against his ribs. He put his arm around her and started scrolling through the streaming menu.

"That one, Daddy, with the horses and the girl," she said, pointing.

"Shocking choice."

"Just play it... please."

He pressed play, and the movie started. Lizzie watched the movie. Mike watched the screen without seeing it.

His eyes drifted to the drawing on the floor. The two tall figures standing side by side. The three small figures beside them. The red house. The blue truck. The dog named Baxter and his unnamed friend.

He held Lizzie a little tighter and sent a silent prayer up to God for guidance.

Chapter 14

Nicole's mom was saddling a horse when Mike and Nicole walked into the barn with the three girls, and the look on her face said she'd been planning something.

"Change of pace today," Tabitha said, tightening the cinch on a tall bay gelding with a white blaze down his nose. Chester, according to the nameplate on his stall. He was bigger than Clover and carried himself with relaxed, unbothered energy. "The girls are ready for a little more independence. I'm going to let them take turns on Clover with me leading, same as before, but I want to get Chester and Jasper into the ring at the same time. I want the girls to get used to riding with other horses moving around them. Good prep for when we start trail rides down the road."

"Trail rides?" Lizzie said, and her voice went up about two octaves.

"Eventually," Tabitha said. "But first, your daddy needs to saddle up."

Nicole was already reaching for Jasper's halter on the wall hook. "Works for me. I haven't been on Jasper in about a week. He probably thinks I forgot about him."

Mike stood in the barn aisle and processed what had just happened. "Wait. Me? On a horse?"

Tabitha looked at him with the same patient, no-nonsense expression she used when the girls tried to negotiate a longer lesson. "You've been standing at that fence for two weeks watching your daughter ride. I think it's time you got in the ring."

"I haven't been on a horse since I was ten years old. That was a long time ago."

"Then it'll come back to you," Tabitha said. "Chester's as gentle as they come."

Three six-year-olds had materialized in front of Mike and were staring up at him with the collective force of children who couldn't fathom why any adult would say no to getting on a horse.

"Daddy, you HAVE to," Lizzie said.

That settled it.

Tabitha walked Mike through a few things while Nicole handled Jasper with the ease of someone who'd done this a thousand times. The contrast was immediate and visible—Nicole moved through the process with muscle memory, adjusting the saddle, checking the girth, and running her hand along Jasper's neck while she said something quietly to him that made his ears flick forward.

They led the horses to the ring. Tabitha got Alicia up on Clover first, adjusted her stirrups, and began walking her in slow circles while Nicole mounted Jasper in one smooth motion.

Mike stood beside Chester and looked up at the saddle, which seemed significantly higher from this angle than it had from the fence.

"Left foot in the stirrup, Mike," Tabitha called from across the ring. "Grab the horn, swing your right leg over. He's not going anywhere."

Mike put his left foot in the stirrup, grabbed the saddle horn, and pulled himself up. It wasn't graceful. His right leg cleared the horse's back by approximately two inches, and he landed in the saddle with enough force that Chester turned his head and gave him a look that clearly communicated his opinion about the situation.

"Sorry," he said to the horse. The horse blinked at him and looked away.

"You're up," Tabitha said. "Now sit tall. Shoulders back, heels down, hands soft on the reins. Don't grip. He can feel everything you're doing up there, so the calmer you are, the calmer he'll be."

Mike sat tall and tried to make his hands soft on the reins, which was difficult because every muscle in his body wanted to hold on to something with the intensity of a man who was very aware that the ground was a long way down.

"Relax your legs," Nicole said, walking Jasper alongside him at an easy pace. "You're squeezing his sides, which tells him to go. Unless you want to go right now."

"I do not want to go right now."

"Then relax your legs."

From the fence, the girls were lined up like spectators at a sporting event. Lizzie had her hands cupped around her mouth. "Daddy, sit up straighter! Tabitha says your back has to be like a board!"

"Like a board, not a noodle!" Amber added.

"You're doing really good, Mr. Hartwell," Alicia said, and the quiet sincerity in her voice was so earnest that Mike almost laughed.

"All right, Mike, give him a gentle squeeze with your calves and a little cluck. He'll walk," Tabitha said.

Mike squeezed gently. He clucked. Chester walked.

The first few steps felt like sitting on a boat—everything shifting underneath him in a rhythm his body didn't recognize yet. His hips moved wrong. His hands pulled on the reins too tightly, and Chester slowed. He loosened them, and Chester picked up the pace again, and for about ten seconds he felt like he was getting the hang of it before the horse drifted toward the fence rail.

"Pull to the left gently," Nicole said from beside him. "Just a little pressure. He'll follow it."

He pulled the left rein. Chester turned away from the fence. Mike exhaled.

"See?" Nicole said. "You're doing fine."

"I'm doing something. I'm not sure fine is the word."

She smiled. "You're on a horse and you haven't fallen off. That's the definition of fine."

The girls took turns in rotation, each one riding with more confidence than the week before, and every time one of them trotted past Mike, they waved or shouted encouragement as if he were the one taking the lesson. Which, he realized, he sort of was.

Lizzie trotted past on Clover and called out, "Daddy, use your legs!"

"I'm using my legs," Mike said.

"Use them better!"

Nicole laughed, and the sound carried across the ring—warm and genuine and completely at ease in a way that made Mike glance over at her. She was sitting loosely in the saddle, one hand resting on her thigh, the late-September sun on her shoulders, her ponytail swaying with Jasper's easy gait.

"Relax your shoulders," she said. "You're hunching. Let your arms hang heavy. The horse does the work. You just sit there and enjoy the ride."

"Easy for you to say. You grew up doing this."

"And you grew up swinging axes and running chainsaws, working for your daddy. If I were standing in the woods right now with a chainsaw in hand, I'd be the one white-knuckling it."

"Fair point."

They rode another lap. Mike's body was starting to figure out the rhythm—hips moving with Chester instead of against him, shoulders dropping, and hands steadying. It wasn't pretty. It wasn't natural. But it was happening, and the fact that he was willing to sit up here and be bad at something in front of his daughter, her friends, and Nicole and not try to hide it—that was its own kind of thing.

Tabitha called the lesson after another twenty minutes. "All right, that's a wrap. I know you all have a festival to get to, and these horses need their dinner."

Mike dismounted from Chester with slightly more grace than he'd mounted and rubbed his neck. "Thanks for not embarrassing me," he said to the horse. Chester snorted, which he chose to interpret as a compliment.

Nicole was standing beside Jasper nearby, watching him with a grin on her face, and the girls were occupied with Tabitha, brushing Clover down near the barn entrance.

"So," Mike said. "Are you and the girls heading to the Harvest Festival today?"

"That's the plan."

"Lizzie and I are heading over around four. We'll probably walk around for a while, grab some very unhealthy festival food for dinner, and hit the rides afterward." He paused. "If you and the twins wanted to meet us there, we could all walk around together."

Nicole was quiet for a second.

"Well, we're all going anyway. Might as well meet up and let the girls have fun together." She smiled. "Just a couple of parents enjoying a friendly evening with their kids."

"Exactly," Mike said. "Town square, around four?"

"We'll find you."

Chapter 15

The town square had been transformed, and Lizzie was already three steps ahead of Mike. Pulling him by the hand toward the thick of it before he'd even gotten his bearings.

Vendor booths lined Main Street in long, colorful rows—hand-painted signs advertising kettle corn, caramel apples, and homemade fudge; craft tables stacked with pottery and candles and knitted scarves; and a bake sale booth run by the women's ministry from Sterling Ridge Community Church with pies and cookies arranged in neat rows under a checkered canopy. The white gazebo at the center of the square had been wrapped in string lights that weren't lit yet but would be soon. A small stage had been set up nearby where a band was tuning their instruments; the sound of a banjo and a fiddle drifted across the crowd in warm, scattered notes. Hay bales and pumpkins were stacked at every corner and in front of every booth. The whole town smelled like apple cider and grilled sausages and the particular sweetness of kettle corn popping in a cast-iron kettle.

The streets branching off from the square had been blocked off with orange barricades, and people were everywhere—strolling between booths, sitting on hay bales eating, and parents chasing children who'd broken free and were weaving through the crowd with the determined speed of kids who knew exactly where they were going.

"Daddy, the pumpkin painting is over there," Lizzie said, pointing. "We should do pumpkins first because last year the good ones got taken early."

"Okay, but we're meeting—"

"I see them!"

Lizzie dropped Mike's hand and took off with the single-minded focus of a child who'd locked onto her target. Mike followed her trajectory and spotted them—Nicole, Amber, and Alicia standing near the gazebo steps. Nicole held a small purse over her shoulder while the twins craned their necks, trying to see everything at once. Nicole was wearing a light jacket over a white top, jeans, and boots, and her hair was down, catching the late-afternoon breeze.

Amber saw Lizzie coming and let out a shout that carried across half the square. "LIZZIE!"

The three girls collided in the middle of the walkway in a tangle of arms and voices. Within five seconds they were talking over each other about what they wanted to do first, each of them making their case with the passionate conviction of tiny diplomats arguing before a summit.

"Pumpkins first," Lizzie said.

"Bounce houses," Amber countered.

"Pumpkins," Alicia said, siding with Lizzie, and the vote was settled.

Mike reached Nicole as the girls began walking toward the pumpkin-painting booth. "Hey," he said.

"Hey," she smiled. "We found each other faster than I thought we would."

"Lizzie's been running reconnaissance since we got out of the truck. She had the whole festival mapped out before we left the parking lot."

Nicole laughed. "Amber wanted to run straight for the bounce houses the second we parked, but I told her we needed to find you first."

"Much appreciated."

They fell into step together, following the girls toward the pumpkin-painting tent. The booth was already busy—a dozen kids of various ages were seated at the long tables, sleeves rolled up, hands covered in paint, surrounded by small pumpkins in shades of orange and white and the occasional pale green. Markers, paint, stickers, and containers of glitter were spread across every surface. Two women from the church were overseeing the operation with the calm efficiency of people who'd done this before and had accepted that glitter was going to get everywhere.

Lizzie, Amber, and Alicia selected a pumpkin from the bins with the seriousness of gemstone appraisers. Lizzie went for the roundest orange one she could find. Amber picked one that was slightly lopsided and declared it "cool." Alicia chose a small white pumpkin and turned it over in her hands twice before setting it down, satisfied.

"All right," Nicole said, sliding into the seat beside Alicia. "What's the plan, artists?"

"I'm doing a sunset," Amber announced, already reaching for the red and orange paint.

"I'm doing flowers," Alicia said, picking up a thin brush and studying it like it were a precision instrument.

"I'm doing a horse," Lizzie said. "Daddy, are you painting one too?"

Mike looked at the table. He looked at Nicole. She raised an eyebrow.

"I guess I'm painting one too," he said, and he picked up a pumpkin and sat down across from Lizzie.

"What are you going to paint?" Lizzie asked.

"I'm thinking about it."

"Don't think too long, Daddy."

Nicole had already claimed a pumpkin of her own and was loading a brush with dark green paint. For the next twenty minutes, all five of them sat at a table in a festival tent and painted pumpkins like it was the most important thing any of them had ever done.

Amber's pumpkin was a riot of color—reds and oranges and yellows swirled together in bold strokes that covered every inch of the surface and spilled onto the table and onto Amber's hands and, somehow, onto the back of her neck. Alicia's pumpkin was meticulous—tiny purple and pink flowers circled the base, each petal painted with the careful precision of a child who'd inherited her mother's patience. Lizzie's pumpkin was a brown horse—or at least that was the intent—standing in a green field under a blue sky, and the glitter she'd added to the sky caught the light every time she turned the pumpkin to show someone a new angle.

"Daddy, what is that?" Lizzie asked, leaning across the table to inspect Mike's pumpkin.

"Mountains."

"It looks like a bunch of triangles."

"Mountains are triangles."

"Not like that, they're not."

Nicole was working on her own pumpkin with quiet focus—an autumn tree with red and gold leaves, clean lines, the kind of simple design that looked effortless because the person painting it had a steady hand and an eye for color. She glanced at Mike's pumpkin and pressed her lips together.

"What?" he said.

"Nothing. Those are very nice triangles."

"They're mountains."

"Whatever you say, Mr. Hartwell."

Lizzie and the twins dissolved into giggles, and Mike shook his head and went back to his triangles.

When the pumpkins were finished, they carried them to the drying area at the back of the tent—a long table covered in newspaper where dozens of pumpkins in various stages of artistic ambition were lined up to dry. Amber placed hers next to Alicia's, and the contrast between the two—explosive color beside delicate precision—was a perfect snapshot of the twins' personalities.

"We'll pick them up before we leave," Nicole told the girls. "They need time to dry, or the paint will smudge."

They stepped back into the festival and let the girls lead them through the crowd. The vendor booths stretched down Main Street and onto the cross streets, and the five of them moved through them at the unhurried pace of people who had nowhere specific to be and were happy about it.

They stopped at a homemade candy booth where an older woman was selling hand-pulled taffy in flavors Lizzie didn't know existed. "What's a salted caramel?" She asked, and the woman gave her a free sample that earned a look of such intense approval that Mike bought a bag.

They stopped at a baked goods table where Nicole picked up a jar of local honey from a farm two valleys over and a small bag of mini apple cider donuts that she opened immediately and offered to everyone. Mike took one. It was still warm and smelled of apples and spices.

"These are dangerous," he said.

"They are... I wonder if I can find these locally. "

They passed the craft booths on the north end—handmade jewelry, woodwork, quilts, and pottery. Nicole paused at a booth selling small handmade ornaments—delicate wooden stars and snowflakes carved from light-colored wood and strung on twine. She picked one up and turned it over.

"These are beautiful," she said to the vendor, a gray-haired man with a leather apron. "Did you carve these by hand?"

"Every single one of them," the man said.

"Mike, look at these," Nicole said, holding one up. "This is your kind of thing, isn't it? The woodworking?"

He took the ornament and studied it. The carving was good—clean lines, a smooth finish, and the grain of the wood running in the right direction. "He knows what he's doing," Mike said, and he meant it as a compliment.

"Takes one to know one," the vendor said with a knowing smile.

Nicole bought two of the ornaments—a star and a snowflake—and tucked them into her purse while the girls dragged them onward.

A woman from church—Mrs. Patterson, who sang in the choir and organized the annual bake sale—waved at them from behind the pie table as they passed. Her eyes moved from Mike to Nicole to the three girls and back, and her smile widened with the particular warmth of someone who was pleased by what she was seeing and wasn't trying to hide it.

Anna, his sister, appeared from behind a craft booth with a clipboard in one hand and a walkie-talkie in the other, her hair coming loose from its ponytail. Her expression carried the intensity of someone who was managing a hundred things at once and thriving on every one of them.

"Mike! You made it," she said, and then she saw Nicole and the girls, and her face brightened. "Oh, hi! You must be Lizzie's friends from school. I've heard so much about you."

"Hey, sis, this is Nicole Sullivan, Lizzie's teacher," Mike said. "And Amber and Alicia, her daughters."

"I'm Anna, Mike's youngest sister. I'm the one running this whole thing, which means I'm the one having a heart attack every five minutes." She grinned at the girls. "Are you having fun, girls?"

"We painted pumpkins," Amber said. "Mine has a sunset."

"That sounds very pretty. Make sure you pick it up before you leave—last year we had about twenty unclaimed pumpkins, and I had to find homes for all of them." Anna's walkie-talkie crackled, and she held up a finger while she listened. "Gotta run... I have to go put out a fire. Possibly a literal one—someone left a grill unattended near one of the stages." She squeezed Mike's arm as she passed. "Have a good time tonight; you deserve it."

Rebecca found them near the lemonade stand ten minutes later. She hugged Mike, hugged Lizzie, and then turned to Nicole with the bright, open warmth that was Rebecca's default setting.

"Nicole! I was hoping I'd see you here." She gave Nicole a quick hug, which Nicole returned easily. "Your hair still looks wonderful, by the way."

"Thank you. I've been getting compliments ever since you dolled me up."

"That's what I like to hear," Rebecca crouched down to the twins' level. "And you two must be Amber and Alicia. Lizzie talks about you every time I see her."

"We know," Amber said, completely unbothered. "We talk about her too."

Rebecca laughed and stood up. "Well, ya'll have a fun evening, and girls, make your parents get you some cotton candy. The strawberry and the blueberry flavors are spectacular."

"Nicole, don't make yourself a stranger; come see me at the salon anytime," she said before looking at Mike and smiling. "And you, dear brother, need a haircut. I expect you in my chair within the week, or I'll hunt you down." She winked at him before walking away.

The festival continued around them—the band had started playing a lively rendition of something bluegrass that had a few couples dancing near the gazebo. The afternoon sun was dropping lower, and the string lights strung between the lampposts were beginning to glow against the sky.

Mike was aware of the picture they made as they walked through town. A man and a woman walking through a festival with three children between them, the girls holding hands and swinging their arms. Like a family.

The thought didn't unsettle him but had him wondering if maybe God had put him on a path he hadn't asked for and hadn't seen coming.

"Daddy, can we go on the hayride?" Lizzie asked.

"Absolutely," Mike said.

"Can we, Mommy?" Amber asked Nicole.

"Of course. Why would we skip the hayride?"

The hayride staging area was set up in the parking lot behind the bookstore on Maple Street—a large green tractor hitched to a wagon filled with hay bales arranged as seats, string lights wrapped around the railing, and a hand-painted sign that read Harvest Hayride—All Ages Welcome! A line of families waited along the rope barrier, and Mike and Nicole and the girls joined the queue just as a wagon was pulling away.

When their turn came, they climbed aboard with about a dozen other families. The girls claimed a hay bale near the front, and Mike and Nicole settled onto a bale beside them.

The tractor rumbled to life, and the wagon lurched forward, pulling out of the parking lot and onto the blocked-off streets that looped through the neighborhoods surrounding the square. The ride was slow and scenic—mostly residential streets lined with old trees that were just beginning to turn, front porches with rocking chairs, and yards with kids' bikes leaned against fences. The evening air was cooler now, and it carried the distant sounds of the festival.

"Look!" Lizzie said, pointing into the distance where the road curved and the tree line opened up. "That's Daddy's work! See it? That big building sticking up into the sky?"

Amber craned her neck. "What is that?"

"The lumber mill," Lizzie said, with the genuine pride of a child who considered her father's workplace one of the most impressive structures on the planet. "That's where my daddy does lumber stuff."

"What's lumber?" Alicia asked.

"It's like big pieces of wood that people use to build stuff. Daddy and Poppa run the whole place."

Amber turned to look at Mike with wide eyes. "Mr. Hartwell, can you show us the lumber mill? I've never seen one."

"Me neither," Alicia said.

"Sure," Mike said. "Maybe one Saturday after your riding lesson. I'll give you the full tour."

"Are there any big machines?" Amber asked.

"There are, and I can show you how they work from a safe distance."

"That's what Daddy always says about everything at the mill... safe this and safe that," Lizzie said to Amber in a stage whisper.

Nicole covered her mouth with her hand, trying to muffle her laugh.

"I heard that," Mike said.

"You were supposed to."

The wagon continued its loop through the quiet streets, and Mike leaned back against the railing and enjoyed the ride. Nicole was beside him, her hands resting in her lap, her face turned toward the mountains that were visible beyond the rooftops—green and gold and amber in the fading light.

"So the mill," Nicole said, turning to him. "You run it with your dad?"

"I do. Dad's semi-retired, though he still shows up most mornings because I don't think he knows how not to. I handle the day-to-day tasks, such as scheduling, orders, and managing the crew. Your brother's my right-hand man and foreman, so he keeps the yard running while I split my time between the office and outside."

"I sense you don't like the office that much."

"I tolerate the office. Too much time behind a desk makes me restless. I'd rather be out in the yard working with the crew, seeing the wood move through the process. Hands-on is more my speed."

"That doesn't surprise me at all," Nicole said, and the way she said it made him smile.

"What gave it away?"

"Nothing really; it's just a feeling I have about you." She paused. "You're an outdoor-type guy, Mike. It shows."

He didn't have a response to that, so he just looked at the mountains and let the wagon carry them around the last turn.

The hayride pulled back into the parking lot, and the families climbed down from the wagon in a slow, easy shuffle. The festival had shifted—the browsing energy of late afternoon giving way to the settling energy of evening. The band was in full swing now; the music carried across the square. The food vendors were busier, smoke rising from their grills. The string lights were glowing between the lampposts, casting everything in a warm, golden wash.

"Daddy, I'm hungry," Lizzie announced the moment her boots hit the ground.

"Starving," Amber confirmed.

Alicia nodded.

Mike looked at Nicole. "Dinner?"

"Definitely."

They started walking toward the food area on the south end of the square—three girls leading the way with their hands linked and two adults walking side by side behind them.

Chapter 16

The pulled pork sandwich was messy and delicious. Nicole had given up trying to eat it gracefully about three bites in. They were seated around a picnic table in the food area on the south end of the town square, paper plates and napkins and cups of lemonade taking up every inch of the table surface. The food vendors stretched along the street in a long row of smoking grills and bubbling fryers, and the smell of barbecue and kettle corn and fried dough hung in the air. String lights glowed above them, crisscrossing the street between the lampposts. The bluegrass band on the stage near the gazebo had shifted into something slower and sweeter, the singer's voice drifting through the festival like background music.

"Okay," Lizzie said, holding up a corncob. "The pumpkin painting was the best. Then the taffy. Then the hayride today."

"The hayride was the best," Amber said, licking barbecue sauce off her fingers. "We saw the lumber mill from the hayride. That was cool."

"The hayride was cool," Lizzie agreed. "But pumpkin painting had glitter. Glitter wins."

"I liked the ornament booth," Alicia said. "The man who carved the stars was really cool."

"The ornament booth was good," Nicole said. "What about you, Mike? What's your number one?"

Mike looked up from the pulled pork he'd been working on. "The apple cider donuts."

"That's food, not a booth," Lizzie said.

"Food counts."

"No, it doesn't."

"It absolutely counts. Those donuts were life-changing."

"They were pretty wonderful," Nicole said. "I'm going to have to track down where that farm sells them locally."

"What about the face-painting booth?" Alicia asked. "Can we do that next?"

"I want a horse on my face," Lizzie said.

"I want a dragon," Amber said. "Like Caleb got last year."

"Let's do the rides next," Lizzie said.

"What about the petting zoo?" Alicia said.

"After the rides."

"But— "

"How about this?" Nicole said, stacking the empty paper plates and gathering the napkins into a pile. "Rides first. Then face painting. Then the petting zoo, if we still have time. Deal?"

"Deal," all three girls said at once.

Mike stood and gathered the cups and the napkin pile and carried them to the trash barrel at the end of the picnic tables. Nicole wiped Amber's face with a wet wipe she'd pulled from her purse because Amber had barbecue sauce on both cheeks and in her hair.

"How did you get it in your hair?" Nicole asked.

"I don't know. It just happened."

"Things don't just happen, Amber."

"This one did."

Mike came back to the table and crouched down to wipe Lizzie's chin with a napkin. She held still for about half a second before squirming away. "Daddy, I'm fine."

"You have butter all over your face."

"It's seasoning."

Nicole caught Mike's eye across the table and held back a laugh.

The ride midway ran down a side street off the town square, and the moment the girls saw it, every thought of face painting and petting zoos evaporated.

Nicole and Mike bought a strip of ride tickets while the girls stood wide-eyed, staring at all the colorful lights.

The street was lined with smaller children's rides on both sides—a spinning teacup ride with candy-colored cups, a kiddie train that chugged along a short loop of track, and a caterpillar coaster with a gentle hill that was just steep enough to make six-year-olds gasp. There was also a fun house with wobbly floors and distorted mirrors, bumper cars, and a set of swinging chairs that spun in a wide circle. In a parking lot further up the road, the bigger rides were set up—a Scrambler, a Tilt-A-Whirl, a Ferris wheel rising above the rooftops, and a carousel lit up and turning slowly at the far end. The whole setup glowed against the evening sky, string lights tracing the perimeter and colored bulbs blinking on every ride. It was a traveling carnival company that came to Serenity Crossing every year—not massive, but more than enough to fill an evening and have children believing they'd walked into the best place on earth.

"Teacups first!" Amber declared, grabbing Lizzie's hand.

"Teacups," Lizzie agreed, grabbing Alicia's hand.

Alicia didn't say anything. She just held on and ran.

Nicole and Mike followed the girls to the teacup ride, where a carnival worker in a red vest helped them into a purple cup. The ride started, and the cup began to spin, and the three girls leaned into the turn and shrieked with the joy of children experiencing centrifugal force and finding it hilarious.

They waved every time they spun past Mike and Nicole, who stood behind the metal safety barrier with the other parents.

After the teacups came the caterpillar coaster, which earned a collective gasp on the hill and a round of applause from Amber when it was over. Then the swinging chairs, where Lizzie pretended she was flying and Alicia leaned back with her eyes closed and her face turned toward the sky. Amber narrated the entire experience at top volume. Then the bumper cars, which resulted in a three-way collision that all three girls considered the highlight of the evening so far.

Between rides, they passed the game booths—a row of carnival games with stuffed animal prizes hanging from the canopy frames. A ring-toss game caught Mike's eye, and he stopped.

"Daddy, win me something," Lizzie said, because subtlety wasn't in her vocabulary.

Mike paid for a round of rings and stepped up to the booth. The game was simple—toss the rings onto a grid of pegs, get one around the neck of a bottle, and win a prize. He missed the first two. The third one caught the edge of a bottle, wobbled, and slid off. The fourth one landed cleanly.

"Winner!" the booth operator called and pointed at the row of stuffed animals. "Pick your prize."

Mike looked at Lizzie. "What do you want?"

"The horse, Daddy."

He pointed at a small brown stuffed horse, and the operator pulled it down and handed it over. Lizzie grabbed it and held it up for Amber and Alicia to see, like she'd won an Olympic medal.

Amber looked at the booth. She looked at the prizes. She looked at Mike.

"Two more rounds," Mike said to the booth operator, already pulling bills from his wallet.

He missed three of the next four rings, but the fourth one landed. He pointed at a small stuffed cat Amber wanted, and she squealed when the operator handed it over. The next round he missed the first two, landed the third, and pointed at a small white stuffed bunny for Alicia, who took it with both hands and held it against her chest. She looked up at Mike with an expression that said more than any six-year-old's words could have managed.

Without warning, Amber hit him from the left. Lizzie hit him from the right, and Alicia came straight in from the front. Three small bodies wrapped around his legs and his waist, jumping and squeezing and laughing, their stuffed animals pressed between them. Mike stood in the middle of the game booth walkway with three little girls hanging off him. His arms around all of them, grinning.

Nicole stood three feet away and watched.

She watched her daughters hug this man without hesitation, with the full-body trust of children who felt completely safe. She watched Lizzie press her face into his side, and she watched Amber squeeze him around the waist with the fearless affection that was Amber's approach to everyone she loved. She watched Alicia—her quiet, careful Alicia—press her stuffed bunny against Mike's chest and lean into him with her eyes closed.

The image tugged at Nicole's heart and sent a flood of warmth through her.

Moments later, after the girls had untangled themselves from Mike, they moved on. The girls led, with the adults close behind. The evening kept going—the lights brighter now, the music louder, and the crowd thicker as the festival shifted fully into its nighttime energy. And at the far end of the parking lot, the carousel waited.

It was a classic traveling carousel—painted horses in rows of three, moving up and down on brass poles; a few bench carriages between the rows; colored lights tracing the canopy; and mirrors reflecting the glow. Calliope music piped through speakers mounted on the center column, and the whole thing turned slowly in the warm evening air like something out of a storybook.

"Horses!" all three girls said at once.

They joined the short line and waited. When the previous ride ended and the gate opened, the girls surged forward and claimed three horses in a single row—three across, side by side. Lizzie picked a white horse on the left end. Alicia picked a blue horse in the middle. Amber picked a red horse on the right end.

Nicole helped Amber up first, making sure her feet were in the stirrups and her hands were on the pole. Then she moved to Alicia and lifted her onto the blue horse, brushing a curl out of her face. Mike had Lizzie settled on the white horse in seconds.

The carousel operator made his way around the platform, checking each rider. Nicole positioned herself standing between Amber and Alicia, one hand resting on the back of Amber's horse behind her daughter, her other hand resting on the back of Alicia's horse on the opposite side. Mike stood between Alicia and Lizzie—one hand on the back of Lizzie's white horse, his other hand on the back of Alicia's horse.

The music swelled—the old-fashioned calliope melody that every carousel in the world seemed to play, tinny and sweet and somehow timeless. The painted horses rose and fell on their brass poles. The lights spun into soft streaks of color against the darkening sky. And the three girls came alive.

Amber held her pole with one hand and her stuffed cat with the other, while she narrated the ride like a horse race announcer. She called out to Lizzie and Alicia as if they were miles apart instead of right beside her. "And they're rounding the turn! The red horse is in the lead! No, wait, the blue horse is catching up! It's going to be close, folks!"

Alicia was laughing, open and loud, with her head thrown back. She called out to Amber, "My horse is faster than yours!" — and the volume of it, the sheer unguarded joy in her voice, made Nicole's breath catch. This was Alicia, her quiet, reserved daughter, feeding off the energy of the carousel and the evening and the two girls beside her. Letting herself be as loud and silly and free as she wanted to be.

Lizzie was pretending her white horse was Clover and narrating an imaginary trail ride that involved mountains, a river crossing, and an encounter with bears, delivered at a volume that suggested the entire carousel had been drafted into her adventure. "Hold on, Clover! We're going through the rapids! Amber, watch out for the bear on your left!"

"I see him!" Amber yelled. "I'll handle the bear! Alicia, you take the rapids!"

"I've got the rapids!" Alicia called back, and all three of them dissolved into the kind of laughter that only happened when children forgot that adults existed and the world belonged entirely to them.

They were happy. All three of them, deeply and completely happy, just feeling it, living inside it, letting it carry them.

Nicole looked across the carousel horse in the middle, and Mike was already looking at her.

Not at the girls. Not at the lights, or the crowd, or the painted horses rising and falling on their brass poles. At her. And Nicole could see it on his face as clearly as she could see the festival lights behind him—this man cared about her. It was right there in the way he looked at her, unhidden and sure.

Nicole held his gaze as the carousel continued turning and the calliope played its tinny, sweet melody into the evening air.

She let it exist—this warm, unnamed thing between them—and she didn't try to overthink it or push it away.

She smiled for the rest of the ride. A real, full, unguarded smile that came from somewhere honest and deep within her. Just a woman, standing between painted horses, with the festival lights spinning and her daughters laughing and a steady, kind man looking at her during a carousel ride like she was the only still point in a turning world.

The calliope slowed. The music wound down to its last few notes, and the painted horses settled to a stop, and the spell of the ride gave way to the noise and the lights and the world around them.

Mike lifted Lizzie down and set her on the platform. Nicole helped Alicia and then Amber. The girls immediately wanted to go again, and when both parents said not tonight, all three of them accepted it with the minimal protest of children who were too tired to fight and too happy to be upset about anything.

The girls moved ahead, the way children do when the night is winding down but their energy hasn't fully surrendered—walking in a loose cluster, comparing stuffed animals, and replaying the carousel ride in real time. Amber was telling Lizzie about the bear she'd fought during Lizzie's imaginary trail ride. Alicia was listening and smiling. Their voices carried back through the warm evening air to Mike and Nicole, who were walking behind them.

"Nicole."

She looked at him as the festival lights caught the angles of his face, and the noise of the festival continued around them.

"Go to lunch with me tomorrow after church," he said. "Just you and me."

Four words. *Just you and me.* Not the girls. Not a riding lesson, or a pizza outing, or an ice cream run engineered by three six-year-olds with a gift for ambush. Just him. Just her.

"I'd like that," she said.

Chapter 17

Mike held the door for Nicole, and they entered Minnie's Diner, scanning the room for an open booth.

Minnie's Diner was packed with the after-church crowd, every red vinyl booth occupied, and most of the chrome-topped counter stools taken. The whole place hummed with the easy noise of people who had nowhere else to be and no particular reason to hurry. The black-and-white checkered floor was scuffed in the places it had been scuffed for thirty years. The jukebox near the door was playing something country and low. Minnie had the kitchen running at full speed, and the smell coming through the pass-through window was roast beef and biscuits and coffee and the warmth of a place that had been feeding this town since before Mike was born.

"I see one," Nicole said, pointing toward a booth near the back window.

"Looks good. I'm right behind you."

She moved through the crowded diner ahead of him, weaving between tables, and slid into the booth. Mike sat down across from her.

Minnie appeared as they settled, a coffeepot in one hand.

"Well, good Sunday afternoon to you both... coffee?" Minnie asked.

"Hi, Minnie, and yes, please, coffee sounds great," Mike said.

"Me, too, please," Nicole said

Minnie poured their coffee. "Just the two of you?"

"Just the two of us," Mike said.

"Well, that's just lovely. You two take your time looking at the menus. I'll be back in a few to get your order." She patted the edge of the table twice and walked away.

"So," Nicole said, picking up the laminated menu and opening it. "This is strange."

"What is?"

"Sitting across from you, and we have no children around us. I keep expecting Amber to knock over a cup or Lizzie to start a debate about ranch dressing."

"Give it five minutes. I might start the ranch dressing debate myself."

"Please don't."

"Ranch belongs on everything."

"It does not belong on everything."

"Name one thing it doesn't belong on."

"Pancakes."

Mike considered this. "I'll give you pancakes."

Nicole laughed. "So what is Lizzie up to this afternoon?" Nicole asked as she looked over the menu.

"Lizzie is baking cookies, and my mom is supervising, which means Lizzie will eat half the dough before anything makes it into the oven, and my mom will let her, and there will be cookies waiting for me when I pick her up but significantly fewer than the recipe intended."

"My mom does the same thing with the girls. The recipe makes three dozen, but by the time Amber and Alicia are done taste-testing, you're lucky to get two." Nicole set her menu aside. "Can I ask you something?"

"Sure, go ahead."

"What do you do when you're not at the mill or not with Lizzie? I realized the other day that I don't actually know what you do in your spare time. Any hobbies? Anything you enjoy doing... you know, 'me time' type things?"

The question caught him slightly off guard. Not because it was unusual, but because no one had asked him that in a long time. Further making him realize how small his world had become since Jenny's death.

"I build things," he said. "I have a woodworking shop behind my home. It's just a hobby, nothing professional. But I spend time out there after Lizzie goes to bed, or when she's with my parents or siblings."

Nicole tilted her head. "What kind of things do you build?"

"Furniture, mostly. Tables, chairs, shelving. I built my dining table and bookshelves for Lizzie's room. I made a rocking chair for my mom last Christmas. Last month I finished a toy chest for Lizzie with her name carved into the lid, and right now I'm working on a coffee table for Jim and Grace for their wedding gift."

"Mike, that sounds like a lot more than just a hobby. That's a craft."

He took a sip of his coffee. "It's peace and relaxation for me. It's the part of my day when I don't have to think about schedules or production numbers or whether we're going to hit our quarterly target at work."

"How long have you been doing that?"

"Since I was a teenager. My dad taught me the basics, and I just kept going. I built a birdhouse when I was fourteen that was so crooked that the birds refused to live in it. My mom still has it on a shelf in the garage."

"She kept a crooked birdhouse for fourteen years?"

"She keeps everything that she feels is special. She has every Mother's Day card all six of us ever made. She has some of our schoolwork that holds special memories for her. Now she keeps anything Lizzie makes, and she won't throw out a single thing."

"Your mom is wonderful."

"My mom is a hoarder of sentiment. But yes, she's wonderful."

"What about you?" he said. "What do you do outside of school and the girls?"

She blew out a breath and then laughed at herself. "That's a shorter list than yours. I read when I have the energy. I help my mom with the animals occasionally. I take walks on the farm when the girls are playing and I need ten minutes of quiet. But honestly, most of my spare time goes to lesson planning or laundry or falling asleep on the couch at nine o'clock because I'm so worn out."

She picked up her mug. "I used to paint. Watercolors, nothing fancy. I took art classes in college as electives, and for a while I had a little setup in our spare room in Knoxville. But I packed it up when the girls were born and never unpacked it."

"You should unpack it."

"I keep telling myself that. I've been checking the community bulletin board for watercolor classes and haven't found any yet, but I'm thinking about asking at the arts co-op I recently heard about."

"You should. My sister Sarah's done some work with them on community projects, and she says they're a good group."

"That's good to know. I miss having something that's just mine. Teaching is mine in a way, but it's also work. Painting was the thing I did because I wanted to, not because anyone needed me to."

"That's how the shop feels to me."

Minnie came back to take their orders. Mike got the chicken pot pie. Nicole ordered the turkey club with a side of Minnie's coleslaw. Minnie wrote it down, refilled their coffee, and left with a grin on her face.

"So, do you miss Knoxville?" he asked.

Nicole looked out the window beside their booth for a moment, watching a truck pull into a parking spot on Main Street. "I miss pieces of it. I miss the coffee shop I used to go to on Saturday mornings when I was out running errands before Derek got sick. I miss the library near our house that had the best children's section.

I miss the friends I made there; we've all gotten pretty bad at keeping in touch."

She turned back to him. "But I don't miss living there. By the end, after Derek passed, the house felt like a museum of a life that didn't exist anymore. Every room had a memory attached to it, and for a while those memories were a comfort, and then they became just too much. I'd walk past his closet, and his clothes were still hanging there, and I couldn't bring myself to move them, but I couldn't stand looking at them either."

Mike nodded; he knew that feeling very well.

"Moving here wasn't running away from that exactly... I mean, it was running away but also moving toward something else, too," Nicole said. "It was walking toward a fresh start. My parents, this town, the job at the elementary school. I needed a place that was mine, not ours. Does that make sense?"

"It makes perfect sense."

She took a sip of her coffee and set the mug down. "I loved teaching in Maryville. The school was bigger, the resources were better, and I had colleagues who became real friends. But teaching here is different in a way I didn't expect. The classes are smaller. I know most of the kids's families in some way. I'm connecting the dots with who's who now that my memory is coming back from growing up here. When one of my students skinned her knee on the playground last week, I knew her mother from when we went to school together. I called her, and we had a real conversation, not a voicemail and a form letter sent home with the child. People here embrace community and engage in real conversations. People care more here. That matters to me a lot; it's comforting. In Maryville, the classes were bigger, the district was bigger, and everything felt like it moved faster. Here I can actually teach the way I always wanted to teach."

"Which is how?"

"Like each kid matters. Because they do."

Minnie brought their food a few minutes later. The chicken pot pie was perfect; the crust was golden and flaky. Mike cut into it and let the steam rise while Nicole arranged her turkey club on her plate and tried the coleslaw.

"So why the lumber mill?" Nicole asked, pointing her fork at him. "You mentioned before that you've worked there since you were sixteen. That's twelve years. You could have done anything."

Mike chewed his bite of food and considered the question. "My dad put me to work the summer I turned sixteen. I spent the first three months hauling boards and sweeping sawdust and thinking it was the hardest thing I'd ever done. And then something clicked. I started learning how the equipment worked, how to read a piece of timber, and how to tell the difference between red oak and white oak by the grain pattern. My dad didn't hand me anything. He made me earn every bit of it, the same as he did with every employee. But I liked the work. I liked that it was physical and specific, and that at the end of the day you could see what you'd accomplished."

"And you just stayed?"

"I just stayed. I moved from the floor to production management, then to operations, and now I handle the daily business, the contracts, and the long-term planning, and work with the crew as much as I can. Dad, even though he claims to be semi-retired, still comes in almost every day, and when he's there, he's outside working with our employees, getting his hands dirty and enjoying the physical work. And honestly, he's in his element and happy, and that makes me happy. He says, One day he'll retire fully and step away completely and hand everything over to me."

"Does that scare you?"

"A little," he said. "My grandfather started that mill, and Dad built it into what it is today. We have just over eighty people working for us. Their families depend on the decisions I'll be making completely on my own. That's not a small thing."

"No, it's not."

"But I'm not afraid of the work. I know the mill. I know the people. I've been in every department, run every piece of equipment, and handled every supplier we work with. I prefer the hands-on work, and I deal with the office work. Maybe in the future I'll hire someone to focus on the office work, which would free me up to do more of what I enjoy. I know the mill will be mine someday when Dad steps all the way back, and that feels right. I've never regretted my career choice, and never once have I thought about doing something else. It's always felt right. It's not glamorous, but I'm proud of what we do there."

"You should be. I knew from a very young age that I wanted to be a teacher. I went to the University of Tennessee in Knoxville after high school graduation, and being away from home broadened my horizons a bit. I realized just how big the world was and how many opportunities I had. Then one thing led to another, and I met Derek my sophomore year. We got married, and we stayed in Knoxville. But we did have plans to move eventually. We lived in a massive subdivision, which was different for me. I liked it, and yet I didn't. It was the same with city life; I liked certain things about it and couldn't stand just as many. Derek and I both dreamed of moving to a small town and having a home with property for the kids to run and play."

"I honestly cannot imagine living in a subdivision or a city. I like space and privacy. I like our smaller community here."

"Can I tell you what surprised me about coming back here?" Nicole said, pulling a piece of turkey from her sandwich.

"Tell me."

"I thought I'd feel like I was going backward. Moving in with my parents at twenty-eight with two kids felt like the opposite of progress at first. My friends in Knoxville were buying bigger houses and getting promotions, and I was packing boxes and driving a moving truck back to the town I'd left at eighteen. I kept waiting to feel embarrassed about it."

"Did you?"

"Not once. And that surprised me more than anything. The first morning I woke up in my old room with the girls sleeping down the hall and my mom making breakfast downstairs and the farm outside the window, I just felt relieved. Like I could stop holding everything together by myself, because there were people around me who wanted to help carry it."

"That's not going backward," Mike said. "That's being smart enough to know where your people are."

Nicole looked at him, and the warmth in her expression was direct and unguarded. "I'm glad I came back," she said.

"I'm glad you came back, too."

"What do you think you'll do long-term? Stay with your parents, or find your own place eventually?"

"Eventually, my own place. The girls love the farm, and my parents love having us here, but I want something that's ours. I've been thinking about it more lately. Maybe next year I'll start looking seriously. There are a few properties in town that come up now and then, or my dad mentioned the possibility of building something on the farm property. I don't know yet. But I'm not in a rush. For now, what we have is working."

"Your parents' place is a good setup for the girls. All that land for them to explore and the animals."

"The girls would live in the barn if I let them. Amber has decided she's going to be a horse trainer, a veterinarian, and a dragon tamer. In that order."

"Solid career plan."

"Very realistic. Alicia wants to be a teacher like me, which she told me last week with the most serious face I've ever seen on a six-year-old."

"Alicia would be a great teacher."

"She would. She already lines up her stuffed animals and gives them spelling tests."

Mike laughed. He could picture it clearly: Alicia sitting cross-legged on the floor with a row of stuffed animals arranged by size, a small whiteboard propped against her knee, teaching a bunny how to spell cat.

"I have to tell you something that happened in my classroom last week," Nicole said.

"Tell me."

"A boy in my class brought a frog to school in his lunchbox. A live frog. I didn't know about it until after morning circle when I heard this sound coming from the cubbies, and seventeen first-graders went completely silent. Which is how you know something is very wrong, because first-graders are never silent unless they're hiding something or witnessing something they know they shouldn't be seeing."

"What kind of frog?"

"A tree frog. The boy, Jackson, walked over to his lunchbox, opened it, and said, This is Gerald. He wanted to see what school was like. And then Lizzie stood up and said, 'Can Gerald sit with us at lunch?' and the entire class erupted."

"What did you do?"

"I conducted an emergency frog relocation. I got a container from the supply closet, caught Gerald, called Jackson's mother, and kept seventeen children from losing their minds while Gerald sat on my desk in a plastic tub and became the most popular student in the building for forty-five minutes."

"Gerald had a good first day."

"I believe you are right."

Minnie cleared their plates and brought the check, and Mike picked it up and pulled his wallet from his back pocket. He left the cash and a generous tip on the table and set the check holder on the edge for Minnie.

The lunch crowd had thinned. A few regulars sat at the counter, nursing coffee. The couple in the booth near the door was sharing a piece of Minnie's pecan pie. The jukebox had cycled through its playlist and started over.

Nicole wrapped her hands around her coffee mug. "This was really nice, Mike."

"It was."

"I can't remember the last time I sat in a restaurant without someone spilling something or asking to go to the bathroom."

"The bar is low."

"The bar is underground." She smiled. "But this wasn't just the bar being low. This was good. I had a really good time."

"So did I."

He looked at her across the booth, and the afternoon felt open and unhurried in a way his afternoons hadn't felt in a long time. Lizzie was happy at his parents' house, surrounded by cookies and grandparents and the promise of his sisters arriving later. Nicole's girls were with her parents on the farm. Neither of them had anywhere to be, and the question that had been forming in the back of Mike's mind came forward.

"Do you have plans this afternoon?" he asked.

She tilted her head slightly. "I don't, actually. I hadn't thought much past lunch."

"There's a place I'd like to take you. A waterfall, part of the national park system. It's on the edge of town, about a fifteen-minute drive from here. Serenity Falls."

"I remember Serenity Falls. I haven't been there since high school."

"It's a good hike this time of year. I go out there when I need to clear my head, and it's one of my favorite places in the area." He set his hands flat on the table. "I'll be honest...I'm not ready for today to end. I'd just like to spend more time with you."

"I'm not ready either," she said. "Let's go."

They slid out of the booth. Mike walked to the front of the diner and held the door open for her. She passed through into the afternoon, warm for late September, with the mountains visible above the rooftops and the first trace of autumn color showing on the highest ridges.

"Thank you, Minnie," Mike called back through the door.

"You two have a beautiful afternoon, and give those girls a kiss and a big 'ole hug for me," Minnie called from behind the counter.

"Will do, Minnie. Enjoy the rest of your day."

Mike walked Nicole to his truck in the small lot beside the diner. He opened the passenger door for her, and she stepped up into the cab with a look that was somewhere between amused and pleased, and he closed her door and walked around to the driver's side and climbed in.

Mike pulled out of the parking lot and turned onto the road that led toward the park. The windows were down. The air was warm and clean. The mountains waited ahead of them, and the afternoon was wide open, and somewhere in the back of Mike's mind, he knew that what he felt sitting next to this woman in the cab of his truck on a Sunday in September was not friendship. It was more than that.

Chapter 18

The road narrowed as Mike turned off the county highway and onto the two-lane park road that curved uphill through the trees. Nicole watched the forest thicken on both sides, the maples and oaks pressing close, their leaves partway through the turn from green to the deep golds and burnt oranges that made the Smokies famous every fall. A wooden park service sign appeared at the entrance that read Great Smoky Mountains National Park in carved lettering. The last time she had driven past that sign, she was eighteen and crammed into the back seat of her friend Lauren's car with three other girls, all of them wearing cutoff shorts and hiking shoes.

Mike pulled into the small parking area at the trailhead, a modest gravel lot with a dozen spaces. Four other vehicles were already there, and Mike eased his truck into a spot near the far end, close to the trailhead marker. He turned off the engine, and the quiet of the mountains replaced the hum of the road.

Nicole stepped down from the cab and stood for a moment, taking in the view. The parking area sat at the base of a ridge, and from here the mountains rose in layers, one behind the other, their peaks softened by the haze that gave the Smokies their name. The sky was a deep, clear blue, and the air was cooler up here than it had been in town, carrying the smell of damp earth and pine and the particular sweetness of leaves just beginning to decay. She had grown up with these mountains outside her bedroom window. She had hiked them as a child, ridden horses along their lower trails, and stared at them from the back porch of the farm on a thousand ordinary evenings. They were as familiar to her as her own name, and it still caught her off guard how beautiful they were when she was standing inside them instead of just driving past.

"I forgot how close it feels up here," she said. "Like you could reach out and touch the ridgeline."

Mike came around the front of the truck and stood beside her. "That's one of the things I like about this spot. You're not looking at the mountains from a distance. You're in them."

They walked to the trailhead, where a wooden post held a laminated trail map behind Plexiglas. The path was well-maintained, packed dirt with a border of flat stones on either side, wide enough for two people to walk side by side.

The forest closed in on them within the first hundred yards. Hardwoods on both sides, their trunks thick and straight, the canopy overhead filtering the afternoon light into soft columns that moved with the breeze. Most of the leaves were still green at this elevation, but here and there a single branch had turned early, a streak of orange or gold against the green that looked almost deliberate, like someone had painted it there to remind you what was coming.

"I haven't been on this trail since senior year of high school," Nicole said, stepping over a tree root that crossed the path. "Lauren Porter and I used to come out here with a group of friends on weekends. We'd hike past the falls and take the trail all the way up to the overlook at the top."

"That's a workout."

"It was. We thought we were so tough. A bunch of teenage girls climbing a mountain because we wanted to sit at the top and talk about boys."

"Did you talk about boys?"

"Every single time."

Mike laughed, and the sound carried easily through the trees. The trail began a gentle uphill climb that Nicole felt in her calves. It wasn't steep, just enough of an incline to remind her body that she spent most of her days standing in a classroom instead of hiking.

"Mrs. Fletcher and I are planning a field trip for the first graders in a few weeks," Nicole said as they rounded a curve where the trail widened near a cluster of boulders. "We're going to take them to the park in town for a leaf-collecting project. The kids will get to have a picnic lunch at one of the shelters, and a couple of park rangers have agreed to come talk to them about what they do, forest fire prevention, and the animals in the area. The kids are going to love it."

"Lizzie will be out of her mind excited about that."

"I know. She asked me last week if we were going to do any field trips this year, and I had to keep a straight face because Mrs. Fletcher and I had just started putting it all together."

"Good luck keeping a secret from Lizzie. She has a sixth sense for surprises."

"Good to know. We're going to need a few parent volunteers to come with us... hint, hint."

He looked at her and grinned. "Subtle, aren't you? Let me know what day, and I'll be there."

The sound of water grew louder as the trail climbed. What had been a distant hush when they left the parking area became a steady, layered sound that filled the space between the trees. Nicole could feel it as much as hear it, a low vibration in the air that told her they were getting close. The trail bent left around a large rock face, and the trees thinned, and then the trail opened, and the waterfall was there.

It was bigger than she remembered. The water came down from a ledge fifty or sixty feet above in a broad white curtain, catching the light where it broke apart over the rock face before gathering into a wide natural pool at the base. The pool was deep and clear, and from there the water narrowed into a stream that ran downhill over smooth stones toward the river far below. Mist hung in the air near the base of the falls, fine enough to feel on her skin.

The flat rocks that edged the pool were just as she remembered them: broad slabs of gray stone worn smooth by centuries of water and weather. Natural seating that angled toward the falls as if the mountain had arranged them on purpose. To the right, a wooden bridge spanned the stream where it left the pool, connecting the trail they stood on to the far bank where the path turned steep and disappeared uphill into dense forest. That was the trail she and her friends had taken all those years ago, the one that climbed to the overlook at the top.

A couple sat on the bridge with their legs hanging over the edge, and a man with a camera and a tripod was set up near the base of the falls, photographing the water. Other than that, the place was theirs.

"This is even more beautiful than I remembered," Nicole said.

Mike led her toward the flat rocks near the edge of the pool, and they sat down on the widest one, a slab of stone that was warm from the afternoon. The sound of the water was constant and full, the kind of sound that wrapped around a conversation and made it feel private even in an open space. Light came through the canopy of leaves overhead in angled shafts that moved across the rock and the water as the breeze shifted the leaves overhead.

Nicole pulled her knees up and rested her arms across them. The mist from the falls was cool on her face, and the air tasted clean. She watched the water come down the rock face and thought about how many times this waterfall had done exactly this, how many people had sat on these rocks and watched it, and how the mountain didn't care about any of them and kept going, anyway. There was comfort in that. The world was bigger than her problems, and it was still beautiful, and it would be beautiful tomorrow whether she had a good day or a hard one.

"This is where I come when I need to think," Mike said. He was sitting beside her, his forearms resting on his knees, his eyes on the waterfall. "I've been coming here since I was fifteen or sixteen. Whenever the noise in my head gets too loud or I've been grinding on a problem too long, I come out here and sit on these rocks and just let the water do its thing for a while. I always feel closer to God here. I don't know if that makes sense."

"It makes sense," Nicole said. "There are places like that. Places where the noise of your life falls away, and it's just you and God and whatever you've been carrying."

"That's exactly what it is." He picked up a small stone from the rock beside him and turned it in his fingers. "Nicole, I want to be honest with you about something."

She looked at him, and she could see his jaw working, as if he were choosing his words with care.

He set the stone down. Then he turned to her.

"I wasn't looking for this," he said. "I wasn't looking for anything. After Jenny died, I built my life around Lizzie and the mill and my family, and it worked. Three years, and I never once thought about dating. I never had the urge. It genuinely never crossed my mind. I went to work, I came home, I showed up for Sunday dinner at my parents' house, and I raised my daughter. And I was fine with that. I was content."

He paused for a moment, looking at the water. "And then I met you and your two girls at the back-to-school bash, and I don't know how to explain it other than to say my world got bigger. It was as if I'd been living inside a house I'd built for two people, and

I didn't realize how small the rooms were until somebody opened a window and I could see how much space was on the other side. I'd kept everything so carefully contained. Me and Lizzie, my job, my family, church. And I thought that was enough because it was all I'd thought to reach for."

"What I feel for you is more than friendship," he continued. "I'd be lying to both of us if I pretended it wasn't. I'm not going to call it something it hasn't had time to become yet, but I know it's real... there is something here between us."

He turned his head and looked at her directly. "I'm worried. Not about me. About you. I know where you are right now because I lived my own version of it. I know what it's like to have a full plate and a heart that's missing a person who was once in your life and isn't there anymore. I don't want to be that someone who walks into your life and makes everything more complicated. I don't want to rush you, Nicole. I don't want to add pressure to a life that's already carrying plenty. I just want you to know what I feel, and I want to hear where you are, and whatever you tell me, I'll respect it."

Nicole looked at him, and the honesty in his face was so complete that it made her want to reach out and hug him. His sincerity and his willingness to speak openly meant so much to her. He was a man sitting on a rock beside a waterfall, telling the truth because he believed she deserved to hear it.

Over the past few weeks, she'd been filing little things away in her mind that she'd noticed about him: every conversation, every small kindness, and every moment where she caught herself thinking about him after the girls were in bed and the house was quiet. She had labeled it friendship because friendship was safe and manageable and didn't require her to examine what was underneath it. She had organized it into neat categories: he's a good dad, he's kind to my daughters, he's easy to talk to, and we have grief in common. The filing cabinet was filling up, and she knew it.

"Can I tell you about Derek?" she said.

"Please."

"Derek was one of the steadiest and kindest people I've ever known. He was funny in that quiet way where you'd miss the joke if you weren't paying attention. He was an electrician, and he came home every day smiling and happy, and he'd pick up both girls at once, one in each arm, and carry them around the kitchen while I finished dinner. He read to them every night in these ridiculous character voices that made them giggle."

She watched the waterfall as she talked, the white curtain of water pouring over the ledge, constant and unhurried.

"We had a good marriage. Not a perfect one, because those don't exist, but a real one. We laughed a lot. We wanted the same things. We had plans. We were going to move to a small town eventually, buy a house with property, and let the girls grow up with space to run. We talked about it all the time."

She paused. "He was diagnosed when the twins were four. The oncologist was honest with us from the beginning, and I appreciated that even when I hated what he was saying. We had eighteen months of treatments and appointments and good days and terrible days and hope and then the slow work of learning to let the hope become something quieter. I had time to prepare for losing him. I planned for it. I organized everything. And then he died, and all that preparation meant nothing. You can watch the wave coming from a mile away, and it still knocks you flat."

Mike nodded. He didn't say anything. He just listened, his body still, his attention on her.

"I went back to teaching in January. I finished the school year in Maryville. I thought the routine would help, and during the day it did. But every afternoon I'd drive back to that house and sit in the driveway for a minute before I went inside because I needed a second to brace myself for the emptiness. The girls were inside with the sitter, so it wasn't actually empty or quiet. But Derek wasn't there. And that absence was louder than anything."

She turned to look at Mike. "I moved here because I needed a place that was mine. Not ours. Mine. And it's been good. It's been really good. The girls are happy, my parents are wonderful, and the school is exactly where I'm supposed to be. I'm building something here that I'm proud of."

"But I've been scared, Mike. Not of you. Of what you represent." She let that sit for a second because it was true, and she wanted him to hear it clearly. "The idea that my heart could do this again, that it could open toward someone new, is the most natural and the most terrifying thing I've felt in a long time. I've been feeling for a while now like God has been opening my heart to the possibility of something more. Quietly, gently, in that way He works where you don't notice it's happening until you're already in the middle of it. And then I look at you, and I see a man who answered my grief question a few weeks ago with more honesty than anyone has given me since Derek died. I see a man who got on a horse yesterday despite not having been on one in years because his daughter wanted him to. I see the way you talk to Amber and Alicia, the way you never treat them like someone else's kids. I see all of that, and I've been telling myself it's just friendship."

She shook her head once, a small movement. "It's not just friendship. I know that. I can feel it. And it's scary, because we both know what it means to love someone and then lose them. That's not something you forget. It's not something that stops informing every choice you make."

The mist from the waterfall drifted across the rocks in a fine veil, and Nicole could feel it on her arms and her face, cool against the warmth of the afternoon.

"But I also believe that God put you in my path for a reason," she said. "And I believe the life He gave me is meant to be lived, not just managed. Derek would want that for me. He told me that, actually, near the end. He said, 'Don't make this house a museum. Live your life.' I didn't understand what he meant at the time because I was too busy trying to hold everything in place... and quite honestly, I didn't want to think of a life without him."

She looked directly at Mike. "I want to see where this goes. I want that. Carefully. With honesty between us every step of the way. I'd like to find out what this is. Slowly. With honesty."

Mike held her gaze, and the look on his face was not relief nor triumph. It was gratitude. The gratitude of a man who had said the hardest thing he'd said in three years and been met with equal honesty in return.

"Slow is good," he said. "I want slow... that's the speed I'm used to. I'm not in any rush, Nicole. This whole thing, this possibility of living fully again, it hit me out of nowhere, and it made me realize how small I'd made my world. I'd kept Lizzie and my routine so close that I'd built, like, a small world or maybe a fortress around us without even knowing I was doing it. Those were things I realize now that I needed at the time. I just didn't realize I was still doing them. My life had become a habit, and I never stopped to think beyond what was right in front of me until you walked into my life."

"We have small human beings watching everything we do, Mike," Nicole said. "They learn from us. They see all of it, and they will absolutely interrogate us the second they suspect anything."

"Lizzie will have a full investigation underway immediately."

Nicole laughed, and the sound mixed with the waterfall, the breeze in the canopy overhead, and the birds calling from the trees on the far bank. It felt good to laugh. It felt good to have said the hard things and still be sitting here, still be easy with each other, still be two people who had chosen honesty over comfort and come through to the other side of the conversation with something that felt like solid ground.

"Can I ask you something?" Mike said.

"Of course."

"Friday evening. Would you want to do this again? Just the two of us. Maybe dinner somewhere, or a walk, or whatever sounds good. I just want to keep spending time with you."

"That sounds wonderful," she said with a smile. The afternoon was stretching out around them, warm and easy, and the waterfall kept pouring down the rock face with the same steady rhythm it had maintained for thousands of years. The couple who had been sitting on the bridge earlier had left, and the photographer had packed up his tripod. The place was theirs now, just the two of them and the water and the mountains and the late September light coming through the trees.

Nicole looked at the waterfall, at the white water crashing into the pool and the mist catching the sunlight, and she felt the goodness of this afternoon in a way that was specific and clear. She was sitting on a warm rock next to a man who had told her the truth of what he felt with honesty, and she had done the same. The life she'd been so carefully rebuilding piece by piece for months had just added a piece she hadn't planned for.

She looked at Mike. He was watching the falls, his face relaxed, the late afternoon light on the angles of his jaw and across the tops of his shoulders. She held her hand out to him, and his fingers closed around hers, warm and sure, and Nicole held on. The waterfall poured over the rocks in front of them, steady and unending, and the mountains rose on every side, and the afternoon was theirs, and she didn't let go.

Chapter 19

Mike held the front door of The 1887 Room open, and Nicole stepped past him into the warmth of the restaurant, the October evening still cool on the back of her neck as the door closed behind them. The first thing she noticed was the ceiling. Pressed tin, original by the look of it, catching the light from the vintage fixtures that hung on long stems above the dining room. The second thing she noticed was the smell. Bread, butter, herbs, and the faint sweet edge of something caramelizing in the kitchen.

The 1887 Room occupied a restored mercantile building on Cedar Street, and the bones of the old structure were everywhere. Exposed brick walls lined with framed black-and-white photographs. Wide-plank hardwood floors that had been refinished to a warm honey color but still showed the wear of a hundred and forty years. A long wooden bar along the far wall served as the host station, its surface polished smooth by decades of use.

In the far corner of the main dining room, a small ensemble was playing, acoustic guitar, upright bass, and a fiddle, the music low and unhurried, filling the spaces between conversations without competing with them.

A young woman at the host stand greeted them and led them to a table near the window. Tablecloth, candles, cloth napkins folded beside the silverware. Mike pulled Nicole's chair out for her, and she sat down and smoothed the napkin across her lap and looked across the table at him.

He looked good. That was the plain truth of it. He was handsome in dark jeans and a white button-down shirt that fit him perfectly.

"This is beautiful," Nicole said, looking around the dining room. "I haven't been here since my parents' anniversary dinner years ago."

"I haven't been here in a while either," Mike said. "Jim and Grace came here for his birthday last month, and he wouldn't stop talking about the food, so I figured it was a good choice."

"Jim has good taste."

"Jim has good taste in food and questionable taste in everything else. Don't tell him I said that."

Nicole laughed. The server came to their table, a young man who introduced himself as David, and went through the evening's menu. Nicole ordered the pan-seared trout with roasted vegetables. Mike ordered the bourbon-glazed pork tenderloin. They both asked for sweet tea. David left with their menus, and the table was just the two of them, the candle between them, the low fiddle and guitar from the corner, and the gentle noise of a Friday evening in a small town.

"So, how was your week?" Nicole asked, resting her chin in her hand.

"Busy. We had a shipment go out Wednesday that was supposed to go out Monday, so the whole crew was scrambling to make up the two days. Your brother was in rare form about it."

"What did Rick do?"

"He gave a speech on the production floor about the importance of scheduling that sounded exactly like my dad, same hand gestures and pauses for effect. Some of the guys who've worked for us long enough and know Dad really well tried their best not to laugh."

She smiled. "My week was good. One of my students brought in a caterpillar he found on the playground and asked if we could keep it in the classroom and watch it turn into a butterfly. So now I have a caterpillar habitat on the shelf next to the reading corner, and multiple students who check on it every fifteen minutes like it's going to transform overnight."

"Do you actually think it will turn into a butterfly?"

"If it's the right species and if it survives the amount of attention it's getting, yes. If not, I'll be having a very different conversation with seventeen six-year-olds in a few weeks."

Mike grinned. "That's a tough lesson."

"First grade is full of tough lessons disguised as small ones."

David brought their sweet teas, and Nicole took a sip and set the glass down. The fiddle player in the corner had shifted into something slow and melodic, and the sound of it drifted across the room. A couple at a nearby table leaned toward each other over their plates. An older pair by the window were eating in the easy, wordless rhythm of people who had been sharing meals for decades. The restaurant was full but not loud, and the candlelight softened everything.

"Can I tell you something?" Mike said.

"Of course."

"I was nervous tonight. Driving over to pick you up, I was genuinely nervous. I can't remember the last time I was nervous about anything that wasn't a quarterly production report."

"Seriously?"

"I changed my shirt twice."

Nicole pressed her lips together to keep from laughing.

"The first one I've had since I was twenty years old, and it's showing signs of age. The second one, Lizzie said I looked like my dad. So I went with the third option."

"Lizzie weighed in on your outfit?"

"Lizzie weighs in on everything. She told me I looked handsome and then she asked me if I was taking you somewhere fancy. I told her that we were going to dinner. She said, good and went back to coloring."

"Amber asked me if I was going out with Mr. Hartwell tonight. I said yes. She said, okay like she'd already known the answer before she asked the question."

"They're keeping tabs on us."

"They absolutely are."

Their food arrived. The trout looked excellent, the skin crisp and the flesh flaky, served over a bed of roasted root vegetables. Nicole watched Mike cut into his pork tenderloin and take the first bite, and the look on his face told her everything she needed to know.

"Jim was right," Mike said.

"Jim was very right," Nicole said after taking her first bite.

They ate and talked, and the conversation moved the way it had moved on the phone this week, the way it had moved at the waterfall, the way it had been moving for weeks now. Easily. Without effort.

"I have a question for you," Nicole said, setting her fork down. "We went to the same high school. Same graduating class. How did we never actually talk to each other?"

Mike leaned back in his chair. "I've thought about that."

"You have?"

"We were in entirely different circles. I was on the basketball team and spent most of my time with those guys. You were in choir, right?"

"Choir and youth group and a small group of friends who were basically attached at the hip. We were not cool."

"I wasn't cool either."

"You were on the basketball team."

"Being on the basketball team in Serenity Crossing does not make you cool. It makes you a guy who shows up to practice and occasionally makes a free throw in front of forty people in a gym that smells like floor wax and sweat."

Nicole laughed. "I remember the gym smelling like floor wax, not so much of sweat."

"That smell is permanently in my memory. I could walk into that gym tomorrow and it would smell exactly the same."

"Do you remember Mrs. Calloway?" Nicole asked.

"Tenth grade English."

"Yes."

"She gave me my first and only D on a paper. I wrote about The Great Gatsby, and she told me my thesis was 'aggressively vague.' I still think about that."

"She told me I had 'a lovely writing voice that would benefit from having something to say.' I carried that around for a year."

"That's brutal."

"She was brutal. But she was also the reason I started paying attention to what I actually thought instead of just writing what I thought the teacher wanted to hear. I came back around on Mrs. Calloway eventually."

"I never came back around on that D."

"Mike, it was one paper."

"It was a formative paper. It shaped my relationship with literary analysis forever. Which is to say, I have no relationship with literary analysis."

Nicole covered her mouth with her napkin because she was laughing and also chewing.

"Okay," she said, recovering. "Here's my real question. Do you remember the senior assembly where they did the awards, and

Tyler Beck won 'Most Likely to Succeed' and gave a speech that seemed to last forever?"

"I remember Coach Davis trying to get the microphone away from him."

"I was sitting in the third row and watched Coach Davis stand up three separate times and sit back down because Tyler just kept going."

"That was the longest morning of my life," Mike said. "We had a game that afternoon and the whole team was sitting in the back row counting the minutes."

"Did you win?"

"We lost by fourteen."

"Was it Tyler's fault?"

"I'm going to say yes, because I've been blaming Tyler for that loss for ten years, and I'm not going to stop now."

Nicole laughed again, and this time she didn't bother covering it. The sound carried, and the couple at the nearest table glanced over, and the woman smiled before turning back to her husband. Nicole didn't mind being overheard. She didn't mind any of it.

"I remember you, actually," Mike said, and his voice was quieter now. "From school. I remember you singing at the spring concert during senior year. You had a solo."

Nicole blinked. "You were at the spring concert?"

"My sister, Anna, was in the chorus. I was there for her. But I remember your solo. You sang something; I don't remember the name of the song, but you were good. Really good."

"I can't believe you remember that."

"I remember thinking you had a nice voice, and then the guy next to me said something about the game that weekend, and I went back to thinking about basketball. I was eighteen. My attention span had limitations."

"That's fair."

"What about you?" he asked. "Did you know who I was?"

"I knew your name. I knew you were Rebecca's brother because Rebecca was in my biology class, and she talked about you occasionally. She said you were the quiet one in the family."

"That sounds like something Rebecca would say."

"She wasn't wrong."

"She's never wrong. She'll tell you that herself."

Nicole smiled and picked up her tea. The candle between them flickered, and the light moved across Mike's face. He caught her looking and held her gaze, and the warmth in it was steady and open, and real.

"I have another question," Nicole said. "Have you ever left Tennessee, like on vacation or anything?"

"I went to Kentucky several times for basketball tournaments in high school. Does that count?"

"Barely."

"Then no. I've never left Tennessee. Never been on a plane. Never seen the ocean."

"You've never seen the ocean?"

"Never. My life went from high school to marriage to Lizzie, and there was never a time when a trip like that came up. Jenny and I talked about going to the coast for our anniversary one year, but then she got pregnant with Lizzie, and we decided to wait, and then…" He paused. "We just never got around to it."

Nicole nodded. "Derek and I went to Myrtle Beach the summer before the twins were born. The water was beautiful, and the sand was so hot I burned the bottoms of my feet walking from the hotel to the shore."

"Was it worth the burned feet?"

"Every bit of it. The ocean is one of those things that's bigger than you expect even when you know it's going to be big. You stand there and you look out and there's just no end to it. It made me feel very small and very grateful at the same time."

"I'd like to see that someday," Mike said.

"You should. You'd love it."

"Where would you go if you could go anywhere?"

Nicole thought about it. "Savannah, Georgia. I've always wanted to see Savannah. The historic squares, the Spanish moss, the old architecture. I've read about it and seen pictures, but I've never been. There's something about a place that holds onto its history instead of tearing it down and starting over that appeals to me."

"You just described Serenity Crossing."

"I described a warmer, flatter, more Southern version of Serenity Crossing. Probably with better seafood."

Mike smiled. His plate was nearly empty, and Nicole's was too, and neither of them seemed in any hurry to flag down the server.

"Tell me something about your mornings," Nicole said. "Before the day starts. What does that look like?"

"My mornings, really?"

"How a person spends their morning is very telling."

Mike thought about it, turning his tea glass slowly on the table. "I get up before Lizzie. Always have. I make coffee, and I take it out to the porch, and I sit there for about half an hour before the day starts. I read my Bible and look at the mountains. If it's the middle of winter, I sit by the window in my living room so I feel as if I were outside. It's the quietest part of my day, and I need it. By the time Lizzie wakes up, I've had my time with God, and I'm ready for the day."

"I love that," Nicole said.

"What about you?"

"My mornings are the opposite of quiet. The twins are up by six thirty, and from that point on it's a sprint to get everyone dressed and fed and out the door. But my version of your porch time is after the girls are in bed. I sit at the kitchen table with a cup of tea or coffee, and I just breathe for a few minutes. Sometimes I write in a journal. Sometimes I just sit there and thank God for getting me through another day. It's not fancy, but it's mine."

"That's all it needs to be."

Nicole was about to say something else when a woman stopped beside their table. She was about their age, dark hair pulled into a low ponytail, a friendly face that Nicole recognized after a second's delay.

"Mike, so good to see you," the woman said.

"Hey, Jess," Mike said, and he stood to give her a brief, friendly hug.

Nicole placed her. Jessica Brewer. They'd had chemistry class together junior year. Jessica had been on the volleyball team and sat two rows ahead of Nicole in Mr. Donovan's class. They hadn't been close, but they'd been friendly, the way most people were in a school that small.

Jessica turned to Nicole, and her face lit up. "Nicole Hanshaw? Oh my goodness, I heard you were back in town. I keep meaning to stop by the school and say hello, but life has been so crazy."

Nicole stood. "It's Sullivan now, but yes. Jessica, it is so good to see you."

Jessica pulled her into a quick hug. "It's been years. You look wonderful. How are you? You have two girls, right?"

"I'm doing really well, thank you for asking, and yes, I have two daughters. They're settling into first grade and loving every minute of it. How about you?"

"Busy. I'm running the physical therapy clinic over on Elm Street now, and my two boys are keeping me humble on a daily basis. We need to catch up. Seriously. Coffee sometime?"

"I would love that."

"I'll find you. I know where you work," Jessica grinned and squeezed Nicole's arm. "You two enjoy your evening. This place is so good." She waved and headed back to her table near the entrance, where a man Nicole assumed was her husband was waiting.

Mike and Nicole sat back down.

"Jessica Brewer," Nicole said. "I haven't seen her since graduation."

"She's been here the whole time. She opened her clinic about three years ago. She's good people."

"It's strange how you can grow up in the same town as someone and then lose ten years without noticing."

"I imagine that's how it goes when you leave. The town keeps going, and when you come back, the pieces don't always line up where you left them. But the good ones reconnect fast."

Nicole looked at him across the table. The candle had burned down by half, and the restaurant had grown a little quieter as the evening settled in. The ensemble in the corner was playing something with a slow, easy melody that the fiddle carried while the guitar kept time underneath. She could feel the music as much as hear it, a low, warm current running beneath the conversation.

"This has been a really good night, Mike."

"It has," he said. "I'm glad we did this."

"Me too."

He leaned forward slightly. "Tomorrow, after the girls' riding lesson, would you and the twins want to come over to my place for a cookout? I'll fire up the grill, the girls can play in the yard, and we can just have a fun, relaxing afternoon. Nothing fancy."

"I would love that," Nicole said.

"Lizzie has been asking to have the girls over for weeks; she wants to show Amber and Alicia her room. I think she has a whole tour planned."

"Of course she does."

David came by with the check, and Mike paid before Nicole could reach for her purse. She gave him a look, and he gave her one back that made it clear the matter was not up for discussion.

They stood up from the table. Nicole reached for her jacket on the back of her chair, and Mike took it from her and held it open so she could slip her arms in. His fingers brushed the tops of her shoulders as he settled the jacket into place, and the touch was brief and warm and deliberate.

The ensemble shifted into a new song as they turned toward the door, something slow and sweet that the fiddle opened with a long, clear note before the guitar came in underneath. A couple near the corner had moved from their table to the small open space near the musicians, and they were swaying in the kind of slow, easy dance that didn't require any skill, just willingness.

Mike looked at the couple, then at Nicole. "Let's dance before we go?"

He took her hand and led her to the open space near the ensemble, and when they stopped, he placed his other hand at the small of her back, and she rested hers on his shoulder. They were close. Closer than they'd been to each other at any point in the weeks she'd known him. She could smell his cologne, clean and warm, and she could feel the steadiness of his hand against her back and the solidity of his shoulder under her palm.

They moved slowly. Neither of them was a dancer, and it didn't matter. The fiddle carried the melody, and they followed it, turning in a small, unhurried circle while the candles flickered on the tables around them and the other couple danced a few feet away with their eyes closed. Nicole's hand was in Mike's, and his grip was firm and gentle, and she was aware of every point where they touched. His hand was on her back. Her fingers rested against the fabric of his shirt. The warmth of him, steady and close.

She looked up at him. He was looking at her, and there was no guardedness in his expression. No careful management. Just warmth and gladness and the particular tenderness of a man who had spent years not reaching for anything and was reaching now.

The song ended. They stopped moving. Mike didn't let go of her hand right away, and Nicole didn't pull it back. They stood there for a breath, two breaths, and then he smiled, a happy, genuine smile that reached his eyes, and they walked toward the door with her hand still in his.

The October night met them on the sidewalk. The air was cool and clean, carrying the faint smell of wood smoke from somewhere and the sharper scent of the mountains. Cedar Street was quiet; the storefronts along the block lit by the warm glow of their display windows, a few leaves skittering across the sidewalk in the breeze. Mike opened the passenger door of his truck for her, and Nicole climbed in.

The drive to the farm was short. Fifteen minutes through the quiet roads on the edge of town, the headlights cutting through the dark, the mountains invisible except where the stars stopped. They talked on the drive the way they'd talked all evening, easily and without agenda, about nothing in particular and everything at once. Nicole told him about a book she'd started reading this week. Mike told her about a piece of cherry wood he'd found at the mill that he was saving for a project he hadn't decided on yet. The conversation filled the cab of the truck the way good conversation always did, naturally, without anyone steering it.

Mike pulled into the gravel driveway of the Hanshaw farm and parked near the front of the house. The porch light was on, casting a warm yellow circle across the front steps, the rocking chairs, and the edge of the porch swing.

He walked her to the front door. The gravel crunched under their feet, and the night was still around them except for the distant sound of a barn owl somewhere on the property and the low hum of insects in the grass.

They stopped at the door. The porch light was above them, and in its glow Nicole could see Mike's face clearly: the line of his jaw and the steadiness in his eyes. She could have reached out and straightened the collar of his shirt if she'd wanted to.

"Thank you for tonight," she said. "I had a wonderful time."

"So did I," he said. "Best Friday I've had in a long time."

"Best Friday I've had in a long time as well."

He looked at her. She looked at him. The night was quiet, the porch light was warm, and Mike was right there, close, real, and solid. He leaned in, and his lips met hers, and the kiss was brief and warm and honest. A goodnight kiss. The kind that said, This is real, and I'm glad. His hand came up and rested against the side of her face for just a second, his thumb brushing her cheek, and then he pulled back and his eyes found hers again.

"Goodnight, Nicole."

"I'll see you tomorrow, Mike. Thank you again for a lovely evening."

He waited until she opened the door and stepped inside before he turned and walked back to his truck. Nicole closed the door quietly behind her and leaned against it, enjoying the giddy schoolgirl feeling racing inside her.

Chapter 20

Mike was standing in the doorway of Lizzie's bedroom, watching her hold up a shirt with the critical eye of a fashion designer preparing for a runway show.

"This one," she said, pressing a pink shirt with a glittery horse on the front against her chest. "No, wait." She tossed it on the bed and grabbed a purple one from the pile. "This one."

"Lizzie, they're coming over for hamburgers. You could wear a paper bag, and Amber and Alicia wouldn't care."

"Daddy, you know nothing about what girls care about."

He leaned against the doorframe and crossed his arms. She had a point. "Go with the purple. It's your favorite color."

She looked at the purple shirt, looked at the pink one on the bed, and then looked at him as if he had just solved a complicated math problem. "Okay." She pulled it over her head, tugged it into place, and smoothed her hair down with both hands. "How do I look?"

"Like a kid who's about to have the best afternoon of her life."

"I already know that, Daddy. I meant, do I look nice?"

"You look great."

She grinned and pushed past him into the hallway, heading for the front door at a pace that suggested Nicole's SUV might already be in the driveway. Lizzie had been like this since they'd gotten home from the riding lesson, a wire of energy that would not sit still. She had cleaned her room without being asked, which in six years of parenting had never happened before. She had arranged her stuffed animals on her bed in a specific order that she'd explained to him in detail and that he had immediately forgotten.

He walked through the living room and into the kitchen to check on the food one more time. The hamburger patties were on a plate in the fridge, seasoned and ready. The hot dogs were next to them. Buns sat on the counter beside a bag of potato chips, a sleeve of paper plates, a stack of paper cups, and napkins. Juice boxes and a gallon of Kool-Aid were in the fridge. Water bottles lined the bottom shelf. The charcoal was in a bag on the back porch, next to the grill.

He wiped down the butcher-block countertop one more time, even though it was already clean. Then he stood in the middle of the kitchen and looked around his cabin with the particular awareness of a man who was about to see it through someone else's eyes.

The living room was tidy. Lizzie's art supply basket was tucked beside the stone fireplace where it always lived, and her crayon drawings were taped to the fridge and framed on the wall near the bookshelf. The walnut dining table he'd built occupied the space between the kitchen and the living area, its surface cleared except for a small vase of wildflowers that Lizzie had picked from the yard this morning and placed in the center with the kind of ceremony that suggested she understood the occasion better than he'd expected. The hardwood floors were swept. The bookshelves he'd built along the far wall were dusted.

The sound of tires on the paved driveway reached him through the open kitchen window, and Lizzie's reaction was instantaneous.

"They're here!"

She was out the front door before he could say a word, the screen door bouncing behind her. By the time Mike reached the porch, she was already at the bottom of the steps, bouncing on her toes as Nicole's silver SUV came to a stop.

The back doors opened, and Amber spilled out first, her feet hitting the ground at a run, followed immediately by Alicia, who was moving just as fast but managed to close the car door behind her. All three girls collided at the base of the porch steps in a tangle of arms, voices, and laughter.

"You have to see my room," Lizzie said, grabbing Amber's hand. "I have the best room. I cleaned it and everything."

"Does it have a bunk bed?" Amber asked.

"No, but it has a toy chest with my name on it."

"That's so cool," Alicia said. She was smiling as she reached for Lizzie's other hand so that all three of them were linked. "Can we see it?"

"Come on." Lizzie pulled them up the steps and past Mike with the urgent efficiency of a tour guide on a schedule, and all three of them disappeared through the front door in a blur of sneakers and ponytails.

Nicole came up the walk carrying a covered glass dish in one hand and a grocery bag in the other, and the sight of her stopped him for a moment. She was in jeans and a soft green pullover, her blond hair down around her shoulders, and she was smiling at the sound of the girls' voices already echoing from somewhere inside his home.

"That was fast," she said, climbing the porch steps.

Mike laughed and held the front door open for her. "Lizzie has been planning this since we left the farm. What can I take?"

"This is the broccoli salad," she said, handing him the dish and the bag. "And in the bag is watermelon I cut up this morning and a container of my mom's chocolate chip cookies, which she insisted I bring even though I told her we had plenty of food."

"Cookies are always welcome in this house."

Nicole stepped through the front door and into the living room, and Mike watched her take it in. Her eyes moved slowly across the room, the way a person looks at a space when they actually want to see it rather than just glance and move on.

"Mike," she said. "You have a beautiful home."

"It's small, but it works for us."

"It's not small. It's perfect." She walked to the dining table and ran her hand across the surface, her fingers following the grain of the walnut. "You built this."

"I did."

"The grain is matched across the whole top. You did that on purpose."

He nodded. Most people wouldn't notice that. He had spent three days selecting and arranging the boards so the grain flowed as a single continuous pattern across the tabletop, and Nicole had seen it in ten seconds.

"It's gorgeous," she said as she turned to look at the bookshelves. "And those. You told me this was a hobby for you."

"It is a hobby."

"Mike, hobbies are collecting stamps or doing crossword puzzles. This is something else."

He set the covered dish and the grocery bag on the kitchen counter and didn't know what to say to that, which Nicole seemed to understand because she just smiled at him and kept looking.

From the hallway, the sound of three girls' voices rose in a chorus of excitement.

Nicole turned to face him fully, leaning one hip against the dining table. "I want to see the shop."

"My woodworking shop?"

"Yep... I have to see where you built all this."

"It's just a workshop. Sawdust and tools."

"Mike."

The way she said his name made it clear that deflection was not going to work. "All right. Let me check on the girls first."

He walked down the short hallway to Lizzie's room and found all three of them on the floor surrounded by stuffed animals, dolls, and the contents of Lizzie's art supply basket, which had apparently migrated from the living room.

"Hey, girls. Miss Nicole and I are going to step out back for a few minutes. We'll be right outside."

"Okay, Daddy," Lizzie said, without looking up.

"Can we stay in here?" Amber asked.

"You can stay right here. Just come find us if you need anything."

"We won't need anything," Lizzie said.

Mike led Nicole through the kitchen and out the back door. The October afternoon opened up around them, cool and bright, the sky wide and blue above the treeline. The creek was audible beyond the yard, with a steady low sound of water over rocks. The trees on the property were in the midst of changing into their fall colors; the maples lit up in shades of orange and red; the oaks held their deeper golds, and the mountains rose behind all of it.

"Oh," Nicole said, stopping on the back porch. She was looking at the yard, at the trees, and at the mountains. "Mike, this view!"

"It's not bad."

"Not bad." She looked at him sideways. "You are the most understated person I have ever met."

He smiled and led her across the yard to the workshop, a solid single-story building with wide double doors and a tin roof that his sister Sarah's crew had built at the same time as his cabin. He unlatched the doors and swung them open, and the smell came out to meet them: sawdust, wood shavings, linseed oil, and the faint sweetness of cherry wood.

Nicole stepped inside and fell silent.

The shop was organized the way Mike's mind worked: everything in its place, every tool hung on the pegboard wall, and the workbench running the length of the left side with clamps and hand planes and chisels arranged by size. A bandsaw and a table saw sat along the back wall. Sheets of sandpaper in various grits were stacked on a shelf. Pencil sketches on scrap paper were pinned to a corkboard above the workbench, rough drawings of furniture pieces, some with dimensions scrawled in the margins.

But it was the furniture that stopped her.

A pair of side tables with tapered legs sat near the entrance, their surfaces stained with a satin finish. A set of picture frames, five of them, leaned against the wall, each one different, each one made from a different wood. A cherry cutting board with an intricate grain pattern rested on the workbench, glowing where the light caught it. A small jewelry box with hand-cut dovetail joints sat beside it, the lid slightly open, the inside lined with felt. And in the center of the shop, raised on a pair of sawhorses, was the coffee table.

It was walnut. The top was a single live-edge slab, the natural bark edge of the wood preserved and sealed while the rest of the surface had been planed and sanded to a finish so smooth it looked like water. The base was mortise-and-tenon joinery, hand-cut, with no visible screws or nails or hardware of any kind. The legs were tapered and slightly angled. The grain in the walnut was rich and varied: dark chocolate running into honey running into amber, the natural pattern of a tree that had been growing for decades before Mike turned it into something new.

Nicole crouched down and looked at the joinery where the legs met the frame. She reached out and touched the live edge with her fingertips, tracing the natural curve of the bark.

"This is the coffee table for Jim and Grace," she said.

"It's not finished yet. I still need to do the final coat of finish on the top and seal the bark edge."

She stood up slowly and looked at him. "Mike, this is one of the most beautiful things I have ever seen."

"It's a coffee table."

"It is not just a coffee table, and you know it." She walked along the side, looking at the way the live edge curved and dipped. "The way you kept this edge. The way the grain runs. You chose this piece of wood for a reason."

He had. He'd pulled that slab from a walnut tree that had come down on the property two winters ago, and he'd known the moment he'd seen the grain pattern that it was meant for something important.

"Jim and Grace are going to lose their minds when you give this to them," Nicole said.

"Jim doesn't get emotional about furniture, Grace; I'm not so sure."

"Jim and Grace will both get emotional about this coffee table."

She moved around the shop, taking her time. She picked up the jewelry box and held it carefully, turning it in her hands.

"Who is this for?" she asked.

"I don't know yet. I build things sometimes, and the right person shows up later."

She set the box down gently and looked at him.

"You're an artist, Mike. I know you don't call yourself that. But this," she gestured at the shop, at the table, at the box, at everything, "this is art."

He held her gaze and let the words land. He wasn't used to someone standing in this space and seeing what she saw. "Thank you."

"Daddy!" Lizzie's voice cut through the air, clear as a bell. "We're starving!"

Nicole pressed her lips together to keep from laughing. "Duty calls."

"Duty always calls at maximum volume in this house."

They walked back across the yard toward the three girls on the back porch. Amber was sitting on the top step with her chin in her hands. Alicia was standing beside her with her arms crossed in a way that looked exactly like Nicole. Lizzie was standing in front of them both with the expression of someone who had been waiting for ages and could not believe the adults had the nerve to be this slow.

"We are very hungry, Daddy," Lizzie announced.

"We just had a snack at the farm two hours ago," Nicole said.

"That was forever ago, Mommy," Amber said.

"Forever," Alicia agreed.

Mike opened the bag of charcoal and poured it into the grill while Nicole took the girls inside to wash their hands and get the food organized. Through the open window he could hear all four of them: Nicole directing traffic while the girls asked questions and offered opinions at the same time.

"Mr. Hartwell, do you have ketchup?" Amber called through the window.

"In the fridge door," Mike called back.

"What about mustard?"

"Same spot."

"What about pickles?"

"Are you building a hamburger or a sandwich shop?"

Amber's giggle came floating out the window, and Mike smiled as he arranged the charcoal in the grill and doused it with lighter fluid. He struck a long match and dropped it in, and the coals caught with a low whoosh.

He walked inside and found Nicole at the kitchen counter transferring her broccoli salad into a serving bowl she'd found in his cabinet. The watermelon was already cut and arranged on a plate. The cookies were in a container, and Alicia was trying to pry the lid off.

"Those are for after dinner," Nicole said without turning around.

"Mommy... you weren't even looking," Alicia asked.

"I'm a mom. I know everything."

Alicia looked at Mike with an expression that said she found this claim both suspicious and plausible, and Mike had to bite the inside of his cheek to keep from laughing.

"Can I help with anything?" he asked Nicole.

"How long until the coals are ready?"

"Ten or fifteen minutes."

"Perfect. That gives us time to get everything else set up."

They moved around each other in the small kitchen with an ease that surprised him. He opened the fridge and handed her the juice boxes. She found the paper plates and cups on the counter and started carrying them to the back porch. It was the kind of coordinated rhythm that usually took years to develop, and they were doing it on their first afternoon in his kitchen like they'd done it a hundred times before.

"Where are your serving spoons?" Nicole asked, opening a drawer near the stove after she'd come back inside. "Never mind."

"You're navigating my kitchen better than I do."

"Your kitchen is organized, and the layout makes sense. I appreciate that about you."

"My kitchen is organized because I own about twelve things."

She laughed, and the sound of it filled the kitchen, and it occurred to him that he enjoyed the sound of her laughter in his home.

The coals turned white, and Mike put the hamburger patties and hot dogs on the grill. The smell of charcoal and grilling meat carried across the yard, and the girls appeared on the back porch like they'd been summoned by a dinner bell.

"Can I have two hot dogs?" Amber asked.

"You can have one and then see how you feel," Nicole said.

"I already know how I'll feel. I'll feel like I want another hot dog."

Mike flipped the hamburger patties and looked over at Nicole, who was leaning against the porch railing with her arms crossed, watching the girls with amusement.

"She makes a compelling case," Mike said.

"Don't encourage her."

"Mr. Hartwell, what's that sound?" Alicia asked. She was standing at the edge of the porch, her head tilted, listening.

"That's the creek. It runs through the back of the property, down past the treeline."

"Can we go see it?"

"After we eat, if your mom says it's okay."

Alicia looked at Nicole.

"After we eat," Nicole said, and Alicia nodded, satisfied with the timeline.

Lizzie had taken it upon herself to set the porch table, which Mike had built two summers ago from the same walnut stock as the dining table inside. She was arranging paper plates at each spot with the focus of someone setting a table at a fancy restaurant, adjusting the placement of each plate until it was exactly where she wanted it.

"Lizzie, do you want me to help?" Alicia asked.

"You can put the cups out. One at each plate."

Alicia took the paper cups and placed one at each setting, and the two of them worked side by side.

Moments later, Mike loaded the hamburgers and hot dogs onto a plate after they had cooked, and then carried them to the table where everyone sat waiting.

"Should we say grace?" Nicole asked once everyone was seated.

Mike nodded. He bowed his head, and the girls followed, and he kept it simple. "Lord, thank you for this food, for this beautiful day, and for the company around this table. Bless this meal and bless these kids who are about to eat us out of house and home. Amen."

As they ate, conversation flowed around the table. Lizzie told Nicole about the drawing she'd been working on, a picture of a horse that she was making for Tabitha as a thank-you for the riding lessons. Amber told Mike about a boy in her class named Oliver who had tried to convince everyone that he could speak to squirrels. Alicia, without any prompting, told a story about a book they'd read in class that week about a deer who lost his hat. She told it with such detail and animation that Mike found himself genuinely invested in whether the deer found his hat.

"What are you going to be for Halloween?" Lizzie asked, turning to Amber.

"A veterinarian," Amber said. "Like Grandpa."

"That's so cool. I'm going to be a cowgirl. What about you, Alicia?"

"I want to be a painter," Alicia said. "With a beret and a paintbrush and one of those boards you hold."

"A palette," Nicole said.

"A palette," Alicia repeated, nodding. "Mommy said she'd help me make one out of cardboard."

"That sounds so cool," Lizzie said.

As Mike reached for the bowl of broccoli salad, he caught Nicole watching the three girls with an expression he recognized because he'd felt it on his own face more than once this afternoon. She was watching her daughters enjoy themselves. She caught his eye and smiled, and her smile said everything.

"This broccoli salad is really good," Mike said.

"Thank you. It's my grandmother's recipe."

"What's in it?"

"Broccoli, bacon, sunflower seeds, red onion, dried cranberries, and a dressing that's basically mayonnaise and apple cider vinegar with a little sugar. It sounds strange, but it works."

"It more than works."

"My mom tried to improve on the recipe once by adding raisins, and my grandmother did not speak to her for three days."

"Over raisins?"

"Over raisins. My grandmother took her recipes very seriously. If anyone tried to change a recipe without her permission, it was treated as a personal offense."

"That sounds like my mom with her biscuit recipe. Jim made the mistake of suggesting she try a different flour once because he was on this healthy eating kick... almond flour, I think it was, and the look she gave him could have peeled paint."

Nicole laughed. "What did he do?"

"He apologized, ate three biscuits, and never mentioned it again."

The conversation kept going, moving from recipes to cooking disasters. Nicole told him about the time she tried to make a Thanksgiving turkey during her second year of marriage and forgot to take the bag of giblets out of the cavity before she put it in the oven. Mike told her about the time he tried to make Lizzie a birthday cake from scratch and the layers came out so lopsided that he had to use an entire second container of frosting just to make it look level.

"Did it taste good?" Nicole asked.

"It tasted like a brick covered in frosting."

"Did Lizzie eat it?"

"Lizzie ate two pieces and told me it was the best cake she'd ever had. Which was either the sweetest thing she ever said or a sign that her taste buds weren't fully developed yet."

"It was the sweetest thing. She said it because you made it."

"She said it because she was four and would eat anything covered in enough frosting."

"Take the compliment, Mike."

He looked at her across the table, and there it was again, that warm, easy thing between them that made every conversation feel like it could go on for hours, and he'd be fine with that.

Cleanup was fast. Paper plates went into a trash bag, leftover food was carried inside, and the broccoli salad bowl was rinsed and set in the sink. The whole process took under ten minutes, which was one of the great benefits of paper plates, and then the girls were free and the yard was theirs.

Lizzie led the charge to the playset Mike had built in the side yard. It was his biggest project outside of furniture, a structure that had taken him most of a summer to design and build, with two swings, a slide, a teeter-totter, a set of monkey bars with a hand-over-hand traverse, and two crawl-through tubes connecting the upper platforms. The wood was cedar, weather-treated and sanded smooth, and the whole thing was anchored deep enough to hold steady.

Amber went straight for the monkey bars, grabbed the first bar, and swung herself forward with confidence. Alicia chose the slide, climbing the ladder carefully and then coming down with a grin that got bigger every time she went. Lizzie was on the swings, pumping her legs, calling out to both of them from across the structure.

"You built that too," Nicole said.

"Last summer. Took me about two months."

"Two months."

"The crawl-through tubes were the hardest part. Getting the angles right so they connected to the platforms without any gaps or rough edges."

She shook her head slowly. "Mike Hartwell, you could build this entire town from scratch, and you'd call it a weekend project."

"That's an exaggeration."

"It's barely an exaggeration."

They watched the girls rotate through every station on the play-set, trading spots, negotiating turns, inventing rules for games that only made sense to the three of them. Amber figured out how to traverse the monkey bars without stopping and celebrated by hanging upside down from the last bar until Nicole told her to come down before the blood rushed to her head.

"Let me ask you something," Mike said as he leaned against the porch railing. "If you could have any superpower, what would it be?"

Nicole looked at him with her eyebrows raised. "Superpower?"

"Superpower. Anything."

She thought about it. "The ability to pause time. Just for a few minutes. So I could catch my breath during the day and not feel like I'm always running."

"That's a good one."

"What about you?"

"I'd want to be able to talk to wood. Ask it what it wants to be before I start cutting."

She stared at him for a beat, and then she laughed, the kind of full, genuine laugh that came from somewhere real. "That might be the most Mike Hartwell answer possible."

"I stand by it."

"You would talk to lumber."

"I would have very productive conversations with lumber."

"Lizzie!" Amber shouted from the top of the slide. "Come do the slide with me!"

Lizzie abandoned the swings and ran to the slide, and the three of them began a complicated game that involved sliding down, running around, and climbing back up in a pattern that seemed to have internal logic, even if the adults couldn't follow it.

The game evolved. At some point, Lizzie found a ball in the toy bin near the porch and kicked it across the yard, and the playset was abandoned instantly as all three girls chased it. They kicked it back and forth, no rules, no teams, just the ball moving between them in the kind of game that children invented on the spot and adults couldn't replicate if they tried.

"Come play!" Lizzie shouted toward the porch.

"Yeah, come play!" Amber echoed.

Mike looked at Nicole. Nicole looked at Mike.

"I should warn you," she said, "I'm competitive."

"I should warn you, Lizzie kicks hard for a six-year-old."

They joined the game, and any structure it might have had dissolved completely. Mike kicked the ball to Alicia, who trapped it with her foot and passed it to Amber, who sent it sideways past Nicole. Nicole chased it down and kicked it back toward Lizzie, who wound up and launched it directly at Mike's shins.

"Ow, Lizzie."

"You're supposed to block it, Daddy."

"I wasn't ready."

"You have to always be ready."

Amber got the ball next and dribbled it past Mike with a move that belonged on a soccer field, not in a backyard. When she scored between two imaginary goalposts, she pumped her fists and did a little spin that made all three girls dissolve into giggles.

"Did you see that?" Amber said to Nicole. "I got past Mr. Hartwell."

"I saw it. Very impressive."

"I let you get past me, Miss Amber," Mike said.

"You did not let me," Amber said with her hands on her hips.

"He definitely did not let you," Nicole said, grinning at him. "You're just faster than he is."

"I am not slower than a six-year-old."

"The evidence suggests otherwise."

The game turned into a chase. Alicia had the ball and took off running across the yard, and Lizzie went after her. Then Amber went after both of them, and then Mike and Nicole were chasing all three girls across the grass while the October light stretched long across the property and the mountains stood quiet behind the trees.

It was the kind of chaos that only children and lazy autumn afternoons could produce, and the yard was full of the sound of it. Lizzie's laugh was the loudest, a bright, rising sound that scattered across the property like birdsong. Amber was close behind, punctuated by shouts of triumph every time she evaded someone. And Alicia was laughing too, running with her arms out, free and easy and unguarded in a way that Mike had watched her grow into over these past weeks.

Nicole was fast. Faster than he'd expected. She caught Amber from behind and scooped her up, spinning her around while Amber shrieked with delight, and then she put her down and took off after Alicia, who saw her coming and zigzagged across the yard like a rabbit.

Mike caught Lizzie, tossed her gently over his shoulder, and she kicked her legs and laughed so hard she couldn't speak. He put her down, and she immediately tagged him and shouted, "You're it!" and sprinted away.

He chased all four of them. He chased Amber, who dodged left. He chased Alicia, who dodged right and then stopped and tagged him back, and took off running before he could react. He chased Lizzie, who ran in circles. He chased Nicole, who tried to hide behind the play set and failed because she was laughing too hard to stay hidden.

The game had no endpoint, which was the beauty of it. It wound down the way all good games wound down, gradually, as legs got tired and lungs needed air. Mike and Nicole were both standing in the middle of the yard with their hands on their knees, breathing hard and smiling, while the three girls continued to run laps around them with the limitless energy that only children possessed.

"I'm out of shape," Nicole said, still catching her breath.

"I run a lumber mill, and I just got outrun by three first-graders."

"We are definitely not as young as we once were."

They sat down in the grass, and then they lay back, and the sky was above them, wide and blue with thin clouds stretching across it in long white lines. The mountains framed the edges of his vision, their ridgelines sharp against the sky, their slopes covered in the fire of October color.

Nicole was beside him, close enough he could hear her breathing, still a little fast from the running, and he could see the edge of her smile from where he lay.

"What a beautiful world God gave us," she said, looking up at the sky.

"I agree."

The girls' voices carried from somewhere behind them, still running, still laughing, still inventing games out of nothing.

"Thank you for today," Nicole said. She turned her head to look at him, and they were close enough that he could see the flecks of gold in her blue eyes. "For inviting us. For this afternoon. For all of it."

"My pleasure."

"I haven't been this happy in such a long time."

"Neither have I."

She held his gaze, and the look between them was quiet and unhurried and full of everything they hadn't said yet and weren't in a rush to say, because afternoons like this one had a way of saying it for them.

Then the girls noticed.

"Get them!" Lizzie yelled from somewhere to the left, and three sets of footsteps came thundering across the grass, and before Mike could sit up, Lizzie launched herself onto his chest, followed immediately by Amber, who landed on his stomach with the precision of a cannonball, and Alicia threw herself across both Mike and Nicole, bridging the gap between them with her entire body, and all five of them were in a pile in the grass.

Elbows and knees and giggles and grass stains and the weight of three small girls who were laughing so hard they couldn't breathe. Mike's ribs were being compressed by what felt like a small army, and Nicole was laughing, her face turned toward him, her hair full of pieces of grass, and she looked beautiful.

"I think we got them," Lizzie said, breathless and triumphant from her perch on Mike's chest.

"You definitely got us," Mike said. He wrapped one arm around Lizzie and reached the other toward Amber, holding them both steady while they squirmed and giggled.

Alicia rolled off Nicole and flopped onto her back between the two adults, staring up at the sky with her arms spread wide. "This is the best day ever," she said.

Mike lay there in the grass with his daughter on his chest and Nicole beside him and two little girls who felt like they belonged here, and the sky was wide and October-blue above them all. Five people in the grass. Laughing and enjoying a simple afternoon without a care in the world. And what he felt wasn't complicated or difficult to understand. It was gratitude, and it was gladness, and it was the clear, simple knowledge that this was what fullness felt like.

Chapter 21

Pastor Warren was talking about ordinary days as blessings and gifts, and Nicole was listening with her Bible open in her lap, the church congregation around her and the man she was falling for sitting beside her.

"We spend a lot of time waiting for the big moments," Pastor Warren said, his voice carrying through the sanctuary. "The promotions. The milestones. The answered prayers we've been holding our breath for. And there's nothing wrong with looking forward to those things. But I want to ask you something this morning." He paused and looked out over the pews. "When was the last time you thanked God for a Tuesday?"

A few quiet laughs moved through the congregation.

"I'm serious," he said, smiling. "Not a Tuesday where something special happened. Just a regular Tuesday. You got up. Your coffee maker worked. You drove to work on roads that someone maintains. You came home to a house with a roof on it and people inside it who were glad to see you." He opened his Bible. "James 1:17. 'Every good gift and every perfect gift is from above, and cometh down from the Father of lights.' Every good gift. Not just the big ones. Not just the ones we prayed for. Every single one."

Mike's hand was around hers on the pew between them, their fingers laced together.

"We overlook the ordinary because it's ordinary," Pastor Warren continued. "We stop noticing the gifts that show up every single day because they've been showing up every single day, and we've gotten used to them. God woke you up this morning and blessed you with another day of life; that's a gift. A quiet home. A shared meal. Health that we didn't have to fight for. A familiar face in a pew. Those are all gifts." He closed his Bible gently. "Psalm 118:24 says, 'This is the day which the Lord hath made; we will rejoice and be glad in it.' Not 'this is the day something incredible happened.' Just this day. The one you're living right now."

On Nicole's right side, Amber, Alicia, and Lizzie were coloring quietly with crayons and the activity pages they'd picked up from the children's table in the foyer. Beyond them, Nicole's mother sat with her Bible in her hands and her father beside her, his attention on the pulpit.

Nicole looked at her hand in Mike's. She thought about last weekend in his backyard, the five of them on the grass, the girls laughing, the wide blue October sky above them. She thought about their date this past Friday at a restaurant in Pigeon Forge, where they had dined on a patio behind the restaurant and enjoyed each other's company. She thought about Derek, and the thought came gently. He had been a gift. A precious, irreplaceable gift that she'd only had for a few years. She missed him. She would always miss him. But he was home with God and free from pain, and she was here, in a church she'd grown up in, holding the hand of a good man while their daughters colored beside them.

"I'm not asking you to pretend everything is perfect," Pastor Warren said. "I'm asking you to notice what's already good. Because gratitude doesn't change your circumstances. It changes how you see them. And sometimes, seeing them clearly for the first time is the thing that changes everything else."

He bowed his head. "Let's pray."

The congregation bowed with him, and Nicole closed her eyes. Mike's hand stayed in hers.

After the prayer, they stood for the closing hymn. Nicole shared a hymnal with Mike, and his voice was low and steady beside hers. She liked the sound of it. She liked the way he held the hymnal so she could see the words without having to lean. She liked all of it.

The service ended, and the organist played a soft postlude as the congregation began to move. Bibles gathered, purses collected, children stretching and wiggling free of the pews they'd been sitting still in for the better part of an hour. The low hum of conversation rose through the sanctuary as people filed toward the center aisle, and the three girls were up and moving before either parent had a chance to stand.

"Can we get cookies at the fellowship hall?" Lizzie asked, already edging past Mike into the aisle.

"After you shake Pastor Warren's hand," Mike said.

"We already know what he's going to say. He's going to say, 'Good morning, young lady, glad to see you today.' He says that every Sunday."

"And every Sunday you shake his hand and say thank you. That's how it works."

Lizzie sighed, the deep, performative sigh of a child who knew the battle was lost. Amber and Alicia fell in beside her, and the three of them moved down the aisle in a tight little cluster, whispering about which cookies they hoped would be at the fellowship hall today.

Nicole and Mike followed, moving with the flow of the congregation toward the back doors. The line was slow and easy, with people stopping to greet each other, to ask about someone's week, to compliment a dress, or to check on a grandchild. Nicole spoke to a couple she recognized from her parents' neighborhood, and Mike exchanged a few words with a man Nicole had seen at the Harvest Festival. It was the rhythm of a town that had been doing this together for decades.

At the door, Pastor Warren stood with his wife, Mary, beside him. He shook Mike's hand and said, "Good to see you, Mike."

"Good sermon today, Pastor. The Tuesday morning line is going to stick with me."

"That's the goal," Pastor Warren said with a warm smile. He turned to Nicole and took her hand. "Nicole, I'm so glad you're here this morning."

"Thank you, Pastor Warren. That was a wonderful message."

"Well, your mother told me last week that I talked too long, so I tried to trim it down. I hope I succeeded."

Nicole laughed. "Your sermon was perfect."

The girls had already filed past with their handshakes completed, and Lizzie was now tugging Amber toward the parking lot with the single-minded focus of a child who had been promised cookies and intended to collect.

Outside, the October morning was crisp and bright. Nicole pulled her cardigan a little tighter and fell into step beside Mike as they crossed the parking lot toward the fellowship hall. The building sat off to the side of the church. A plain, practical building that hosted everything from potlucks to youth group to vacation Bible school, but on Sunday mornings it belonged to coffee and conversation and whatever the women of the church had decided to bake that week.

"Your mom actually told Pastor Warren he talks too long?" Mike said.

"My mother has opinions about everything, and she shares them freely."

"I respect that about her."

"You say that now. Wait until she has opinions about you."

He looked at her. "Does she have opinions about me?"

"Mike, everybody in this town has opinions about you and everyone else for that matter; it's practically a civic duty around here."

He laughed, and she loved the sound of it. Easy and real and unhurried.

The fellowship hall was filling up by the time they walked in. Long tables lined one wall with coffee urns, pitchers of sweet tea and lemonade, juice boxes stacked in a plastic tub, and a spread of homemade baked goods that could have stocked a bakery. Banana bread, cinnamon rolls, a plate of brownies, a tray of cheese straws, and cookies in numerous varieties. Women in this church took their Sunday fellowship contributions seriously, and it showed.

The room buzzed with conversation and laughter. Men stood in clusters near the coffee, talking about the weather, about the Tennessee Volunteers, and about whatever project somebody's cousin was working on that wasn't going right. Women gathered at tables and along the walls, catching up on the week, trading recipes, and planning the next church event. Children wove between the adults like small, fast-moving obstacles, and a table in the corner had been set up with juice boxes and a plate of cookies specifically for them. Lizzie spotted it first and led the charge, with Amber and Alicia right behind her. Within thirty seconds they were seated at the kids' table with cookies in hand and two other children from church already deep in conversation with them.

Nicole and Mike moved through the room together. His hand found the small of her back as they navigated around a cluster of men near the coffee.

They were pouring coffee when Rebecca appeared.

She came from the direction of the refreshment table, carrying a plate with a cinnamon roll on it and a smile that was working very hard to be casual and not quite managing it.

"Hey, Nicole," she said, giving her a hug. "That dress is gorgeous, girl. Is it new?"

"Thank you. I've had it forever, actually. It just doesn't get out much."

"Well, it should." Rebecca turned to her brother. "And you. Look at you."

"What about me?"

"You're smiling."

"I do smile sometimes, Rebecca."

She took a bite of her cinnamon roll and studied him with the particular attention of a twin sister who had been watching her brother for twenty-eight years and noticed every single shift in his baseline. "I like it. You look happy."

"I am happy."

"Good," she said, and then turned her attention away from him. "Nicole, you simply must have one of these cinnamon rolls. Mrs. Everett makes them, and they're dangerous."

"I grabbed one," Nicole said, holding up her plate. "I remember Mrs. Everett's cinnamon rolls from when I was a kid. They haven't changed."

They talked for a few minutes, the three of them standing near the coffee with their plates, and the conversation was easy. Rebecca asked Nicole how the week had been, and Nicole told her about a science project her class was doing with caterpillars that had become the most closely monitored insects in the history of first grade. Rebecca laughed and said she'd heard about the caterpillars from three different mothers at the salon, which meant the entire town was now emotionally invested in whether or not they turned into butterflies. Mike stood beside Nicole and listened, and every now and then he added something dry and quiet that made both women laugh.

Rebecca squeezed Nicole's arm before she left and leaned in to whisper in her ear. "I'm glad you're with my brother; you've brought such joy into his life."

Nicole smiled as she watched her walk away.

They drifted through the room after Rebecca left. Mike refilled both their cups of coffee, and Nicole added cream to hers. They stood together near the wall and watched everyone in the room.

"I love this," Nicole said.

"The coffee?"

"All of this. Church, and then this afterward. I missed it so much when I was in Knoxville. Derek and I went to a good church there, but it was big, and we never really knew anyone beyond the people in our small group. It wasn't like this."

"There's nothing like a good small-town church where everybody knows everybody and half the congregation is related to the other half."

"That's exactly what I missed. The warmth and community feel of this congregation is amazing."

"As are you, Nicole," he said as he looked at her. She held his gaze and smiled, and he smiled back, and the fellowship hall and its hundred conversations continued around them.

"Nicole!"

She turned. Winona Fletcher was crossing the room toward them, weaving through the crowd with a coffee cup in one hand and her church bulletin tucked under her arm. Winona was a small woman with short brown hair and the kind of energy that left you dizzy sometimes. She was one of the first people Nicole had connected with when she'd started at the school, and their partnership on the upcoming field trip had turned professional respect into a genuine friendship.

"Hey, Winona," Nicole said.

"Hey, honey. Hey, Mike." She looked up at Mike with a grin. "I saw your name on the parent volunteer list for our field trip next Wednesday. I'm thrilled."

"Happy to help," Mike said.

"You say that now. Wait until you're responsible for a group of rambunctious first-graders with butterfly nets in an open park."

"Should I be nervous?"

"A little fear is healthy, Mike. It keeps you sharp." She turned back to Nicole. "I've got the ranger station confirmed; I spoke with them yesterday. They're sending two rangers, and they said they'd bring some animal pelts and track molds for the kids to look at. The kids are going to lose their minds."

"That's perfect," Nicole said. "I talked to the cafeteria on Friday about the sack lunches, and they're all set. Thirty-five lunches, packed and ready for pickup Wednesday morning before we leave."

"Two classes' worth of six-year-olds loose in a park. What were we thinking?"

"We were thinking it would be educational and fun."

"It'll be educational and chaotic. The fun is debatable." But Winona was grinning as she said it. She looked at Mike again. "Seriously, Mike, we appreciate you volunteering. Nicole tells me you're good with kids, which is exactly what we need. Just wear comfortable shoes, bring a sack lunch, and a lot of patience."

"I've been raising Lizzie for six years. Patience is a skill I've developed."

Winona laughed. "You'll be fine. Nicole, I'll email you the final schedule tomorrow so we can go over it at lunch."

"Sounds good."

Winona patted Nicole's arm and headed back into the crowd, stopping to talk to someone else before she'd made it three steps, because that was how the fellowship hall worked. You never got anywhere in a straight line.

"She's something else," Mike said, watching Winona disappear into a conversation.

"She's the best. I'm lucky to work with her."

"Lizzie hasn't stopped talking about the field trip since you told the class about it. She asked me last night if she could bring binoculars."

"Does she have binoculars?"

"She has a pair of toy ones from a birthday party goodie bag. They don't actually magnify anything, but she doesn't know that."

Nicole laughed. "Let her bring them. It'll make her day."

They were still standing together near the wall when Olivia Hartwell came across the room.

She moved through the fellowship hall the way she moved through every room she entered, with warmth, elegance, and the comfortable confidence of a woman who had been part of this church for years and knew every person in the building by name. She had a cup of coffee in one hand, and she was smiling.

"Nicole, how are you doing, sweetheart?"

"I'm doing really well, Mrs. Hartwell. How are you?"

"Oh, I'm wonderful. Busy week, but the good kind of busy." She sipped her coffee. "How are the girls settling in? Lizzie tells me Amber is reading chapter books like they're going out of style."

"She is. She's burning through them faster than I can keep up. Alicia is more into drawing right now, and she's been filling sketchbooks since school started."

"Talent runs in the family. Your mother is one of the most artistic women I know. She made me a wreath for my front door last Christmas. And how about you? How are you feeling about being back home? Still enjoying yourself?"

"Honestly, it feels like I never left. I mean, things are different, obviously, and there are new faces I'm still getting to know. But this town has a way of pulling you back in."

"It does. It certainly does." Olivia smiled. "Listen, I wanted to ask you something. We're doing Sunday dinner at the house this evening. I'm putting a ham in the oven. Dinner will be around five, but the girls and I usually start cooking around two. Rebecca, Sarah, Anna, and Grace will all be there, and we'd love for you and the twins to join us."

"I would love that," Nicole said. "And I'd love to come early and help cook, if that's all right. I enjoy being in the kitchen."

Olivia's face lit up. "Well, that's even better. Come whenever you'd like. The more, the merrier."

"Can I bring anything?"

"Honey, you can bring whatever you'd like, but please don't feel like you have to bring anything but yourself and those two girls."

"I'll bring something," Nicole said. "My mom would have my head if I showed up to someone's dinner table empty-handed."

Olivia laughed. "Your mother raised you right. Tabitha and I are cut from the same cloth on that one." She reached out and touched Nicole's arm. "We'll see you this afternoon then."

"You will. Thank you, Mrs. Hartwell."

"Oh, sweetheart, call me Olivia. I think we're past formalities, don't you?"

Nicole smiled. "Thank you, Olivia."

Olivia gave Mike a look that was brief and knowing and full of the particular satisfaction of a mother who was watching something she'd hoped for come together exactly the way she'd imagined. Then she headed back into the fellowship hall, stopping to talk to Nicole's mother near the refreshment table, the two women falling into conversation as naturally as breathing.

Mike put his arm around Nicole's shoulders.

"So," he said. "You're coming to Sunday dinner."

"I'm coming to Sunday dinner."

"I should probably prepare you."

"For what?"

"The Hartwell clan. There are a lot of us. We're loud. We're opinionated. Everybody talks at the same time and nobody listens, and my mom will try to feed you until you physically cannot eat another bite, and then she'll wrap up a plate for you to take home. Rebecca will ask you a hundred questions. Anna will say something that makes everyone laugh. My dad will sit in his chair and drink his coffee and say about four words all evening, but they'll be the best four words anybody says."

"That sounds wonderful."

"It is wonderful. It's also a lot."

She leaned into him slightly, her shoulder against his chest, and the weight of his arm around her felt steady and right. Across the room, the three girls were still at the kids' table, Lizzie talking with her hands the way she always did while Amber listened and Alicia drew something on the back of a napkin.

"I think I can handle it," Nicole said.

Mike looked down at her and smiled, and what she saw in his face was simple and clear. He was glad she was here. He was glad she was coming to dinner. He was glad about all of it, and he didn't need to say so because his arm around her shoulders and the smile on his face said it better than words could.

"Yeah," he said. "I think you can too."

Chapter 22

The Hartwell brothers were running football routes in the front yard like a group of grown men who had never quite accepted that high school was over. Jim threw a spiral to Dave, and Ethan, Sarah Hartwell's boyfriend, cut between them trying to intercept with the kind of effort that suggested he'd been losing this battle all afternoon and had no intention of quitting.

Nicole pulled to a stop and turned off the engine. Bill Hartwell was on the front porch in one of the rocking chairs with Lizzie on his lap, and the second Nicole's SUV came into view, Lizzie was on her feet.

"They're here!"

Lizzie was off the porch and across the yard before Nicole had her seatbelt undone, her ponytail bouncing and her sneakers barely touching the grass.

Both back doors opened at once. Amber and Alicia tumbled out, and within seconds all three girls were talking over each other, grabbing hands, and spinning in a circle of noise and excitement that carried across the yard. Lizzie pulled them toward the front yard and the football, and the three of them scattered into the game without a backward glance.

Nicole gathered the broccoli salad she had made from the passenger seat and reached for the red velvet cake she'd picked up at the grocery store. She'd wanted to bake something herself, but the window between church and coming here had been too narrow, and the cake in the bakery case had been too pretty to pass up.

Mike was walking toward her from the yard. He had a grass stain on one knee of his jeans, and his face was flushed from running. When he reached her, he kissed her cheek and took the salad dish from her hands.

"You brought the broccoli salad," he said.

"I did. And a cake I didn't make myself, in case anyone asks. I feel bad because I really wanted to bake something."

"Nobody will ask. They'll be too busy eating it."

She handed him the cake box, and they walked together toward the porch. Bill was still in his chair, and he nodded at Nicole as she came up the steps.

"Nicole. Glad you could make it."

"Thank you for having us, Mr. Hartwell."

"Bill," he said. "And you're welcome here anytime."

She smiled at him and followed Mike through the front door.

The kitchen was loud with five women working and talking at the same time. Olivia was at the stove checking the ham. Rebecca was at the island chopping vegetables with more enthusiasm than precision. Sarah was shucking corn at the counter. Anna was arranging a fruit tray and taste-testing every third piece. Grace was beside her, peeling potatoes, her sleeves rolled to the elbows, comfortable and unhurried.

Mike set the broccoli salad and the cake box on the counter near the refrigerator.

"Red velvet," Rebecca said, leaning over to peek into the box. "Nicole, you are officially my new favorite person."

"She brought the broccoli salad too," Mike said.

"Michael," Rebecca pointed her knife at him. "We are in the middle of something in here. Go back outside."

"I just carried in her—"

"Out."

Sarah didn't look up from her corn. "She's right. You're in the way. This is girl territory."

Mike looked at Nicole, and the expression on his face was pure resignation, the look of a man who had grown up with sisters and had learned a long time ago which battles to fight. Nicole pressed her lips together and grinned. "Go on back to your fun outside... I'm fine."

He shook his head, grinning, and walked back toward the door. Rebecca watched him go and then turned to Nicole with a satisfaction that only a twin sister could produce.

"He's been circling this kitchen for the past half hour."

"He has not been circling," Olivia said from the stove. "He came in twice, and both times I sent him back out."

"That's circling, Mom. He not so subtly wanted to make sure we were all in a decent mood for when Nicole arrived."

Olivia gave Rebecca a look that was patient and unhurried and did not dignify the accusation with a response. She turned to Nicole. "Sweetheart, make yourself at home. There's sweet tea in the fridge, and we've got plenty to do if you're up for it."

"Put me to work," Nicole said. "What hasn't been started?"

"The green bean casserole," Grace said. "Everything for it is on the counter by the fridge."

Nicole moved to the counter where the canned green beans, cream of mushroom soup, and a bag of French fried onions were already set out. She washed her hands and then opened the first can and started draining the beans into the sink.

"Grace, how are the reservations at the inn looking for November?" Anna asked from her spot at the fruit tray.

"Full," Grace said. "Every room. I had to turn away three couples last week for Thanksgiving weekend alone."

"I told you," Rebecca said. "This town in the fall is the best-kept secret in Tennessee, and people are finally catching on."

"It's not a secret anymore if people are catching on," Sarah said.

"That's my point, Sarah."

Sarah shook her head and kept shucking.

"Nicole, I have to ask you something," Rebecca said, setting her knife down and turning to face her fully. "And I need you to be honest with me."

Nicole looked up from the casserole dish. "Okay."

"How is Lizzie in the classroom? Because here... that child runs this family."

Nicole laughed. "She has strong opinions. I'll say that."

"Strong opinions are the Hartwell family motto," Anna said.

"Last week, during our community helpers unit, I asked the class if anyone could name a community helper in Serenity Crossing. Lizzie raised her hand and said, very seriously, 'My Aunt Rebecca, because she knows everything that happens in this town before it happens.'"

Rebecca's mouth dropped open. Anna let out a laugh that carried across the kitchen. Sarah stopped shucking. Grace covered her mouth with her hand.

"She did not," Rebecca said.

"She absolutely did. And the whole class just accepted it. Nobody questioned it."

"Because it's true," Sarah said.

"It is true, and I want that quote framed and hung in my salon," Rebecca said. She put her hand over her heart. "That is the greatest thing anyone has ever said about me."

"You realize she basically called you the town gossip," Anna said.

"She called me an essential community resource, Anna. There's a difference."

Olivia was shaking her head at the stove, but she was smiling. "That child has no filter."

"She's honest," Nicole said. "She says what she sees. I love that about her."

"She gets that from her daddy," Olivia said. "Mike was the same way as a boy. Quiet most of the time, but when he did speak up, he said exactly what he meant and not a word more."

Nicole spread the French-fried onions over the top of the casserole and slid it into the oven alongside the ham. She wiped her hands on a kitchen towel and moved back to the counter where the tossed salad still needed assembling.

"Oh, I should mention," she said, tearing lettuce into a large wooden bowl. "We have a field trip this Wednesday for both first-grade classes. We're taking the kids to the park for a nature walk with two rangers from the station."

"Lizzie must be beside herself," Grace said.

"She's been counting the days. She asked Mike if she could bring binoculars."

Anna grinned. "Does she have binoculars?"

"Mike said she has toy ones from a birthday party goodie bag. They don't magnify anything, but she doesn't know that, and I told Mike to let her bring them."

"And," Nicole said, glancing around the kitchen, "Mike signed up to come as a parent volunteer."

The reaction was immediate and unanimous. Rebecca stopped chopping. Anna looked up from the fruit tray. Sarah paused with an ear of corn in her hand. Grace raised her eyebrows. Even Olivia turned from the stove.

"Mike volunteered," Rebecca said.

"He did."

"Mike. My brother. Voluntarily going on a first-grade field trip in an open park."

"With butterfly nets," Nicole added.

Rebecca looked at Sarah. Sarah looked at Anna.

"He's always been wonderful with children. He has patience with them that many people don't. I'm glad he's doing that," Olivia said.

The conversation moved the way conversations in a full kitchen always do, threading from one topic to the next without anyone steering it. Rebecca asked Grace about the menu for the inn's Thanksgiving dinner and whether she'd finally decided on a pie selection. Anna mentioned that the Chamber of Commerce was already planning the town's Christmas tree lighting for the first week of December. Sarah said something dry about being recruited to build the stage again this year, and Anna told her she could complain or she could volunteer, but she couldn't do both.

Nicole moved to the sink to rinse the tomatoes and looked out the window.

The front yard was full of activity, and she could see all three girls. They were running with Lizzie in the lead and Amber close behind. Alicia was trailing by a few steps, and Dave had the football tucked under his arm and was letting them chase him in wide, lazy circles while Jim called out plays that nobody was following.

As she watched, Mike stood near the edge of the yard, and Alicia had stopped running and was crouching near the fence line, looking at something on the ground. Mike crouched beside her.

Whatever Alicia had found, he was giving it his full attention, his head tilted toward her, listening.

Nicole watched her daughter point at something in the grass and Mike lean closer, and Alicia's whole face opened up the way it did when someone took her seriously.

"She found a bug," Nicole said. "I guarantee it."

Olivia was beside her at the sink. She had come to fill a pot for the corn, and she followed Nicole's gaze through the window.

"Lizzie told me all about the fun you had at the Harvest Festival," Olivia said, turning the faucet on.

Nicole turned from the window.

"And Lizzie told me last week that her daddy is humming," Olivia said. "While he's making breakfast. She said she didn't know he could hum because he's never done it before."

The image of Mike standing over scrambled eggs, humming something while Lizzie sat at the kitchen table and noticed, hit Nicole with a specificity she wasn't prepared for.

"I don't say this to put pressure on you," Olivia said. She set the pot on the stove and turned the burner on. "I say it because I want you to know that what you've brought into his life matters. And into Lizzie's."

"I haven't done anything special," Nicole said.

"You showed up. Sometimes that's the most special thing a person can do." Olivia adjusted the flame under the pot. "He had a very hard time after Jenny died. I don't know how much he's shared with you."

"He told me she passed away three years ago. And he told me he'd realized he'd been keeping his world small without noticing he was doing it."

Olivia nodded. "That's the short version." She was quiet for a moment, and when she spoke again, her voice carried the particular steadiness of a woman who had lived through something hard and come out the other side whole. "Jenny was in a car accident."

Nicole went still. She had known Mike's wife had died. She had known it was three years ago. But for some reason she had imagined something gradual. Something with time to say goodbye, the way she and Derek had been given time, hard as those months were.

"I didn't know that," she said.

A thought surfaced then that she had never put together before. Jenny Mitchell. She remembered a dark-haired, bright, and friendly girl who had been with Mike a lot during high school. She now remembered how everyone in school just knew he was going to marry Jenny.

"I remember her," Nicole said quietly. "From school. We weren't close; we hung around in different groups, but I remember her."

Olivia nodded. "She was hard to forget."

"I never put it together that she was his Jenny. I just never made that connection."

"Most people who've been away probably wouldn't. You come back and the town is mostly the same, but the people have lived whole lives in the years you were gone."

Nicole leaned against the counter. "How bad was it for him? After."

"Bad. He was numb for months. He went to work, and he took care of Lizzie, but there was an emptiness in his eyes for a long time. We all took turns going to his house. Cooking, watching Lizzie, making sure he ate. Rebecca moved into his guest room for months."

Nicole thought of Derek. Of those last few months when she'd known what was coming and had tried every day to be ready for it. She'd said goodbye. She'd had time. And it had still knocked the ground from under her the day it actually happened.

"With Derek, I knew," Nicole said. "I had a few months of knowing his death was coming. And I thought that would make it easier, having time to prepare." She paused. "It didn't. Not really. It just changed the shape of it."

Olivia looked at her with the clear, unhurried attention of a woman who had raised six children and learned a long time ago that listening was more important than answering.

"I at least had the opportunity to hold his hand as he passed away," Nicole said. "I was able to tell him everything I needed to tell him. The idea of a phone call, of it just being over without any warning at all, that's..." She shook her head.

"You don't have to compare your road to his," Olivia said gently. "Yours was hard enough, and you walked it with grace, I'm sure."

Nicole nodded. The kitchen was still busy around them, Rebecca and the girls talking about something at the far counter, but this conversation had its own space, and both women were honoring it.

"He's different now," Olivia said. "He makes plans again. He looks forward to things. He's happier, and I see parts of my son coming alive again that have been missing for far too long. And I know that has a lot to do with you and those two girls out there."

Nicole looked out the window again. Mike had stood up from his crouch near the fence, and Alicia was pulling him by the hand back toward the football game. He let himself be pulled.

"He's a good man," Nicole said.

"The best of them," Olivia said. "And I'm his mother, so I'm allowed to say that."

The pot on the stove began to bubble, and Olivia turned back to it and dropped the corn in piece by piece.

Nicole went back to the salad and began listening to Rebecca telling Grace about a woman who had come into the salon last week wanting her hair color to match a picture on her phone. The picture turned out to be a photo of a golden retriever.

"Are you serious?" Grace said.

"One hundred percent serious. She wanted 'that color and that volume.' I said, Ma'am, that's a dog. She said she knew it was a dog; she just wanted her hair to look like that. So I gave her a warm honey hair color makeover and a blowout, and she left happy as a clam."

"Did it look like the dog?" Anna asked.

"It looked fantastic color-wise, but quite a bit different from the dog's hairstyle."

Nicole laughed, and so did everyone else.

The back door opened, and Mike appeared. His hair was ruffled, and he had a fresh grass stain on his left knee to match the one on his right.

"Just checking in," he said.

"Check in number two," Rebecca said without looking up.

"What?"

"You peeked in the window earlier too… I caught that."

"I was just asking Dad something."

"Sure… whatever you say, Mike."

Nicole caught his eye across the kitchen as he grinned

"Go keep an eye on those girls, Michael," Olivia said. "Nicole is fine; we'll call you if we need you."

"Yes, ma'am."

He gave Nicole a wink before turning to leave.

Anna watched the door close and shook her head, smiling. "He's a different person, you know that? Back in August, the most exciting thing in Mike's week was a lumber order. Now look at him. Volunteering for field trips. Checking in on us… or should I say… checking in on you, Nicole." She pulled a piece of fruit from the tray and ate it. "It's amazing how fast everything has changed this fall. God's timing really is something. Everything just lined up exactly when it was supposed to."

Nicole nodded. "It's been a wonderful fall."

And it had. It had been the best fall she could remember.

But the word timing stayed with her a beat longer than it should have. Not because Anna had said anything wrong. Not because

Nicole disagreed. But because everything lining up also meant everything that came before it, and November was just a few weeks away. November seventh.

She shook the thought loose, rinsed her hands under the faucet, and dried them on the towel.

The biscuits went into the oven. The corn was boiling. The salad was tossed and sitting in its bowl on the counter. The vegetable tray was finished; the fruit tray beside it was too. The kitchen was reaching that particular point in a meal's preparation where everything was either done or in its final minutes, and the energy shifted from work to anticipation.

The back door banged open, and Lizzie appeared, red-cheeked and out of breath, with grass in her hair and one shoe untied. "Uncle Dave said he's going to eat the whole bowl of corn on the cob, and there won't be any left for anyone."

"Uncle Dave is just giving you a hard time; he knows it's your favorite," Olivia said.

"Is it almost ready? I'm starving."

"You are not starving, Elizabeth Anne Hartwell. You had a snack an hour ago."

"That was a whole hour ago, Grammy."

Nicole crouched to tie Lizzie's shoe. "There's plenty of corn for everyone, and it should be ready in about ten minutes," Nicole said.

"Ten minutes is forever."

"I think you'll live, Lizzie."

Lizzie sighed the long, elaborate sigh of a six-year-old who had been told to wait and considered it a personal injustice. Then she turned and ran back out the door, letting it bang shut behind her.

Nicole stood and looked out the window. Mike was in the yard, watching the door Lizzie had just run through. Alicia was hanging from one of his arms. Amber was beside them, holding the football and grinning as if she'd just scored the winning touchdown. Mike looked up right then, toward the window, and his expression was one of pure joy. There was no denying she was falling for him.

Chapter 23

Tyler held up a leaf the size of his face and said, "Mr. Hartwell, is this one poisonous?"

Mike took the leaf from him and turned it over in his hands. "That's a sycamore. Not poisonous. The bark peels off the tree in patches, so it looks like it's wearing camouflage. They use the wood for butcher blocks and crates."

"But could it be poisonous if I wanted it to be?"

"No, Tyler. That's not how trees work."

Tyler considered this for a moment, clearly disappointed, and then stuffed the leaf into his paper bag. He ran back up the path to where Sophia and a boy named Jackson were crouching over a pile of leaves near the base of a white oak.

Mike's group of six first-graders had been on the wooded trail for about twenty minutes, and in that time he had identified several tree species, answered questions about bears twice, settled a disagreement about which leaf was the biggest, and explained three separate times that no, they were not lost, and yes, he knew the way back. The trail wound through a section of the town park where the hardwoods grew thick and tall, and on a Wednesday morning in late October, the canopy overhead was a layered ceiling of red and orange and gold that made the whole path feel like walking through the inside of a painting.

He was enjoying himself more than he'd expected to. Nicole had assigned him a group of six from her class, and the kids had figured out within the first ten minutes that he could name every tree on sight. After that, the leaf-collecting project became a game. They brought him every leaf they picked up, and he told them what it was and what the wood was used for. Red oak makes floors and barrels. Sugar maple is the kind that gives you syrup. Tulip poplar is Tennessee's state tree and grows taller than any other hardwood in these mountains. The kids treated every answer like a discovery, and Mike found that he liked being their walking field guide. He knew trees the way some people knew constellations, by shape and color and the way they held their branches, and it was a kind of knowledge that rarely came in handy outside the mill. Here, with six fascinated six-year-olds, it was the most useful thing about him.

Lizzie was at the front of the group with her toy binoculars around her neck, scanning the woods on either side of the path with the serious intensity of someone conducting a wildlife survey.

"Daddy, I see a woodpecker," she said, pressing the binoculars to her eyes as she pointed.

Mike looked. There was, in fact, a downy woodpecker working its way up the trunk of a dead hickory. "Good eye, Lizzie."

Sophia appeared at Mike's elbow with her paper bag held open for inspection. She had organized her leaves by size, smallest to largest, and each one was placed flat and uncrumpled inside the bag with the kind of precision that made Mike think she probably organized her crayons by color, too.

"Mr. Hartwell, can you check mine?" she said. "I want to make sure I have all the different kinds."

He looked through her bag. "You've got red oak, white oak, sugar maple, hickory, and tulip poplar. That's five different species. That's a good collection, Sophia."

"Tyler's bag is just a big mess," she said. "He's crumpling all of them."

"Tyler's bag is Tyler's bag. You worry about yours."

"I'm not worried," she said. "I'm just sayin'... his bag's a mess."

She walked back to the group with the dignified air of a person who had made her point and didn't need to belabor it.

Mike kept his eyes on all six of his kids as they moved along the trail. Jackson and a girl named Maya were walking together a few yards ahead, comparing leaves and having a conversation about whether caterpillars had bones. Harper, the girl who had moved to Serenity Crossing from Bristol at the beginning of the school year, was walking by herself near the edge of the path, collecting leaves quietly. She'd been like that all morning, not unhappy, just self-contained. Mike had made a point of checking in with her a few times, and each time she'd given him a small, serious smile and shown him her latest leaf.

The trail opened up at a junction where two paths met in a wide clearing, and coming up the other path was another group. Pastor Warren was walking at the back of a cluster of seven kids, wearing jeans, a flannel shirt, and a pair of hiking boots that looked like they'd seen a decade of Saturday mornings. His granddaughter, a small girl with dark curly hair, was beside him, holding his hand.

"Mike," Pastor Warren said, raising a hand as the two groups merged in the clearing.

"Pastor Warren. How's your group doing?"

"Well, I've learned that worms don't have feelings, and that someone named Jackson put a frog in his lunchbox last month, and it's still the most exciting thing that has ever happened at Serenity Crossing Elementary."

Mike laughed. "Jackson is up ahead; he's in my group. I heard all about the frog in school episode."

The two groups fell in together as the trail continued into a stretch of older hardwoods where the path was wide enough for the kids to spread out comfortably. Pastor Warren's group fanned out ahead alongside Mike's, and the children moved through the trees in loose clusters, bags rustling, voices carrying back and forth in the particular pitch of first-graders who had been given permission to explore.

"Beautiful morning for this," Pastor Warren said. "I told Mary last night that this field trip would probably wear me out, and I'd come home ready for a nap after wrangling a bunch of little ones all day, and she laughed at me. Said I'd be asleep on a park bench by eleven."

"Are you worn out yet?"

"No... but the day's still young."

Tyler came running back down the path, holding a pinecone. "Mr. Hartwell, does this count as a leaf?"

"That's a pinecone, Tyler."

"I know, but does it count?"

"I'm afraid not."

Tyler looked at the pinecone, looked at Mike, and then looked at Pastor Warren as if seeking a second opinion.

Tyler sighed and dropped it on the path and ran back to the group.

"How's the mill running these days?" Pastor Warren asked as they walked.

"Good. Really good, actually. We just finished a big order for a development in Gatlinburg, and we've got two more big projects lined up through December. Dad's still coming in most days. I don't think he's grasped what semi-retirement is."

"I think Bill's at a point in his life where it's hard to let go. A man works his whole life, and then it's time for retirement, and that can be tough. I've seen many a man not know what to do with himself at that point in life."

"Dad still enjoys the hands-on work at the mill. It seems to make him happy, and I'm glad to have him around still. I take care of all the office work and run the mill, and honestly... I'd be fine if Dad continued to come in every day and just do whatever he wants to do."

"You've got a lot more responsibility nowadays, from what I've heard. You're carrying it well from what I can see."

"I'm trying. Some weeks are easier than others."

They walked in step, and ahead of them Lizzie had stopped to show Pastor Warren's granddaughter her binoculars. The little girl took them and held them up to her eyes, and then announced, very seriously, that she could see a bear. Lizzie told her it was probably just a big rock. The little girl said she was pretty sure it was a bear. They agreed to disagree and kept walking.

"How about outside of work?" Pastor Warren asked. "Life treating you good?"

Mike was quiet for a few steps. A yellow leaf drifted down from a hickory branch and landed on the path between them.

"Things are good," he said. "Really good."

"You've had a different look about you the last few weeks. There's a little more pep in your step these days."

Mike nodded. He picked up a twig from the path and turned it in his fingers.

"Nicole and I are seeing each other," he said. "I imagine you've noticed us together at church. It's going well... great, actually."

"I'm glad to hear that."

They walked toward a cluster of milkweed plants growing along the edge of the trail, and Maya called out that she could see a caterpillar. Several kids from both groups crowded around, and Mike stepped over to make sure nobody was grabbing at it. The caterpillar was striped black, yellow, and white, a monarch larva, curled on the underside of a milkweed leaf. Sophia informed everyone that it would turn into a butterfly, and Tyler asked if it could bite. Mike told them they could look but not touch, and he waited until they'd had their fill before herding them gently back to the path.

When he fell back into step with Pastor Warren, the conversation picked up where it had left off, the way conversations do between two men.

"I love her, Pastor Warren. I know it with everything in me," Mike said.

Pastor Warren looked at him. "That's a big step, Mike... I'm happy for you."

They kept walking. The kids were ahead of them, spread across the trail, Harper walking with Lizzie now, the two of them examining something Lizzie had spotted through her binoculars. Pastor Warren's granddaughter had found a red maple leaf the size of her hand and was carrying it like a prize.

"She's a wonderful woman," Pastor Warren said. "I've watched her with those girls of hers, and I've watched her in this community since she came back. She's kind, she's steady, and she loves the Lord. You chose well, Mike."

"I didn't choose anything. It just happened."

"The best ones usually do."

Mike dropped the hickory twig and put his hands in his pockets. The trail curved ahead through a stand of birch trees, their white bark bright against the reds and oranges around them.

"Can I tell you what worries me?" he said.

"You can tell me anything."

Mike watched his daughter up ahead. She had the binoculars up again, narrating her observations to Harper, who was listening with the quiet patience of a girl who was still figuring out where she fit and had found someone willing to include her.

"It's not Nicole that worries me," he said. "It's not us. What we have is right. I know that the way I know hickory from oak just by the feel of it."

He paused, and when he spoke again, his voice was steady but quieter. "What worries me is how much I want this. All of it. Her. The girls. The life I can see when I let myself picture it. I want it with everything I have, and that's the part that scares me. Because I know what it costs to lose someone you love. I learned that in one afternoon when Jenny died, and that lesson tore me apart."

"I built my life back," Mike continued. "It took me a long time. I realize now how small I had made my world." He let out a breath. "And now my life is expanding again. And it's wonderful. Nicole is incredible. But if I lose this, Pastor, I won't just be losing it for me. I'll be losing it for Lizzie, who already lost her mother. And for Amber and Alicia, who already lost their father. And for Nicole, who has already buried a husband. The stakes aren't just mine. They belong to five people. And the weight of that keeps me up some nights."

He shook his head. "I know I shouldn't think that way. I know worrying doesn't do a bit of good. I know that. But knowing it and feeling it are two different things."

They walked in silence for a few steps before Pastor Warren spoke. "Mike, I want to tell you something, and I want you to hear it as a man who has loved the same woman for thirty-six years and been terrified of losing her at times too."

Mike looked at him.

"The fear you're describing is not a warning sign. It's not God telling you to slow down or pull back. It's the natural cost of loving someone after you've learned what loss feels like. A man who didn't feel fear would be a man who wasn't paying attention to what he has."

"But here's what I've learned," Pastor Warren continued. "If you wait until the fear is gone before you move forward, you'll wait forever. The fear doesn't leave. It just stops being the loudest voice in the room. And that only happens when you decide to trust God with the things you can't control. Not because the risk disappears, but because you believe that whatever comes, He'll be there in the middle of it. The same way He was there three years ago, even when it didn't feel like it."

Tyler's voice carried back to them from up the trail. He was telling Jackson that he'd found a leaf bigger than his head, and Jackson was informing him that wasn't possible, and both of them were absolutely certain they were right.

"Faith has never been the absence of fear, Mike," Pastor Warren said. "It's the decision to keep walking anyway."

Sophia appeared at his side. "Mr. Hartwell, I found a leaf I don't recognize. Can you tell me what it is?"

He took the leaf from her. Small, oval, with a smooth edge and a waxy surface. "That's a black gum," he said. "Also called a black tupelo. They turn the most beautiful shade of red in the fall, darker than any other tree out here."

"Thank you," Sophia said, and she placed it carefully in her bag.

Pastor Warren smiled as she walked away. "You're pretty good at that."

"I just know trees."

"That and you're good with kids. You're a natural with them."

They walked on. They discussed the church's Christmas tree lighting in December and whether the sound system in the sanctuary was finally going to get replaced. Pastor Warren mentioned that his youngest grandson had started pee-wee football and was showing real promise.

The trail curved back toward the main path that led to the park's picnic shelters, and Mike could see Mrs. Fletcher in the distance. She blew two short bursts on her whistle, the signal Nicole had told him about that meant all groups should start heading toward the shelters for lunch and the ranger presentation.

Mike turned to his group. "All right, everybody, time to head to the shelters for lunch. Make sure you've got your bags. If you set your bag down somewhere, we'll need to all go as a group and look for it."

Sophia, Harper, and Lizzie had theirs. Jackson held his up. Maya had hers tucked under her arm. Tyler was patting his pockets like a man who'd lost his keys, and then spotted his bag on the ground three feet behind him and ran back for it.

Pastor Warren gathered his own group, his granddaughter immediately taking his hand again. "Mike, it was good talking with you today."

"You too, Pastor. Thank you."

"Nothing to thank me for. Just two men walking in the woods." He put his free hand on Mike's shoulder for a moment, a brief, firm touch, and then he turned and led his group up the path toward the main clearing.

Lizzie fell into step beside him as they walked, her binoculars bouncing against her chest, and a few small pieces of bark clinging to her hair from a tree she had apparently inspected at very close range.

"Daddy, did you know that caterpillars eat milkweed?" she said. "A girl from the other class told me, and I told her that Mrs. Sullivan has real caterpillars in our classroom, and some of them already made their crysta... their chry..."

"Chrysalis."

"Their chrysalis. And they're going to be butterflies soon, and Mrs. Sullivan said we might get to watch them come out."

"That sounds cool, Lizzie."

"Tyler found a worm and tried to name it. He wanted to call it Steve."

"Did the worm seem like a Steve?"

"It seemed like a worm, Daddy."

Mike laughed. Lizzie grinned up at him, pleased with herself, and then she looked ahead toward the shelters where the other groups were already converging. Kids were finding seats at the long wooden picnic tables, teachers were distributing sack lunches from cardboard boxes, and across the clearing Mike could see Nicole. She was standing near one of the tables with a clipboard, directing students toward their seats and handing out lunch bags. She had her hair pulled back, and she was smiling at a student who was talking to her with animated hands.

"Daddy, there's Mrs. Sullivan," Lizzie said. She tugged the hem of his shirt. "Can we sit by her for lunch?"

Mike looked at his daughter. "Yeah, Lizzie. I think that's a great idea."

They walked toward the shelters, Lizzie pulling ahead to catch up with the rest of the group, and Pastor Warren's words walked with him. Faith has never been the absence of fear. It's the decision to keep walking, anyway.

Chapter 24

Lizzie was three steps ahead of the twins when she marched up to the next porch, her cowgirl boots loud on the wooden steps, the brim of her hat tilted at an angle. She rang the doorbell before Amber and Alicia had even reached the bottom step. When the door opened and an older woman appeared holding a plastic cauldron full of candy, Lizzie tipped her hat and said, "Trick or treat, ma'am," in a voice that carried all the way back to the sidewalk.

"Well, look at you," the woman said. "A real cowgirl."

"Yes, ma'am. And that's my sheriff." Lizzie pointed back toward Mike, who was standing on the sidewalk beside Nicole with a tin star pinned to his chest and a brown hat that sat a little too far back on his head. He tipped it when the woman looked his way.

"Very handsome sheriff," the woman said, dropping candy into Lizzie's bag.

Amber came up the steps next, her white coat buttoned over a long-sleeved shirt, the toy stethoscope swinging from her neck. "I'm a veterinarian," she said. "Like my grandpa."

"A veterinarian. That's a big job."

"I already know how to give a horse a shot," Amber said. "Grandpa showed me. You have to be very careful."

"I'll remember that," the woman said, and dropped a handful of candy into Amber's bag.

Alicia was last, stepping up to the door with her beret tilted to one side and the cardboard palette Nicole had helped her make held against her hip. She had painted six circles of color on the palette with real paint, and she carried a clean paintbrush tucked behind her ear the way she had seen artists do in a picture book.

"And what are you, sweetheart?"

"I'm a painter," Alicia said. "A real one."

"You certainly look like one. I love your palette."

"My mom helped me make it, but I picked the colors myself."

The woman smiled and gave Alicia an extra piece of candy. Alicia said thank you and turned back down the steps with her bag held open so she could see what she'd gotten.

Nicole watched all three of them from the sidewalk, and the pride she felt was the specific kind that comes from seeing your children be polite, confident, and happy in the world without any coaching from the wings.

Mike's hand found hers as the girls ran ahead to compare their latest haul under a streetlight. His fingers were warm, and Nicole leaned into him slightly as they walked. The fake police shirt he'd ordered looked convincing enough from a distance, and up close the plastic badge caught the light from the porch lamps they passed. The holster on his belt was empty because Lizzie had informed him that a good sheriff doesn't need a gun; he just needs to be brave, and Mike had agreed with this assessment without argument.

Nicole had drawn her cat whiskers with eyeliner in the bathroom mirror before they left, and Amber had stood on her tiptoes and told her that the left side was thicker than the right side. Nicole had said that was because cats are never perfectly symmetrical, and Amber had accepted this with the seriousness of a girl who intended to be a veterinarian and therefore respected animal anatomy.

The residential streets near downtown Serenity Crossing were full of families. Porch lights glowed on both sides of the block, and jack-o'-lanterns lined the steps of the homes, their carved faces flickering with candles that made the shadows jump. Someone had strung orange lights through the boxwoods in front of a Victorian with a wide front porch, and a motion-activated ghost on the railing let out a low moan every time a child walked past. The first time it went off, Alicia had grabbed Amber's arm. The second time, she walked past it on purpose and laughed when it moaned again.

The October air was cool against Nicole's face, and overhead the sky was clear and full of stars, the kind of sky you only got in the mountains where the nearest city lights were miles away. The dark shapes of the ridgeline rose beyond the rooftops, and somewhere a few streets over a dog was barking at the steady stream of costumed children passing its yard.

"All right," Lizzie said, appearing in front of them with her bag held open. "I have tons of chocolate bars, gummy bears, one thing I don't know what it is, a bunch of lollipops, and a pencil."

"A pencil?" Mike said.

"The man at the green house gave out pencils, and we got to pick out which color we liked."

"That's really cool."

Amber and Alicia crowded in to show their bags.

"Lizzie, do you want to trade one of your gummy bears for my lollipop?" Amber asked.

"What flavor is it?"

"Grape."

"Yep... purple is my favorite color!"

"Deal."

The exchange was made, and then all three girls took off toward the next house.

Mike and Nicole continued to follow them, and a couple from church passed on the other side of the street and waved. The woman called out that the girls looked adorable, and Mike waved back and said, thank you. A little boy dressed as a dinosaur ran past them on the sidewalk with his father jogging to keep up. Two houses ahead, a group of older kids in matching skeleton costumes were posing for a photo on someone's front lawn while a mother counted to three.

"What was your favorite Halloween costume from when you were a kid?" Nicole asked.

"A lumberjack," Mike said. "Three years in a row. My mom took a flannel shirt and added padding so I looked like a bulky, muscled lumberjack, and I carried a plastic axe. Dad thought it was the funniest thing he'd ever seen."

"Three years? You didn't want to try something different?"

"Nope."

Nicole laughed. "I remember two of my favorite costumes. One was a ballerina the year I was eight. Pink tutu, the whole thing. And then the next year I told my mom I wanted to be a farmer, and she found a pair of overalls for me at the resale store, and I carried a toy pitchfork."

The girls reached the next house and went up the steps in their usual order: Lizzie first, then Amber, then Alicia. A woman opened the door with a bowl of candy.

When the door closed and the girls came back down the steps, Alicia turned to Lizzie on the sidewalk and said, "Last year Grandma and Grandpa took us trick-or-treating."

"How come?" Lizzie asked.

"Because Mommy and Daddy stayed home. Grandma let us stay out really late, and our bags got so full of candy. Grandpa kept sneaking candy out of our bags when he thought we weren't looking." Alicia grinned. "Amber caught him eating a Snickers."

"He said he was making sure it tasted okay," Amber said.

Alicia laughed. "That was the bestest Halloween ever."

Nicole's foot caught on a crack in the sidewalk as the memory of last year came to her. It arrived complete, like a photograph pulled from a drawer, every detail intact.

The house in Knoxville. October thirty-first, one year ago. Her parents loading the girls into the car in the driveway. Amber in her princess costume waving from the backseat. Alicia blowing a kiss through the window. Her mother's face as she closed the car door, the careful way she smiled at Nicole, the look that said I love you and I'm sorry and go be with him all in one glance. The car pulling away. The taillights turning at the end of the street. Then Nicole going back inside to the quiet house where Derek was in their bed, propped on pillows because lying flat made the pain worse. The pill bottles lined up on the nightstand. The world outside their bedroom moving forward while inside that room the man she had married at twenty-two was running out of days, and both of them knew it.

That was one year ago tonight.

One year ago she was sitting in a dim bedroom holding the hand of a dying man. Tonight she was in Serenity Crossing with cat whiskers on her face and the hand of a man she was falling in love with wrapped around hers. The distance between that night and this one was both infinite and thin enough to tear.

Her grip on Mike's hand tightened. She blinked fast twice, three times. Her eyes stung, and she looked up at the stars scattered across the sky. Her throat closed. She pressed her lips together and took a breath through her nose, slow and controlled. The kind of breathing she had taught herself during the months when falling apart wasn't an option because someone had to hold everything together. Someone had to make sure the girls ate breakfast, the bills got paid, and the hospice paperwork was filled out correctly.

Mike stopped walking. He turned toward her, his hand still holding hers, and he stepped closer.

"Are you okay?"

She shook her head. She opened her mouth, but nothing came out. She looked at the ground and blinked, and two tears slid down her cheeks, cutting through the eyeliner whiskers on her face.

Mike glanced ahead at the girls. They were on the next porch, all three of them, occupied with the door opening and the candy and whatever Lizzie was saying to the homeowner. He pulled a folded handkerchief from his back pocket and pressed it into Nicole's free hand. Then he put his arm around her and drew her close. He didn't say anything. He held her, and she pressed her face against his shoulder for a moment, the badge on his shirt cool against her cheek, as she breathed and steadied herself.

"I'm sorry," she said. "I'm sorry, that just hit me out of nowhere."

"You don't need to apologize."

She wiped under her eyes again. The girls were coming down the porch steps now, comparing candy, and Nicole took a breath and put on her Mommy face, the one that said everything is fine.

Lizzie ran up to them. "That house gave out full-size candy bars. The big ones. This is the best Halloween ever."

"A full-size candy bar? You girls are so lucky, Lizzie," Nicole said.

"Come on, there's more houses," Lizzie said as she grabbed Amber's hand, and the three of them ran ahead to the next walkway.

Nicole watched them go. Her face was damp where the tears had run, and the cool air felt sharp against the wet tracks on her skin.

"Do you want to talk about it?" Mike asked.

She nodded. They started walking again, keeping the girls in sight.

"Last Halloween," Nicole said. "Alicia was talking about last Halloween."

"I heard."

"My parents drove up to Knoxville and took the girls trick-or-treating. That's what my girls remember, and that in itself is a good thing. Grandma and Grandpa and candy and staying out late." She paused. "What I remember is sitting beside Derek in our bedroom while they were gone."

Mike walked beside her and listened.

"He was bedridden by then. Had been for a few weeks. The hospice nurse came every day at that point, sometimes twice. The pain was constant for him. His medication took the edge off, but that's all it did. He couldn't get out of bed. He couldn't eat anything solid. He weighed maybe a hundred and thirty pounds, and when I married him, he was two-ten."

She kept her eyes on the girls ahead of them, their shapes moving under the streetlights: Lizzie's hat, Amber's white coat, and Alicia's beret.

"My mom and dad loaded the girls into the car. Amber was a princess. Alicia was a ladybug. Amber waved at me from the backseat, and Alicia blew me a kiss. That tore me up to know I was missing trick-or-treating with my babies."

"I remember closing the door, walking back to our bedroom, and sending up a prayer thanking God I had good parents who dropped everything and came when I asked them for help. I sat next to Derek in our bedroom and held his hand. The window was open because he liked the fresh air, even in October, and I could hear the neighborhood outside. Kids on the sidewalk. Doorbells. Parents talking. All the normal Halloween sounds." She glanced at Mike. "And I sat there listening to all of it, and I told him what I imagined the girls were doing. I made it up, house by house. I told him Amber was probably being very polite and Alicia was most likely asking every person what their costume was, and he smiled, Mike. He smiled with his eyes closed because smiling was about all the energy he had left. And I just kept talking because I thought if I stopped talking, I would fall apart, and I couldn't fall apart, not in front of him."

She took a breath. "I didn't cry that night. I learned not to. My tears scared him more than the cancer did. He'd see me upset, and he'd try to comfort me, and he didn't have the energy for that, and I refused to be the reason he used what little he had left on making me feel better."

"After I ran out of imaginary houses to describe, I asked him if he wanted to watch a movie. He said yes and watched The Princess Bride because it was his favorite movie. He'd seen it a hundred times, and it still made him laugh. And I held his hand through the whole thing."

She stopped walking. They were between houses, standing on a stretch of sidewalk where the streetlight didn't quite reach and the shadows from a large maple tree made the pavement dark. The girls were a house ahead, ringing a doorbell, their voices carrying back on the cool air.

"And then November seventh came, and my husband died. I held his hand and watched him take his last breath. I will never forget that moment. Never."

She wiped her eyes with the handkerchief again. "I'm sorry. I thought I was past the point where it could hit me like that."

"Don't apologize," Mike said. "You loved him. That doesn't go away because the calendar turned."

She nodded. She pressed the handkerchief against her cheek and then lowered it. "The tears just came. I heard Alicia talking about last year, and it was like the whole night came flooding back. I could smell the bedroom. I could hear the sounds through the window. I could feel his hand. I am so sorry... I hope I haven't ruined your evening."

"Mommy!" Amber's voice carried from the porch ahead. "That lady said she likes my stethoscope, and she asked if I could listen to her heart!"

Nicole looked up. Amber was standing on the porch, holding her stethoscope out with both hands, beaming.

"Did you listen to it?" Nicole called back.

"Yes! She said, I'm a good vet!"

"That's wonderful, baby. I'm proud of you."

Amber turned back to her sister and Lizzie, and they compared bags once more before heading to the next house.

Nicole and Mike started walking again. His hand found hers, and the warmth of his grip was steady and real.

"Can I ask you something?" she said.

"Anything."

She looked at the sidewalk in front of her as she walked. "Do you think we're moving too fast?"

"Where did that come from?"

"Because it's been less than a year. Derek died on November seventh, and that's one week from today. I'm walking down the street on Halloween holding another man's hand, and my girls are out there laughing and having the best night. Part of me is so happy I don't know what to do with it, and part of me is sitting in that bedroom in Knoxville holding Derek's hand. I'm just wondering what kind of woman moves on this fast."

"I loved him, Mike. I need you to know that. I loved Derek with everything I had. Our marriage was good. He was a good man and a wonderful father. I would have spent the rest of my life with him if that had been an option. I didn't come back to Serenity Crossing looking for anything except a fresh start for me and the girls. I wasn't looking for you. I wasn't looking for any of this."

"I know," Mike said.

"But here I am. And it happened so fast. And I worry about what people think. I worry about what it looks like from the outside: a woman whose husband has been gone less than a year already dating, already falling for someone. I worry that people look at me and think, She must not have loved him that much if she could move on that fast."

"And I worry about what it says about me," she said. "Not to other people. To myself. I worry that being this happy this soon means I didn't grieve the right way, or that I'm trying to skip past the hard part, or that I'm filling the hole in my heart instead of doing the real work of healing. I don't want to believe any of that is true. But the questions keep coming, and right now they're louder than they've been."

Mike was quiet for a few steps. Then he said, "Can I tell you what I see?"

"Please."

"I see a woman who loved her husband very much. Who sat beside him and held his hand and described their daughters' Halloween to him because he couldn't be there. I see a strong woman who didn't cry because she was more worried about him than she was about herself. I see a woman who buried that man, is raising their two girls on her own, and made a massive move back to her hometown to be near her family. I see an amazing woman who started a new job and built a new life."

He looked at her. "I don't see someone who moved on too fast. I see someone who kept living. There's a difference, Nicole. A big one. And who's to say what's too fast and what's too slow? I don't think there's a right timeline for this. I don't think God hands us a chart that says grieve for this many months, and then you're cleared for the next thing. I think He gives us what we need when we need it, and sometimes the timing doesn't match what we expected."

"I see a woman who had the courage to let something new grow," he continued. "And that doesn't erase what came before it. It doesn't mean you loved Derek any less. It means you're still here, and you're brave enough to keep your heart open, and that's not a failure of grief. That's the opposite."

Nicole looked at him. "I know God put you in my life. I believe that. I believe He had a plan for me that I couldn't have drawn up on my own, and that you and Lizzie being part of it is not an accident. I believe all of that with the same faith I've carried my whole life."

She paused. "But believing it and feeling settled about it are two different things. And right now, seven days from the anniversary of Derek's death, I feel the gap between what I believe and what I'm afraid of. And I don't know how to close it."

"Maybe you don't have to close it right now," Mike said. "Maybe the gap is just where you are right now, and that's okay."

"I don't want to pull away from you," she said. "That's not what this is."

"I didn't think it was."

"I just needed to say it out loud. I needed you to know what's in my head so you're not wondering."

"I'm not wondering. I understand, and I'm not going any-where."

The girls came running back, bags bouncing against their legs, Lizzie's rope swinging, Amber's stethoscope catching the light.

"Mommy, my bag is getting really heavy," Alicia said.

"That's because you're a very good trick-or-treater."

"Can we do that street?" Lizzie pointed to a block where the houses had even more decorations: porch lights blazing, fake cobwebs thick on every railing, and a yard with a glowing inflatable pumpkin that was taller than any of them.

"Absolutely," Mike said.

The girls took off, and Nicole watched them go. Three small figures running down a sidewalk in Serenity Crossing on the last night of October, their candy bags swinging, and their costumes slightly askew from two hours of porches and doorbells.

Mike took her hand again as they started following the girls

The cool air moved against her face, against the tear tracks she had wiped away with his handkerchief. She folded it and tucked it into her jacket pocket as she thought about two Halloween nights. The one she had lived a year ago in a quiet bedroom in Knoxville with a man who was leaving, and the one she was living right now on a sidewalk in the mountains with a man who was staying. Both nights belonged to her. Both were true. One hadn't replaced the other. They sat side by side inside her, the way grief and hope had learned to share the same space without asking permission.

November seventh was seven days away. She could feel it the way you feel weather before it arrives: a pressure in the air, a shift in the light. She didn't know what that day would ask of her. She didn't know if she would hold it together or if the tears would come again the way they had tonight, sudden and sharp and beyond her control.

For now, she knew she was holding the hand of a good man on a clear October night, and her daughters were laughing ahead of her, candy bags heavy and full. And she knew that Derek was in heaven and no longer in pain. He was no longer lying in a bed, listening to the world move past his window. He was in the arms of Jesus, whole and healed and free. And the life she was living right now, walking this sidewalk with whiskers on her face and love in her chest that she hadn't planned for, was beautiful and complicated and entirely hers.

Chapter 25

Nicole had the phone to her ear before she'd even sat down, standing at the porch railing with her jacket still on and her school bag dropped at her feet.

Mike picked up on the second ring. "Hey, you."

"Hey." She leaned one hip against the railing and watched Amber push Alicia on the swing set. "Listen, I'm going to take a rain check on date night tonight. Is that okay?"

"Of course. Everything all right?"

"Everything's fine. I just had a long day at school, and I'm worn out. Actually, it's been a long week with challenges every day. I just want a quiet night at home."

"Are you feeling okay? You're not getting sick?"

"No, I'm fine. Honestly. Just tired. A hot bath and an early bedtime kind of evening. I'll see you tomorrow for the girls' riding lesson."

"Okay. Get some rest, Nic. You deserve it."

"Thank you. Give Lizzie a hug for me."

"I will."

"Bye, Mike."

"Bye."

She pulled the phone from her ear and held it in both hands and looked at the screen until it went dark. Then she set it on the porch railing, wrapped her arms across her middle, and stood there watching her daughters play on the swingset.

The screen door opened behind her, and Tabitha stepped onto the porch, carrying two mugs. She was still wearing her barn jacket and her work jeans, her hair pulled back and streaked with the silver that had been gaining ground for years. She set one of the mugs on the railing beside Nicole's phone and kept the other in her hands.

"Coffee," Tabitha said. "You look like you could use some."

"Thank you, Mama."

Tabitha sat down in the wooden rocker nearest the railing and took a sip from her own mug. She rocked, slow and steady, and watched the girls on the swing set.

Nicole picked up the mug. The coffee was hot and strong, the way her mother always made it, and the warmth of the ceramic against her palms felt so good.

"I heard a little bit of that phone conversation," Tabitha said. "Sounded like you canceled your standing date night with Mike."

Nicole took another sip and kept her eyes on her girls. "I did."

"That conversation didn't sound like a woman who's tired, baby. That sounded like something else."

"I am tired."

Nicole pressed her thumb against the rim of the mug. Out in the yard, Amber had jumped off the swing at the top of its arc and landed in the grass with both feet. Alicia clapped and yelled, "Do it again," and Amber climbed back onto the seat and started pumping her legs once more.

"I don't want to go out tonight and pretend I'm having a good time when my head is somewhere else. Mike doesn't deserve that. He'd know something was wrong in five minutes, and I would rather not be the reason his evening is ruined." She paused. "I just want to be here. I want to sit somewhere quiet and feel whatever I'm going to feel without worrying about how I look while I'm feeling it."

Tabitha nodded slowly. "That makes sense to me."

"I have been up and down all week, Mama. Happy one minute, sad the next. I was laughing with my students this morning during read-aloud, and then an hour later, while the kids were at recess, I was hiding in a bathroom stall because my eyes were burning and I just wanted five minutes to myself." She shook her head. "I keep wondering if there's something wrong with me. Like some kind of chemical imbalance or something. I feel like I've been on this emotional roller coaster all week, and I want off."

"There's nothing wrong with you, Nicole."

"Then why can't I keep it together?"

"Because tomorrow is November seventh, and your heart knows what that date means even when your head is trying to keep busy."

Nicole looked at her mother. Tabitha was watching her with eyes that held no judgment, no urgency, and no agenda. Just love, steady and clear.

"Talk to me," Tabitha said. "Whatever is going on in that amazing mind of yours, let me have some of it. Give it to me. I can take it."

Nicole looked back at the yard. Amber had jumped off the swing again, and this time Alicia followed, and the two of them were sitting in the grass now, picking at something on the ground, their heads close together.

"Do you know what I remember most about this day last year?"

"Tell me."

"November sixth. One year ago tonight." She held the mug in front of her with both hands and looked at the steam curling off the surface. "The girls were asleep. It was late, nine or nine-thirty. I was sitting in the chair beside Derek's bed. He'd been in and out all day. In and out for the better part of forty-eight hours, really. Awake for a few minutes, then gone again, then awake for a few more. The hospice nurse had been there twice that day. She told me privately that we were close to the end and that it could be hours or it could be a few days, but that his body was shutting down."

She took a breath. "I was sitting there in the chair, turning pages in a magazine. I looked up, and his eyes were open and clear, and he was looking right at me. Not confused, not foggy like he'd been. Just present. And he said three words, Mama."

Nicole's voice had thinned, and she took a moment to swallow and steady herself.

"He said, 'Love you, Nic.' His voice was so thin, Mama. So thin. But he meant every syllable. I could see it in his face. And I took his hand, and I told him I loved him too, and he closed his eyes. And that was the last thing he ever said to me. Three words, and then he went to sleep, and he never woke up again."

She pressed her lips together and breathed through her nose.

"I sat beside that bed all night. I didn't sleep. I held his hand, and I listened to him breathe, and I prayed. I prayed for God to heal him, and I prayed for God to take him, and I know those two prayers can't both be answered, but I said them both because I meant them both." She glanced at her mother. "Is that terrible? To have prayed for both?"

"No," Tabitha said. "That's honest."

"He passed the next morning. November seventh. A little after six. I was holding his hand. I watched him take his last breath, Mama, and I will carry that moment with me for the rest of my life. I will never forget it. The room was so quiet. And I just sat there holding his hand, and then he was gone."

Tabitha set her mug down on the porch floor and reached over and laid her hand on Nicole's arm. Her grip was firm and warm.

"Watching someone take their last breath," Nicole said. "It changes you. It's the most devastating thing and the most sacred thing at the same time, and I don't know how both of those can be true in the same second, but they are."

"I know they are," Tabitha said. "I held my mother's hand when she passed away. I was right there beside her, just like you were beside Derek. And you're right. You never forget a moment like that. It lives in you. It rearranges something inside you, and you go on living, but you're different after. The world looks different."

Nicole nodded. Tears were building behind her eyes, and she blinked, trying to hold them back. Then one fell, tracing a line down her cheek to the corner of her jaw. She wiped it with the back of her hand.

"There's something I've never told anyone," she said.

Nicole watched her daughters in the yard. They had moved from the grass to the base of the sycamore tree and were collecting the fallen leaves, holding them up to compare shapes and sizes, their voices a distant, bright melody against the quiet of the farm. Two six-year-old girls doing exactly what six-year-old girls should be doing on a Friday afternoon, oblivious to the weight of the conversation happening forty yards away on the porch.

"When Derek took his last breath," Nicole said, "I felt two things at the exact same time. I felt devastated. The man I loved was gone. The father of my girls was gone. The life I had built and planned and counted on was over in that one breath, and the grief hit me like nothing I've ever experienced."

She turned to face her mother. "And I felt relieved."

She watched her mother's face for something—a flinch, a flicker of surprise, anything that would confirm the thing she had been telling herself for a year. But Tabitha's expression didn't change. Her hand stayed on Nicole's arm. Her eyes remained steady.

"I felt relieved, Mama. Because he wasn't in pain anymore. Because the months of watching him fight and lose were over. Because he wasn't lying in that bed struggling to breathe. He was with

God. He was whole and healed and free from all of it, and there was a part of me that was grateful it was finished." Her chin trembled. "And I have been carrying the question of whether that makes me a horrible person for a year. I have never said that out loud. Not to anyone. Not to Mike, not to my friends, not to my counselor in Knoxville. I have held it inside and wondered every single day if something was wrong with me for feeling relief when my husband died."

Tabitha stood up from the rocker. She turned to face Nicole and took the mug from her hands, and set it on the railing. Then she took both of Nicole's hands in hers and held them. Her grip was the grip of a woman who had helped her husband deliver calves at midnight and rebuilt fences in storms and held her own mother's hand in a hospital bed.

"Nicole Marie Hanshaw Sullivan," Tabitha said. "You listen to me. Feeling relief does not make you a horrible person. It makes you a human being who loved her husband enough to care more about his suffering than her own loss."

"I watched you, baby. I watched you carry that man's illness. I saw what it was doing to you. The only time throughout his entire illness you asked for help was last Halloween because you couldn't bear the thought of your girls missing trick-or-treating. That's the only time you picked up the phone and said, Mama, I need you. One time. In eighteen months, child."

Tabitha squeezed her hands. "You managed his medications. You drove him to every appointment. You handled the insurance and the paperwork, and the bills, and you kept those two little girls' lives as normal as you could while the ground was crumbling under your feet. You held your family together. You did it with a grace I have never seen matched in another person, and I'm including myself in that."

"Mama."

"I'm not done." Tabitha's eyes were wet now too, but her voice didn't waver. "The relief you felt when Derek passed was not a betrayal of your love. It was the cost of your love. You loved him enough to stand beside him through it all, and you watched him suffer, and when the suffering ended, your body and your heart did the only thing they could do. They exhaled. That's not selfishness. That's not weakness. That is what happens when you have been holding on so tight and for so long that the only thing left to feel when it's finally over is the release."

Nicole's face crumpled. She pulled one hand free and pressed it over her mouth and closed her eyes, and the tears came, fast and furious, the kind that burn like fire.

"The Bible tells us in Revelation that God will wipe away every tear," Tabitha said. "That there will be no more death, no more sorrow, no more crying, no more pain. Those things pass away. And when Derek took that last breath, he walked straight into that promise. He is whole, Nicole. He is healed. He is in the presence of Jesus with no more pain and no more fear, and the relief you felt was your heart recognizing that truth. That's not something to be ashamed of. That is your faith telling you what your mind wasn't ready to hear."

Nicole opened her eyes. She looked at her mother through the blur of tears, and Tabitha was right there, close, solid, and unshakable. The same woman who had bandaged her knees when she was five and taught her to ride a horse when she was six and held her when she cried at seventeen over a boy whose name she no longer even remembered.

"I miss him, Mama," Nicole said. "I miss him and still love him, and I'm in love with Mike, and those things live in me at the same time, and I don't know what to do with that."

"You don't have to do anything with it. Love isn't a limited resource. God didn't design our hearts to hold only one person and then shut the door. First Corinthians says love bears all things, believes all things, hopes all things, and endures all things. It doesn't say love replaces all things. What you feel for Mike doesn't erase what you had with Derek. It grows beside it. Grief and joy are not enemies. They're seasons, and sometimes they share the same soil."

"Am I moving too fast? Does falling in love with someone this soon after losing Derek mean what I had with him wasn't as real as I thought?"

"You know the answer to that."

"I'm asking you."

Tabitha let go of one of Nicole's hands and reached up and brushed a tear from her daughter's cheek with her thumb. "From where I'm sitting, watching my daughter over the past several weeks, I haven't seen someone who is moving too fast. I've seen someone come back to life. I've seen the girl I raised start to look like herself again. I've seen you laugh, really laugh, for the first time in two years. I've seen my granddaughters get their mama back in a way they haven't had her since before Derek got sick. And I've seen a good man walk into your world and treat you and your girls like you are the most important and most precious people on this earth."

She tilted her head. "What would Derek think if he could see you right now? You told me once that near the end he told you not to turn your house into a museum. He told you to live your life. That man loved you enough to say those words when saying anything at all cost him everything he had. Do you think he'd look at what you're building with Mike and those three girls and be angry? Or do you think he'd look at you and say, 'That's my girl?'"

Nicole pressed her lips together. A sound came out of her that was half laugh and half sob, and she shook her head because she knew the answer.

"I think he'd say, 'That's my girl,'" she said. "And then he'd say, 'Now buckle up and enjoy the ride.'"

"I think so, too."

Nicole wiped her face with both hands. She took a long, uneven breath and picked up her coffee and took a sip. It was lukewarm now, but she drank it anyway.

"I don't have all the answers for you," Tabitha said. "I wish I did. But I can tell you this. You loved Derek Sullivan well. You were the best wife that man could have asked for. And the fact that your heart has room for someone new doesn't diminish a single day of what you and Derek had. It honors it. Because you learned how to love from that marriage, and you are carrying everything it taught you into whatever comes next."

Nicole nodded. She looked at her mother, and the gratitude she felt was so specific and so large that she couldn't find words for it, so she just held her mother's gaze and let her eyes say what her voice couldn't.

Tabitha stood up straight and looked out at the girls, then back at Nicole. "Here's what I want you to do. I want you to take the rest of this evening for yourself. Turn off your cell phone and put it away. Go hike the mountains. Go for a horseback ride. Go inside the house and sit. Do whatever you want. But I want you to feel everything you need to feel. Cry if you need to cry. Yell and holler and scream if that helps. Then I want you to draw yourself a long, hot bubble bath and sit in it until the water goes cold. I want you to have some peace and quiet and just be Nicole for a few hours. Not Mommy. Not a teacher. Not anyone's girlfriend. Just you."

"What about the girls?"

"Your father and I will take them into town for dinner. Then we'll go get some ice cream. Then we might ride into Pigeon Forge and catch a movie or do some shopping; we'll see what the girls are in the mood for. Don't expect us home until late."

"Mama, you don't have to do that."

"I know I don't have to. I want to. That's what grandparents are for." She looked at Nicole with the steady, no-nonsense warmth that had been the foundation of every good thing in Nicole's life since the day she was born. "You have spent months being strong for everyone else. You are entitled to an evening where you don't have to be strong for anyone. Including yourself."

Nicole stood up and wrapped her arms around her mother and held on, her face against Tabitha's shoulder, and Tabitha held her back.

"I love you, Mama."

"I love you more, baby girl. And I am so proud of the woman you are."

Chapter 26

Lizzie had been talking about farm animals for the entire drive, and Mike was only catching every third sentence. His mind kept circling back to the phone call last night, the one where Nicole's voice had been just a little too careful and her reasons had been just a little too tidy.

"And Tabitha said next time she might let us brush the miniature horses by ourselves, which means we'd be in charge of them, Daddy, like actual horse people," Lizzie said from the back seat.

"That sounds great, Lizzie."

"Are you listening to me, Daddy?"

"I'm listening."

"You're doing your thinking face. You always do your thinking face when you're driving and not listening."

He glanced at her in the rearview mirror. She was sitting in her booster seat in jeans and the boots Olivia had bought her, her hair pulled back in the ponytail Mike had managed this morning on his third attempt. She was watching him with the particular scrutiny of a six-year-old who had figured out that adults weren't always paying as much attention as they claimed.

"I'm listening and thinking," he said. "I can do both."

"Grammy says boys can't do both."

"Grammy says a lot of things."

Lizzie went back to her preview of the morning's agenda, which apparently included not just goats but also a plan to convince Tabitha to let her ride Chester instead of Clover because Chester was taller and Lizzie had decided she was ready for taller.

Mike turned onto Ridge Road and followed it to the end, where the Hanshaw property opened up on both sides of the gravel drive. The white fence ran along the pasture. The red barn stood solid against the foothills.

He pulled into the gravel area beside the barn and parked. Tabitha was already in the riding ring with Amber and Alicia; the three of them were standing near Clover.

"Lizzie!" Amber yelled, waving both arms above her head.

Lizzie jumped down from the truck and ran toward the ring, and the three girls collided near the gate in the noisy, full-body greeting that had become their Saturday ritual.

Mike climbed out and closed his door and stood beside the truck for a moment, watching the girls. Then he looked toward the farmhouse.

Nicole's car was parked in its usual spot near the front porch. But the porch was empty.

He walked toward the riding ring. Tabitha looked up as he approached. She gave Clover's neck a pat and stepped away from the horse to meet him near the fence.

"Morning, Mike."

"Morning, Tabitha. Where's Nicole?"

Tabitha glanced at the three girls. They were occupied, Lizzie pointing at something in the pasture while Amber leaned sideways to see what she was pointing at and Alicia watched them both with her quiet, attentive expression.

"She's not joining us for the lesson today," Tabitha said. She kept her voice even, unhurried. "She's up at the house. I think she could use a friend right now, and I think that friend is you."

Mike stood still. The date landed on him like a hand on his shoulder. November seventh. One year. Nicole had canceled last night. She wasn't here this morning. Tabitha was choosing her words with the care of a woman who was very aware that three six-year-olds were ten feet away with ears that missed nothing.

"Go on up to the house," Tabitha said. "The girls are fine with me. I was thinking today's lesson might run a little longer than usual. Maybe we'll visit the animals afterward, spend some time with Earl and the minis. Take whatever time you need. Don't worry about a thing."

"Thank you, Tabitha."

She nodded once, the way she did when a thing was settled and didn't need more words.

Mike turned and walked toward the farmhouse.

The distance from the barn to the house was maybe a hundred and fifty yards, and the gravel path curved past the garden and the old sycamore tree, and the swing set in the back. The only sounds were the girls' voices behind him growing fainter as he walked, and somewhere out in the pasture a horse blowing air through its nose.

He climbed the porch steps. Through the screen door, he could see the living room, the couch, the bookshelf, and a hallway that led to the kitchen. The house was still. No radio, no television, no sound of anyone moving.

"Nicole?" he called through the screen.

He stepped back from the door and looked out over the property. The front yard, the gravel drive, the pastures stretching toward the foothills. He didn't see her. He turned and walked along the porch to the corner of the house, then down the steps and around to the backyard.

She was lying on a quilt in the grass about twenty yards from the swing set. The quilt was a patchwork of blues and greens, spread flat on the ground. Nicole was on her back with her arms at her sides and her face turned toward the sky. Her hair was loose and fanned out on the fabric. She was wearing jeans, a pullover sweater, and her boots were sitting on the edge of the quilt. Her eyes were closed.

He walked across the grass toward her. She didn't move until he was about ten feet away, and then she opened her eyes and looked at him.

"I heard your truck," she said. "And then I heard you call my name through the screen."

"Your mama sent me up."

"I figured she would."

He stopped at the edge of the quilt. "You okay?"

She looked at him for a moment, and what he saw in her face wasn't sadness. It wasn't red eyes or tear-streaked cheeks or the tight, held-together expression of someone fighting to keep it in. Her face was calm. Open. The skin around her eyes was relaxed, and there was the faintest trace of a smile at the corner of her mouth.

"I'm good," she said. "Sit down."

He lowered himself onto the edge of the quilt and sat with his legs stretched out and his hands resting on his knees. The grass around the quilt was cold with morning dew, and the sky above them was a pale, washed-out blue, the kind of November sky that looked like it couldn't decide between clouds and clearing.

"Do you want to talk about it?" he said.

Nicole turned her head on the quilt and looked at him. "I do, actually. If you're willing to listen."

"I'm always willing to listen."

She looked back up at the sky. "Today is one year."

"I know."

"Today is just for myself," she said. "Not because I'm falling apart. I'm not. I'm taking the day to remember Derek. The real Derek. Not Derek with cancer, not the hospital bed, nor the medications, nor the hospice nurse. I want to remember the man I married."

She folded her hands across her stomach. "This is just how I work, Mike. Sometimes I need to be still and sit with things. Feel whatever needs to come up. Talk to God. Let it all land without trying to organize it or fix it or put a bow on it."

"That makes sense."

"I'm in a good place right now. I need you to hear that. I'm not sad. I'm not angry. I woke up this morning, and I made a choice to spend this day remembering the good, and that's what I'm going to do."

A pair of sparrows landed in the sycamore tree behind the swing set and chattered at each other for a few seconds before going quiet.

"Tell me about him," Mike said. "The good stuff."

Nicole smiled. A real smile, warm and easy, and it changed her whole face. "He couldn't cook worth a lick. Not even a little. He tried to make the girls scrambled eggs one Saturday morning and somehow burned them and undercooked them at the same time. I still don't know how that's physically possible. He stood in the kitchen holding the pan and looking at the eggs like they had personally betrayed him, and I laughed so hard I had to sit down."

Mike grinned. "That takes real skill."

"It does. It's a gift. He also made toast once that set off the smoke detector. The girls were eighteen months old, and both of them started crying. Derek was standing on a chair waving a dish towel at the smoke detector while the toast was still smoking in the toaster, and I walked in from the laundry room to absolute chaos." She was laughing now, the memory playing behind her eyes. "He looked at me from the chair and said, 'Nic, I think the kitchen is trying to kill me.'"

"Sounds like a man who should've been kept away from the stove."

"He should have... trust me. But he kept trying. I remember sometimes he'd announce that this was the day he was going to master breakfast, and every time something went wrong. The girls loved it. They thought it was the funniest thing in the world. They'd sit in their high chairs and watch him like he was putting on a show."

She was quiet for a moment.

"He used to dance with them in the kitchen," she said. "After dinner, while I was cleaning up, he'd put on music and pick them both up, one in each arm, and just spin around the kitchen. They were so little. They'd hold on to his shirt and giggle, and he'd sing along to whatever was playing. He had a terrible voice, Mike. Just awful. But he didn't care. He sang loudly and off-key, and the girls thought he was the greatest singer in the world."

"What kind of music?"

"Everything. Country mostly. He loved old Garth Brooks. But he'd also put on Frank Sinatra sometimes, or whatever came up on the radio. The song didn't matter. It was the dancing. That was his thing with them. That was the part of the day that was just his."

She turned her head to look at Mike. "He took me to Gatlinburg for our anniversary the year before he got sick. We left the girls with his parents and drove down for the weekend. We stayed in this little cabin up in the hills; nothing fancy, just a bedroom and a fireplace, and a porch with a view. And on the second night, we were sitting on the porch, and he looked at me and said, 'Nic, I think we've got this whole life thing figured out.' Just like that. Like it was the simplest truth in the world."

She turned back to the sky. "We didn't have it figured out. Nobody does. But in that moment, sitting on that porch, I believed him. And I'm glad I did. I'm glad I let myself believe it, even if it turned out to be a lot more complicated than either of us thought."

Mike listened. He didn't try to fill the pauses. He sat on the edge of the quilt and let her talk, because he understood that this was what she needed today, not comfort, not counsel, just someone to hold the other end of the conversation while she laid out the memories and looked at them in the light.

"Last night my mama said some things to me that I needed to hear," Nicole said. She sat up slowly, drawing her knees toward her and wrapping her arms around them. She turned to face him. "Can I tell you what I told her?"

"You can tell me anything."

She reached for his hands and held them in her lap, her fingers laced through his, and she looked straight at him. Her eyes were clear and steady. Blue, direct, and fully present.

"When Derek took his last breath," she said, "I felt devastated, and I felt relieved. At the exact same time. And I have carried the guilt of that relief for an entire year. I never told a soul until last night. I was afraid of what it meant about me. I was afraid it meant I didn't love him enough, or that I wanted it to be over, or that I was selfish in a way I couldn't forgive. I had even begun to wonder if some part of me was cruel and heartless."

She squeezed his hands. "And my mama looked me in the eye and told me that the relief I felt wasn't a betrayal of my love for Derek. She said it was the cost of it. She said I had been holding on so tight and for so long that when it was finally over, the only thing my heart could do was exhale." Nicole's chin lifted. "And she was right. A year of carrying that question, and she answered it on the back porch in five minutes. Just hearing those words helped me."

Mike held her hands and said nothing, because nothing he could say would be better than what Tabitha had already said, and he knew it.

"My parents took the girls into town last night," Nicole said. "Dinner and ice cream and whatever else grandparents do when they're giving their daughter a night off. And I was alone in the house for the first time in I don't know how long, and at first I just stood in the kitchen and had no idea what to do with myself."

She let go of one of his hands and tucked a strand of hair behind her ear. "So I went to the barn and saddled Jasper. And I rode. I rode out along the fence line and up into the foothills where the trail cuts through the trees, and I talked to God the whole way. Out loud, Mike. Just me and Jasper and the mountains and God, and I said every single thing I've been holding in for the past week, longer than that if I'm honest. I told Him I was angry and grateful and confused and at peace, and I asked Him why this year has been the way it's been, and then I stopped asking and just listened."

"What did you hear?"

"Nothing specific. No voice from the sky. But there was a point, maybe an hour into the ride, where the questions just stopped mattering. I was sitting on Jasper at the top of the ridge where you can see the whole valley, and the sky was turning that deep blue it turns right before it goes dark, and I just felt held. Like God had me exactly where He wanted me, and He wasn't letting go."

She picked up his hand again. "I came home and ran a bath and sat in it until the water went cold, and the whole time I just thought about the good. Every good memory. Every good day. The dancing in the kitchen and the burned eggs and Gatlinburg and the girls' birth and the way Derek looked at me when he held them both in the hospital for the first time. And somewhere in the middle of all that remembering, I realized something I hadn't been able to see before."

"Tell me."

"I realized that God didn't just give me Derek. He gave me the privilege of being the person who walked beside Derek through the hardest part of his life and into the moment he stepped into the arms of Jesus. That's not a burden. That's a calling. And He prepared me for it. Every hard thing, every long night, every moment where I held it together when I wanted to fall apart, He was building something in me. Strength I didn't know I had. And then He took that strength and He put me on a new road, and that road was long and bumpy, and it led me here." She looked at him. "Right here. To this town, to this farm, to this quilt in the backyard on November seventh, talking to a man who understands every word I'm saying because he's walked his own version of this road."

Mike's throat was tight, and he swallowed against it.

"He's had me in the palm of His hand the whole time," she said. "I just couldn't see it until last night."

She held his gaze for a long moment, and the look on her face was the steadiest, most settled expression he had ever seen on her. Not the careful, held-together composure of a woman managing her emotions. Real peace. The kind that came from having sat with the hardest questions and found answers that held weight.

"I want you to leave," she said.

He tilted his head.

She smiled. "I can see your mind spinning. I'm okay, Mike. I'm more than okay. But I want to finish this day the way I started it. I want to see it through. I want to spend the rest of today remembering Derek and praising God for every blessing He's put in my life. And I want to do that alone."

He looked at her for a moment longer. Then he stood. He bent down and pressed his lips to the top of her head, and her hair was soft and smelled like lavender. He held the kiss for a second before he straightened.

"Nicole."

She looked up at him.

"Do you have any idea how amazing you are?"

Her eyes went bright, and she pressed her lips together, and she didn't answer, but the way she looked at him was answer enough.

"Take all the time you need," he said. "I'm not going anywhere."

She nodded.

He turned and walked across the grass, past the swing set and the sycamore tree, along the side of the house and back down the gravel path toward the barn. The air was cool on his face.

He could hear the girls before he saw them. Lizzie's voice carried across the property, followed by Amber's, followed by Tabitha's calm instruction. He came around the corner of the barn and saw them walking from the riding ring toward the barn, the lesson finished, all three girls talking at once while Tabitha led Clover by the halter.

Tabitha saw him first. She stopped and looked at him, and whatever she saw in his face told her what she needed to know, because she gave a small nod and waited.

"Tabitha," Mike said, "would you mind if I hung around for a while? I'd love to visit the animals with you and the girls."

"I'd love that," she said.

Chapter 27

Lizzie had been talking about Clover for the last five minutes, and Mike had heard every word. Every sound his daughter made felt vivid and close, like someone had turned the volume up on his whole life and he was only just noticing how good the music was.

"And Tabitha said I was the best rider she's ever had in the ring, Daddy. I love Clover. I hope someday I'll have a horse just like her."

"Maybe someday you will."

"I will, Daddy. I just know it."

Mike turned the truck onto the driveway that led to his parents' property. He hadn't planned on coming here today. He and Lizzie had gone home after the farm, had a snack, and spent the afternoon doing little things. Lizzie drew at the kitchen table while Mike sat and watched her. Then they had gone outside, and he'd pushed Lizzie on her swing for a little while and then kicked a ball around for a bit. It had been a quiet afternoon, but not an empty one. Mike had spent most of it thinking, and the thinking had been the kind that didn't make a man restless. It made him still. It made him certain.

At four-thirty, when the sunlight started pulling back from the mountains, he'd stood in his backyard and looked out over the property. The creek. The half-bare trees. And he'd thought about his parents, the way he sometimes did. But today his thoughts had a different quality. Today he wanted to be near them. He wanted to sit on the porch where he'd sat a thousand times and tell them what he'd witnessed this morning, because what he'd seen this morning was the kind of thing a man needed to say out loud to the people who raised him.

Bill and Olivia were sitting in their chairs on the front porch, Olivia with a mug in her hands, Bill beside her with his legs stretched out and his boots crossed at the ankles.

Mike stopped the truck and sat there for a moment. He watched them through the windshield. His dad's big hands rested on the arms of the rocker. His mom's silver-threaded hair caught the porch light.

"Daddy, Grammy and Poppa are on the porch!" Lizzie was already unbuckling her seatbelt.

"I see them."

She was out the door in a flash. She crossed the yard and took the porch steps at her usual pace, which was full speed, and Olivia was on her feet before Lizzie reached the top step.

"Well, look who's here," Olivia said, catching Lizzie and pulling her close. "This is a nice surprise."

Bill stood, and when Lizzie turned to him, he lifted her up with one arm and settled her against his side. "Hey, little bit."

"Poppa, I rode Clover today. Tabitha said I was the best rider she's ever had."

"Is that right?"

"Yep. And I brushed two of the miniature horses by myself, and Amber fell in the goat pen, and Alicia found three eggs, and we visited Earl and he ate hay right out of my hand."

Bill looked at Olivia over the top of Lizzie's head. "Busy day."

"The busiest," Lizzie said.

Mike climbed out of the truck and walked across the yard. He climbed the porch steps, and Olivia pulled him into a hug before he could say a word. She was warm, and she smelled like coffee and the vanilla hand lotion she'd been using for as long as he could remember.

She pulled back and looked at his face, and whatever she saw there made her tilt her head slightly, the way she did when she was reading one of her children and deciding whether to ask or wait.

"Thought we'd stop by for a bit," Mike said.

"I'm glad you did. Let me get you some coffee."

"I'd like that."

Olivia went inside. Lizzie was still in Bill's arms, telling him about the goats and how one of the baby goats had climbed onto Amber's lap and fallen asleep, and Bill was listening with his steady, patient attention, nodding in the right places, his eyes crinkling when Lizzie described the baby goat's ears.

"Poppa, can I go play in my room? I want to set up the farm animals Grammy got me so I can show you how the riding ring works."

"Go ahead," Bill said, setting her down. "I'll come see it in a bit."

She disappeared through the front door, and Mike could hear her footsteps moving through the house toward the room his parents kept for her. Olivia had decorated his old room with a bookshelf and an art table, and a toy-box that overflowed.

Bill settled back into his rocker. Mike took the chair beside him. The two of them sat for a moment, looking out at the property. The old red barn near the treeline. The mountains rose behind everything, their ridges sharp against the sky. The sunlight was fading. Another ten minutes and the valley would be in shadow.

"You look like a man who's carrying something good," Bill said.

Mike leaned back in the chair. "I am, Dad."

Olivia came back through the front door with two mugs and handed one to Mike. She sat down in her chair and pulled her sweater tighter around her shoulders. "Lizzie's in her room arranging plastic horses in a circle. I think she's running a riding school."

"She probably is," Mike said.

He held the mug in both hands and felt the warmth of it against his palms. He looked at his mom, and then at his dad, and he took a breath.

"This morning, when I arrived at the Hanshaw farm for Lizzie's riding lesson, Nicole wasn't anywhere in sight. Normally she'd be outside waiting for us. Tabitha sent me up to the house to check on her," he said. "It's one year today. Since Derek passed away."

Olivia's hand went still on the arm of her chair. Bill's eyes stayed on Mike.

"I found her lying on a quilt in the backyard. And I thought she'd be upset. I thought maybe she'd been crying, or that she needed someone to sit with her while she worked through a hard day. But that's not what I found."

He paused, not because he was searching for words, but because the memory of Nicole's face on that quilt was so clear and so present that he needed a moment to let it settle before he could talk about it.

"She was at peace, Mom. Complete peace. She was lying there with her eyes closed and her face was calm and open, and when she looked at me, she smiled. And she told me she'd made a choice to spend today remembering the good. Not the hospital, or the medications, or the hard parts of her husband's illness. The real Derek. The man she married."

"That takes strength," Olivia said.

"It does. And she told me about him. The good stuff. The way he couldn't cook and he burned eggs and set off the smoke detector trying to make toast. The way he danced with the girls in the kitchen. She was laughing when she told me these things. Real laughter. And I sat there and listened, and she let me in on these memories like she was giving me a gift, like she trusted me to hold them."

Bill's gaze hadn't moved from Mike's face.

"And then she told me about her evening on Friday," Mike said. "She saddled Jasper and rode up into the foothills alone. And she talked to God the whole way. She told Him she was angry and grateful and confused and at peace, all of it, and then she stopped talking and just listened."

"What did she hear?" Olivia asked.

"That's what I asked her. She said nothing specific. No voice. But she said she got to the top of the ridge where you can see the entire valley, and she felt held. Like God had her exactly where He wanted her and wasn't letting go."

Olivia pressed her lips together and looked down at her coffee.

"She told me she realized that God didn't just give her Derek," Mike said. "He gave her the privilege of being the person who walked beside Derek through the hardest part of his life. She said that it wasn't a burden. She called it a calling. And she said God prepared her for it. Every hard night, every moment she held it together when she wanted to fall apart, He was building something in her. And then He took that strength and put her on a new road."

His throat tightened, and he swallowed against it, and he kept going because he needed to finish.

"And she looked at me and said that road led her here. To Serenity Crossing, to the farm, to that quilt in the backyard on November seventh, talking to me. Because I've walked my own version of that road."

The porch was quiet. The only sound was a bird somewhere in the pines near the barn, calling twice and then going silent.

"I almost lost it," Mike said. "Sitting right there on that quilt, I almost completely fell apart. I held it together because that was her moment, not mine, and she needed me to be steady. But I want you both to know that, aside from the day Lizzie was born, this morning was one of the most important moments of my life. Watching a woman who has been through the hardest years a person can go through, sitting in the grass with that kind of peace on her face, praising God for every blessing in her life, including the ones that came wrapped in pain. I have never seen anything like it."

Olivia reached up and wiped her eyes with the back of her hand. Bill was still. He hadn't moved since Mike started talking. His coffee mug sat in his hands like he'd forgotten it was there. He looked at his son for a long moment, and then he looked out at the mountains, and then he looked back.

"A woman who can be that honest with God," Bill said, "is a woman who will be that honest with you. That's a rare son. Your mother has been that honest with me for thirty-six years, and I'm still grateful for it every single morning."

He reached for Olivia's hand. She gave it to him. Bill held her hand and lifted it, and pressed his lips to her knuckles, and then he held it against the arm of the rocker between their two chairs.

"Your daddy told me something once," Olivia said. "Right after we got married, I was worried about something. I don't even remember what, probably money, probably the house, probably everything. And I asked him how he knew it was going to work. And he looked at me and said, 'I don't know if it's going to work. I just know I'm not going anywhere because God put me right here for a reason.' And that was enough for me."

Mike looked at his parents. His dad's hand around his mom's. The life they'd built, the family they'd raised in this house on this land with this view, and he felt the full weight of what they had given him. Not just a good childhood, or the lumber mill, or the faith they'd shown him. The example. The living, daily proof that two people could choose each other and keep choosing each other and build something that lasted.

"I need to tell you both something," Mike said.

Olivia looked at him.

"I'm going to marry her."

He said it the way he'd said everything that mattered in his life. Quietly. Without drama.

"I know it with everything in me. I've known for a while, if I'm being honest. But this morning made it real. This morning I watched the woman I love sit in the grass and praise God for a road that led her to me, and I am not going to stand on that road and do nothing."

Bill nodded. "She's a good woman, Mike, and you're a good man. I'd say God knew what He was doing when He put you two on the same road."

"He usually does," Mike said.

Olivia stood up from her rocking chair. She walked over to Mike's chair, leaned down, and wrapped her arms around his shoulders from behind, her cheek pressed against the side of his head. She held him. She didn't say anything for a moment, and when she finally spoke, her voice was steady and warm.

"I have prayed for this," she said. "I have asked God to bring you peace and put someone in your life that could help ease the pain of losing Jenny. My prayers have been answered."

She kissed the top of his head and held on for another moment before she straightened up, wiped her eyes again, and looked out at the yard. "I'm going to go check on Lizzie, and then I'm going to start dinner, because apparently my son is getting married and I need to feed somebody."

Mike laughed, and Bill smiled beside him

The screen door closed softly behind her. Mike heard her footsteps moving through the house, and then Lizzie's voice rising in the happy, animated pitch that meant Grammy was being given a tour of the plastic horse riding school.

Mike sat with his father on the porch. The last of the light was slipping behind the mountains. The sky above the ridgeline was deep blue, darkening at the edges, and the first star had appeared above the barn.

He thought about Nicole on that quilt. The peace on her face. The steadiness in her eyes when she'd looked at him and told him where the road had led. He thought about what he'd said to her before he left. Do you have any idea how amazing you are? He thought about the way she'd looked at him when he said it, her eyes bright and clear.

He thought about the life that was coming. The one he hadn't planned, hadn't expected, hadn't gone looking for. The one that had found him anyway, because God had a way of doing that, of putting two people on a road and letting them walk it until they looked up and realized they'd been walking toward each other the whole time.

Bill rocked slowly in his chair. The runners creaked against the porch boards in a rhythm as steady and familiar as a heartbeat.

"Dad?"

"Yeah, son."

"Thank you."

Bill looked at him. "For what?"

"For showing me what it looks like. You and Mom. Every single day, my whole life. You showed me what it looks like. Love. Strength. Compassion. Forgiveness. Faithfulness. A good life. A strong marriage."

Bill was quiet for a moment. Then he reached over and put his hand on the back of Mike's neck, the way he'd done when Mike was a boy, big and warm and sure, and he held it there.

"Love you, son," Bill said.

Chapter 28

Mike had been sitting on his front porch for the better part of an hour, watching the sky above the mountains change colors like it were trying on outfits and couldn't decide what to wear.

Lizzie was still asleep. She'd been worn down by a full day yesterday at the Hanshaw farm and an evening of showing her grandparents every detail of her plastic horse riding school, which had grown to include a waiting list and a second barn made out of a shoebox. Mike had carried her from the truck to her bed last night after they'd gotten home, and he'd pulled the covers up to her chin and stood there for a moment, watching her sleep.

Now the house was quiet behind him, and the sky was putting on a show: layers of pink and amber building above the ridgeline, the color deepening as it spread. He thought about church this morning. He thought about Sunday dinner at his parents' house afterward, the way his mom would already be in the kitchen by the time they arrived, and the way his dad would be on the porch in his rocker with his coffee and his view and his steady, unhurried presence. He thought about inviting Nicole and the girls to join them, and then he thought about yesterday, about the quilt in the backyard and the peace on her face and the way she'd asked him to leave so she could finish the day alone. Maybe she'd want another quiet day. Maybe she'd want space. He would give her whatever she needed, for as long as she needed it, because that was what you did when you loved someone. You let them be who they were at their own pace.

His phone buzzed on the arm of the chair.

He picked it up and looked at the screen. A text from Nicole.

Meet me at the waterfall. Around nine.

He read the message twice. Then he smiled and typed his reply.

I'll be there.

He set the phone down and took a long sip of his coffee and looked at the mountains. The pink was fading into the pale blue of a November morning, and the first real light of the day was reaching the tops of the trees along the creek. He had about two hours. He'd need to get Lizzie up and dressed and over to his parents' house, and he'd need to let his mom know he wouldn't be at church this morning. He imagined his mom might have a question or two about that because he rarely missed church, but she'd take one look at his face and she'd know, and she'd smile, and she'd tell him to go.

He stood and carried his mug inside. He walked through the living room and into the kitchen and set the mug in the sink, and as he turned to head down the hallway to wake Lizzie, a piece of paper on the refrigerator caught his eye.

He stopped.

It was Lizzie's drawing. The big one, the one she'd made on the living room floor that Friday night a few weeks ago while the cartoon played on the TV above the fireplace and her crayons were scattered around her in a rainbow of organized mess. He'd taped it to the fridge the next morning, and it had been hanging there ever since, tucked between a school lunch menu and a reminder card for Lizzie's next dentist appointment.

Two tall figures stood in the center of the page. One with dark hair and very long arms. One with yellow, wavy hair past her shoulders and a pink shirt. Beside them, three smaller figures held hands in a line, each one in a different colored dress, each one with a wide U-shaped smile. A red house with a triangle roof and a chimney sat behind them. A blue truck with black circular wheels was parked in the yard. A brown four-legged dog stood near the truck, and beside it a second dog with no name yet. A big yellow sun filled the upper-right corner. And behind everything, a line of green, jagged triangles ran across the top of the page.

Mike stood in his kitchen and looked at the drawing his daughter had made.

She had drawn a family. Not the one she'd been given. The one she saw coming.

I'm making art, Daddy.

He reached up and pulled the drawing carefully from under the magnet. He held it in both hands for a moment, looking at the two tall figures standing side by side and the three small ones beside them. Then he folded it in half, and folded it once more, and slipped it into his back pocket.

***

The sound of water grew with every step Mike took, building from a faint hush into a layered rush that filled the space between the trees. The forest had gone spare since September; the canopy thinned out; the hardwoods stood in their bare architecture against the sky. But the light came through without obstruction now, falling in broad planes across the trail and the rocks and the forest floor, and the air smelled like cold earth and pine and the clean mineral scent of moving water.

He came around the last bend where the trail curved past the large rock face, and the trees opened, and the waterfall was there.

The water came down from the ledge fifty or sixty feet above in a broad white curtain, catching the light where it broke apart over the rock face before gathering in the wide pool at the base. The pool was deep and clear, and the stream that left it ran downhill over smooth stones, passing beneath the wooden bridge to the right before disappearing into the forest below. Mist hung near the base of the falls, fine enough to see through, and the air near the water was cool and alive.

Nicole was sitting on the flat rocks at the edge of the pool. The same broad slab of gray stone where they had sat in September, the one that angled toward the falls as if the mountain had placed it there on purpose. Her Bible was open on her lap. Her hair was down, loose around her shoulders, and the light was coming through the bare canopy above and falling across her in wide, clear shafts. She was reading, her head bowed slightly over the page, one hand resting on the open Bible. She hadn't heard him yet.

Mike stood at the edge of the clearing and watched her. The falls poured behind her in their broad white curtain, and the mist caught the light and scattered it, and Nicole sat in the middle of all of it with her Bible open and her face calm and the whole November morning arranged around her like it had been built for this single moment. He felt the full weight of what he was looking at. A woman who had walked through the hardest years of her life and come out the other side with her faith intact and her heart wide open. A woman who had chosen this place, this morning, to be with him.

He walked toward her. His footsteps on the rock reached her before his voice did, and she looked up from her Bible and saw him, and the smile that came across her face was warm and unguarded.

She closed the Bible and set it on the rock beside her.

"Hey," she said as she stood.

"Hey."

She reached out and took the front of his shirt in her hands; the fabric gathered in her fingers, and she pulled him toward her and kissed him. It was brief and sweet and sure, and when she pulled back, her eyes were bright and clear and looking straight into his.

"Thank you for coming," she said.

"You could've told me to meet you at the bottom of a mine shaft and I would've shown up."

She laughed and picked her Bible up from the rock and sat back down, tucking her legs to the side. "Sit with me."

He lowered himself onto the rock beside her. The stone was cool, but the sun was on it, and the falls poured in front of them with the same steady, constant sound they had been making for thousands of years. The pool caught the light and held it, and the mist drifted across the rocks in a fine veil.

"I'm guessing this means we're not making it to church this morning," Mike said.

Nicole looked at him sideways with a half-smile. "I think God will understand."

"Pastor Warren might have questions."

"Pastor Warren will survive."

Mike grinned. She leaned into him slightly, her shoulder against his, and they sat for a moment looking at the water.

"When you brought me here in September," Nicole said, "I fell in love with this place all over again. I'd been here as a teenager and I thought I remembered it, but I didn't. Not really. I didn't understand what it was until you showed me." She turned to look at him. "Do you remember what you said to me that day? When we first sat down right here on these rocks?"

"I do," he said. "I told you this is where I come when I need to think. When the noise in my head gets too loud, I come here and sit. This is where I feel closer to God."

"That's exactly what you said." She looked at the waterfall. "I wanted to come here today. Just you and me. I wanted to sit in this place where you've been coming since you were a teenager and feel what you've always felt here. I wanted us to be closer to God, right here, in this exact spot."

She opened her Bible to the first slip of paper she had inserted as a marker. "I marked a few passages last night. Will you let me read them to you?"

"I'd like that."

She smoothed the page with her hand. The sound of the waterfall wrapped around them, steady and full, and Nicole began to read.

"Isaiah, chapter forty-three, verses eighteen and nineteen. 'Remember ye not the former things, neither consider the things of old. Behold, I will do a new thing; now it shall spring forth; shall ye not know it? I will even make a way in the wilderness, and rivers in the desert.'"

"Rivers in the desert," she said. "That's what He did for us, Mike. We were both walking through our own deserts, and we didn't even know it. We thought we were fine. We thought the lives we'd built were enough. And God looked at us and said, I'm not done yet. I have a new thing for you. And He put it right in our path, and it sprang up like water in a place where we didn't think water could grow."

She turned to the next slip of paper and found the second passage.

"Psalm thirty, verse five. 'For his anger endureth but a moment; in his favour is life: weeping may endure for a night, but joy cometh in the morning.'"

Her voice was steady as she read, and when she looked up from the page, her eyes were full but not overflowing, and her face held the same settled peace he had seen on the quilt yesterday morning.

"Three years for you," she said. "One year for me. I'm not saying our weeping is over forever, because grief doesn't work that way. But I am sitting here on a Sunday morning in November, beside a man I love, at a waterfall that has been pouring water over these rocks since before either of us was born, and I am telling you that joy came. It came. Just like He promised."

She turned to the last marked page.

"Isaiah, chapter forty-three, verse two. 'When thou passest through the waters, I will be with thee; and through the rivers, they shall not overflow thee.'"

She closed the Bible and held it in her lap, and looked at the waterfall. "Look at it, Mike. Look at all that water. It's been coming down that rock face for centuries. It didn't stop when Derek got sick. It didn't stop when Jenny died. It didn't stop during the worst nights of our lives, when we were lying awake asking God why. It just kept going. Steady and constant, and faithful. And we passed through the waters, both of us, and they did not overflow us. He was with us the whole time."

Mike sat beside her and listened to the falls and felt the truth of what she was saying in a place deeper than words could reach. He thought about the times he had spent on these rocks, sitting alone with his grief and his questions, watching this water and trusting that God was somewhere in the sound of it. He thought about the afternoon in September when he had brought Nicole here and told her the truth of what he felt for her, and she had met him with the same honesty. And he thought about yesterday, November seventh, one year, and the woman beside him who had spent that day remembering the good and praising God for every road He'd put her on, including the one that led her here.

"I'm not carrying guilt anymore," Nicole said. "Not for the relief I felt. Not for how quickly this happened between us. Not for any of it. God carried me through the waters, and He set me down right here, and I am grateful, Mike. I am so grateful to be sitting beside you in this place."

He reached into his back pocket.

"I want to show you something," he said.

He pulled out the folded piece of paper and held it out to her.

She took it. "What's this?"

"Open it."

She unfolded it once, and then again, and looked at it.

The drawing lay open in her hands. Two tall figures in the center. Three tiny figures beside them, holding hands. A red house. A blue truck. A brown dog named Baxter and his friend who didn't have a name yet. A big yellow sun. Mountains across the top.

Nicole's lips parted, and she smiled, and the smile grew as her eyes moved across the page, taking in every crayon stroke, every detail that a six-year-old had placed there with the careful, certain hand of someone who was drawing something real.

"Lizzie drew this?" she said.

"She did. A few weeks ago, on a Friday night. She was lying on the living room floor with her crayons spread out everywhere, and I sat down beside her and asked her what she was coloring." He paused. "And she corrected me. She looked up at me and said, 'I'm making art, Daddy.'"

Nicole looked at the drawing. She traced the three small figures with her fingertip: the one in the purple dress and the one in the pink, and the one in the blue, all three of them holding hands and smiling. Then she looked at the two dogs, and the red house, and the blue truck, and the mountains, and she pressed her lips together, and her eyes filled.

"She saw it before any of us did," Nicole said.

"She did."

Nicole held the drawing and looked at it for another long moment, and then she looked at Mike. "The Art of Starting Over."

Mike looked at her. "What do you say we find out if the artist got it right?"

Nicole's face broke open, the tears and the smile arriving at the same time, and she nodded once, quick and certain, the way a woman nods when the answer has been yes for longer than the question has been asked.

Mike took the Bible gently from her lap. He held it in his hands and turned the pages until he found what he was looking for, and when he found it, he smoothed the page and read aloud.

"Song of Solomon, chapter eight, verse seven. 'Many waters cannot quench love, neither can the floods drown it.'"

His voice was steady. The waterfall poured over the ledge in front of them, white and constant, and the sound of it filled the air, and the words he had just spoken sat beside that sound as if they had been written for this place.

He closed the Bible and set it on the rock beside them.

He turned to Nicole. He brought his hands up and cradled her face, his palms against her cheeks. Her skin was cool from the mist and warm beneath it. Her eyes were blue and steady and full of the kind of trust that only comes from a woman who has walked through the flood and found the other side. He looked at her, and he held her face in his hands, and he said what he had come here to say.

"Nicole. I have built a lot of things in my life with these hands. Tables and chairs and bookshelves and a life that I thought was complete. But I have never built anything as important as what I want to build with you. I love you."

He leaned in and kissed her.

The waterfall poured. The mist drifted across the rocks. The mountains stood on every side, steady and ancient and sure, and Mike Hartwell kissed the woman he loved beside the water that never stopped.

Leave A Review

If you enjoyed this book, please consider leaving an honest review on Amazon

Visit Our Website:

www.tarabaisden.com

Visit Our Amazon Author Page HERE

Find Us On Social Media:

Facebook

Facebook Author Page

Instagram

Scan the QR code above to sign up for our newsletter!

Scan the QR code above to sign up for our newsletter!

Also by Tara Baisden

<u>Serenity Crossing: The Hartwell's Series</u>

#1 Hometown Sweethearts

#2 Hearts Restored

#3 The Art of Starting Over – coming April 3, 2026

#4 Love in God's Timing – coming May 1, 2026

#5 Wildflower Heart – coming June 5, 2026

#6 Brave Enough to Love – coming July 3, 2026

<u>Laurel Ridge Series</u>

#1. Season of Hope

#2. Finding Grace

#3. His Perfect Plan

#4. Love Redeemed

#5 Snowbound Blessings

#6 Sheltered Hearts

#7 Restoring Faith

#8 Love Rekindled

#9 Where She Belongs

#10 Shelter in His Arms

#11 Where Love Stands

#12 The Pieces We Mend

#13 Where Love Grows

#14 Where Hearts Heal

#15 Harvest of the Heart

#16 Heart of the Season

#17 Season of Forgiveness

#18 Threads of Grace

Riverbend Valley Series

#1 A Cowboy's Second Chance

#2 Wanderlust & Wild Horses

#3 Heartstrings on the Horizon

#4 Runaway in Riverbend Valley

#5 Mended Hearts

#6 Healing Hearts

#7 Home to Lost Creek

Mistletoe Falls Series

#1 Whisk Me Under the Mistletoe

#2 Once Upon a Christmas

#3 The Mistletoe Express

#4 Candy Canes & Sweet Dreams

#5 Wrapped Up in Christmas

#6 Jingle All the Way Home

About The Author

Tara Baisden is a Contemporary Christian Inspirational Romance author who proudly calls the beautiful state of West Virginia her home. Nestled on a sprawling mountainous property, she is surrounded by the peace and serenity of nature. Her days are happily spent in the quiet of country life, writing heartwarming stories of love, faith, and second chances. Tara also enjoys quilting, working in her garden, tending to her beloved pets, and soaking in the beauty of her surroundings.

With deep roots in West Virginia, family is everything to Tara. One of her favorite pastimes is gathering on the front porch with loved ones, sharing stories, laughter, and enjoying the simple, meaningful moments that life offers. When she's not crafting her novels, Tara can often be found exploring the rich history of her home state, visiting local historical sites, and, of course, stopping by every bookstore she passes! Her passion for reading and discovery always fuels her next adventure.

Tara is the author of the Laurel Ridges series of novels, as well as the Riverbend Valley series of novels, of which have been beloved by fans of inspirational romance. Her novels reflect her love for faith, family, and the timeless beauty of the world we live in.

Known for her sweet and clean romances, she creates characters that feel like family and settings that make readers want to visit again and again.

You can find out more about Tara and her latest releases at www.tarabaisden.com or follow her on social media for updates and behind-the-scenes glimpses of her writing process. Stay connected—you won't want to miss the heartfelt stories of love and family she has in store!